Praise for the work of PAUL THOMAS

DIRTY LAUNDRY

'Thomas is a true original, energetic, scintillating and quite mad. I devoured [*Dirty Laundry*] in one gulp, then suffered the indigestion of laughter for a week.'
Vincent Banville, *The Irish Times*

'*Dirty Laundry* reaffirms that Thomas is a master storyteller and rapidly becoming one of the yardsticks by which contemporary Australian crime fiction is measured.'
Stuart Coupe, *The Sydney Morning Herald*

'A master of plot, pace and the killer one-liner.'
Marele Day

'The most explosively funny New Zealand novel yet written.'
Tom Scott, *The Sunday Star-Times*

INSIDE DOPE

'Fast, funny, multi-layered – a cracking good read.'
Alan Hill, *The Daily Telegraph*

'Paul Thomas is a top talent with skill to burn.'
Robin Wallace-Crabbe, *The Australian*

'Tightly plotted, studded with eccentric characters, roars along like an express train, refreshingly literate.'
Susan Geason, *The Sun-Herald*

GUERILLA SEASON

'Fast-paced, irreverent, tightly plotted and often very funny. Not to be missed.'
Susan Geason, *The Sun-Herald*

'One of the funniest writers in this part of the world.'
Neil Jillett, *The Age*

'Paul Thomas's murders are among the best that money can buy. When you're reading [him], you've just about got everything: thrills, laughs, social comment and – irrespective of genre – a very good book.'
Bernard Carpinter, *New Zealand Books*

FINAL CUT

'A delightfully paced caper, full of serious cleverness, cracking dialogue, deadpan one-liners that would make Raymond Chandler's jaw drop in admiration, and perceptive and insightful observations on various stratas of the Sydney milieu. A book that pulp/noir masters such as David Goodis, Peter Rabe and Charles Willeford would be proud to call their own if they were writing about Sydney in the late 90s. Tough, intense, dry, oh so very sharp, and a cracker-jack distillation of our city.'
Stuart Coupe, *The Sydney Morning Herald*

'A very knowing exposition of sexual obsessi
Robin Wallace-Crabbe, *The Bul*

THE EMPTY BED

PAUL THOMAS

HarperCollins*Publishers*

HarperCollins_Publishers_

First published in Australia in 2002
by HarperCollins_Publishers_ Pty Limited
ABN 36 009 913 517
A member of the HarperCollins_Publishers_ (Australia) Pty Limited Group
www.harpercollins.com.au

HarperCollins_Publishers_
25 Ryde Road, Pymble, Sydney, NSW 2073, Australia
31 View Road, Glenfield, Auckland 10, New Zealand
77–85 Fulham Palace Road, London, W6 8JB, United Kingdom
Hazelton Lanes, 55 Avenue Road, Suite 2900, Toronto, Ontario M5R 3L2
and 1995 Markham Road, Scarborough, Ontario M1B 5M8, Canada
10 East 53rd Street, New York NY 10022, USA

National Library of Australia Cataloguing-in-Publication data:

Thomas, Paul, 1951–.
  The empty bed.
  ISBN 0 7322 7170 3.
  1. Marriage – Fiction. 2. Crime – Fiction. I. Title.

NZ823.2

Cover and internal design by Darian Causby, HarperCollins Design Studio
Cover photograph: photolibrary.com/nonstock
Typeset by HarperCollins Design Studio in Sabon 11.5/18
Printed and bound in Australia by Griffin Press on 80gsm Bulky Book Ivory

5 4 3 2 1   02 03 04 05

To Hank's Table and all who gathered there.

CHAPTER 1

I'm not sure of anything any more. Except this: ignorance is bliss. What we don't know can't hurt us. And what we find out can erase our certainties, like words wiped off a blackboard.

You can make up your own mind but, for what it's worth, I don't think I deserved it. I followed the rules; I did my best. That's how I see it most of the time, anyway. Now and again – when I've had a few, say – I blame myself. As you do.

I divide my life into BC and AC. C is for cat, the cat that got out of the bag.

We made love the last night of BC. She'd been out – dinner with clients. She had a lot of those. I was in bed pretending to read a book when she got home. She came into the bedroom sparkle-eyed, flushed with drink and flattery. I'd always assumed that these client dinners were frisky affairs. The men would play up, chance their arm, and who could blame them? A woman like my wife beat the hell out of the usual idiot-savant marketing types or some grey-faced financial controller with permanently clenched eyebrows.

She was usually up for it, as they say, after these evenings of wine and flirtation. I didn't attach any particular significance to that – I gather the same applies to a lot of women. But I had to be quick: once her head hit the pillow, the wine took her down fast. Give her a couple of minutes to nestle in and she wasn't a taker for that swelling lump nudging her buttocks. She'd murmur, 'Honey, I'm gone.' And thirty seconds later she would be, snorting softly as she drew away.

That night, I left nothing to chance. When she stretched out to switch off the bedside light, I slid questing fingers down her spine into the first of the warm splits. She gave a little shudder and said, 'Oh, like that is it?' My fingers hurried on, dipping into hot fluid. She said, 'I'm ready.' She stayed on her side with her back to me, lifting her upper leg so that the knee was almost touching her shoulder, and fumbling for me. She was as ready as she'd ever been, purring, wide-open, a film of sweat popping on her flared back. I put it down to the wine and the fact that sometimes, for no reason that I understand – hormones? Biorhythms? – lust comes over us with special violence. Afterwards I asked, 'What got you going?' but she was already shutting down. She flopped onto her front, subsiding into the mattress, and went to sleep.

Our last conversation BC was less remarkable. In fact, it was mundane to the point of bathos. She was on her way out to play tennis; I was staying in to work. The subject was what we were going to have for dinner. I offered to barbecue and she said, 'I don't feel like meat.' I laugh about that sometimes. I don't imagine it's a pretty sight.

I said, 'We could go out.'

She said, 'I was out last night.'

'I wasn't.'

'Why don't we just have pasta?'

I said, 'I had pasta last night.'

She looked at her watch. 'I'm going to be late. Whatever.' She blew me a kiss and walked out, swinging her racquet and her fine behind.

I tried to work. I have everything I need to work at home: the tranquillity of a child-free household in a gracious neighbourhood, a study which gets the afternoon sun, a squat PC which hums with latent power, a wall of reference books. Everything except the will. I go into the study, close the door, and ... muck about. The only thing that can keep me in there for more than half an hour at a time is getting lost in a maze of pornography while roaming the internet, a doubly unproductive exercise given that the boys I teach hardly need my help to get their gelled and bepimpled heads around that subject.

That weekend I had the excuse of a cold. A pretty good excuse it was too; I had a sore throat, a headache, and a constant flow of oily, olive mucus which meant that I couldn't leave home without a stack of handkerchiefs. On my way out for a coffee, I went to the handkerchief drawer but my wife had got there before me. She'd been sniffling and dribbling for a few days and had no time for those pointless, lacy scraps with which women are supposed to cope with everything their noses throw at them.

I didn't make a habit of going through my wife's pockets but this was an emergency. These days, only urchins and senior citizen street-people can get away with wiping their noses on their sleeves. The hip-pocket of a pair of Dolce & Gabbana trousers gave up an unmarked white linen handkerchief and a folded piece of paper. I suppose some men, some prissy souls, would have put the piece of paper back where they found it and gone sniffing and hawking on their way. It never occurred to me to do that. We had, after all, been married for fifteen years. We were on record as claiming that we didn't keep secrets from each other, a boast which, now that I come to think of it, usually met with scepticism. So for no other reason than casual curiosity, I unfolded the piece of paper. The period of my life that I think of as BC was about to end. As were a few other things.

It was a note, handwritten: *My darling Anne, You are out of this world. I can't wait till next time.* It was signed, if you can call it that, *Jxxx.*

Nothing too enigmatic about that, I think you'd agree. Not a text which was open to a barrage of jostling interpretations.

Needless to say, I couldn't call on such sardonic resilience at the time.

To begin with, I went into denial. It didn't make sense: this 'darling Anne' couldn't be my darling Anne. There had to be some explanation – bizarre, perhaps, discomforting, maybe, anything but the catastrophe those words signified at face-value. Our marriage had stood the test of time. We were better at it than most. Many of our married friends were on their second and some of them still hadn't got the hang of it. And we were more than just quietly fond of each other as couples with sturdy, convenient marriages can be. We loved each other. We said so regularly. Maybe I said so more often than she did but there wasn't much in it.

Look, I don't mind admitting that I wasn't the greatest catch. There were those in my wife's circle who'd failed to see the attraction fifteen years ago so god knows what recent acquaintances made of us. Certainly, if professional status and remuneration were their criteria, they'd have to conclude that she'd married down. She'd long since swerved confidently into the fast lane while I've puttered along a dreary back-road these days used only by the timid and the unworldly, my heart no longer in the journey but too far gone to turn back.

I defy anyone in that position not to have the odd spasm of insecurity. I sometimes fished for reassurance in the guise of wry self-deprecation as in, 'One of these days, you'll trade me in for a flasher model.' And she'd smile and shake her head and say things like 'Where do you get these daft ideas?' or 'You'll do me.' All the indicators were positive. She was happy. She was flourishing. Life was good. We still had fun. We still had sex. She still enjoyed it.

And then I remembered the previous night, how she'd breathed, groaned almost, 'I'm ready.' That wasn't my doing. I didn't get her ready – she was already ready. She'd walked in the door with a glow between her legs, wanting more where that came from. But she'd had to settle for me, anything to soothe that burning itch. She hadn't kissed me, hadn't even turned her head. She'd just grasped the nearest cock and backed onto it.

I stormed through the house, cursing and shaking. Eventually, I managed to calm down. I had to get a grip on myself; I couldn't afford to lose control. My wife was formidable in our rare confrontations precisely because she kept her cool whereas I tended to burst into flames. She was skilled at exploiting my combustions. She'd say calmly, 'Well, if you're going to be like that, there's no point in continuing this discussion.' Or, if I'd thoroughly demeaned myself, her face would set like stone and she'd maintain an arctic silence until I withdrew and apologised. This time, I vowed, I would not overreach myself, I would not lapse into obscene incoherence. There was no need. The thing spoke for itself.

In the midst of this maelstrom of humiliation, self-pity and jittery anticipation, I realised that part of me was deriving a weird kind of pleasure from the situation. I actually blushed. Until that moment, it had never occurred to me that I might have a masochistic streak.

Let's face it, we all relish occupying the moral high ground, even though it usually involves sacrifice. Up until that moment, nearly all the shameful behaviour within our marriage could be laid at my door. While I'd done nothing which could be termed vile, I had, for instance, ruined Christmas Day for young and old by arguing poisonously with my father-in-law across the table. And as I've mentioned, there was a school of thought, in which my wife's family was heavily represented, which held, in a nutshell, that I wasn't good enough for her. Exhibit A was my inadequacy as a provider, exhibit B my physical appearance and personality. There's no accounting for taste but only the radically unconventional could find me a more attractive human being than my wife. This time, though, no-one could point the finger at me. The fault was all hers. The damage was all mine.

My wife didn't hurry home. Perhaps they were playing Wimbledon rules – no tie-breaks in the deciding set. For all her easy grace on and off the court, she was one of those people who needed to win and I found myself wondering if the previous night's exertions would catch up with her if it 'went down to the wire'. That should give you some idea of how disoriented I was.

The waiting got to me. I was spinning out, all appeasement one minute, willing to overlook a posse of lovers, and psychotic the next, wanting to break her neck.

I went for a drive, to fill in time and occupy my seething mind. Ironing shirts was an alternative but, fastidious as I was, that didn't require quite enough concentration. Failing to give Sydney traffic due respect, however, was akin to autocide and it was a little early to be contemplating that.

I found my way to the airport. There was no conscious decision involved; no mystery either. The urge to trade in my life for a new one in a faraway place was my standard reaction to professional setbacks and domestic unpleasantness. Feeling unappreciated at work, I'd picture myself living off the land among grimy, grinning peasants in some overlooked corner of Europe. After one of our rare, no-holds-barred rows, I'd lay awake in the spare bedroom imagining the man from Interpol doing his painful duty, informing my wife that the trail went cold in Vientiane; it looked like I'd gone bamboo, melted into the jungle or headed up river to places from where white men came back changed out of all recognition – if they came back at all.

This ludicrous fantasy was an old friend. I'd been devising variations on it since I was a teenager. Back then, the basic storyline was a blend of the Charles Atlas sales pitch and *Kung Fu* – 140 lb weakling spends five cruel years in mountaintop martial arts academy, emerges as wire-hard warrior with supernatural penis. Par for the course, I suppose, for a lonely, mildly fucked-up seventeen year old. One expects more of forty-three year olds, even forty-three-year-old cuckolds in the first flush of humiliation.

A mini-bus pulled up behind me, disgorging a cabin crew from an Asian airline. One of the stewardesses, a willowy beauty, as alert as a wild animal after years of sidestepping bottle-nosed foreign devils at 30,000 feet, examined me gravely as she filed past. I ventured a rueful half-smile but her eyes slid away without a flicker of response and she disappeared into the terminal, dragging her little luggage trolley behind her.

I drove back into town, to the school where I taught. There were plenty of people about, mainly parents and browsing girls come to cheer on their jock sons and boyfriends-to-be. I made it to my study without bumping into any of the tweedy fanatics among my colleagues who regarded time spent in the classroom as an irksome distraction from our true mission – to nurture champions. I was in no mood for their clod-hopping mateyness or their homoerotic raves.

I shut the door and rang my parents, down on the farm.

My mother answered. 'I thought you'd be watching the game.'

'Eh?'

'The big match.' Christ, I couldn't get away from it. 'Your father's gone over to the Curtises to watch it.'

'I forgot it was on.'

'Oh, well.' There was disappointment in my mother's voice: sport and gardening were subjects my father and I could discuss calmly, even amicably. I didn't have strong views on either. 'Anyway, how are you, dear?' Without waiting for an answer, she added, 'How's Anne?'

I should have expected that. Unlike me, my wife had never suffered the Chinese water torture of parents-in-law's disapproval. My mother admired her as wholeheartedly as everyone else did. It brought home to me, though, that this was a pointless exercise. My parents couldn't help me. This sort of ugliness didn't feature in their lives; it was something that happened to other people, unsound people. Besides, trouble on the home front was a matter for one's vicar. He had the answers at his fingertips.

'We're okay. Look, sorry Mum, but I'm actually at work and someone's just walked into my office. I better go. Talk to you soon, okay?'

'All right, dear. I'll tell your father you rang.' She wasn't put out; she was of a generation who accepted that work came first. 'Give our love to Anne.'

You bet. I'll slip it into the conversation first chance I get.

I rang my sister at the waterfront dream-home she shared with her husband, a sleek financier with the Midas touch, and their three pulverisingly loud children. Rosie allowed me to flounder through a conversation with her seven year old – 'So, Arabella, what have you been up to today?' 'Are you being nice to your little sister?' – before coming to the phone. I was sufficiently deranged to tell her what I thought of parents who encouraged their sprogs to answer the phone.

'Thank you for that,' she said sweetly. 'Was there anything else?'

'It happens to me all the fucking time. I mean, if I want to talk to Arabella, I'll come over and ...'

'What's the matter, Nick?'

'It's Anne.'

'What's happened?' It came out in a rush. Rosie and Anne were more like sisters than sisters-in-law.

'I think we've got a problem.'

'What sort of problem?'

'The sort that involves a third party.'

There was a long silence before Rosie said, 'Oh god, you don't think Anne's having an affair, do you?'

'I think it's a distinct possibility.' When she didn't say anything, I said, 'Aren't you going to tell me it's out of the question?'

'I've seen too many apparently rock-solid marriages go belly-up to say that about anyone, even Anne. So what set this off?'

I lied. I told her there was nothing concrete, I just had a nagging suspicion. And I didn't pay too much attention to her advice which consisted of a string of banalities, rattled off as if she could smell something burning: I shouldn't jump to conclusions, maybe it was just a communication thing, Anne wasn't that sort of person, she was probably under pressure at work.

My sister couldn't help me either.

I sat at my desk. Nothing moved except my brain. For the first time since I'd found the note, I thought beyond the betrayal and the looming confrontation. I thought about the consequences. Was this it for us, was this the end of the line? Well, that could be up to me. Getting back to tennis for a moment, the ball was in my court. Could I live with it? Could I forgive her?

I'm not a hater and I don't bear grudges. I don't have the energy. I'm not saying I like the creeping jesus who brown-nosed his way into the head of department's job at my expense but I don't sit around thinking of ways to get my own back. If short-fuse Steve throws a tantrum on the golf course or tight-arse Tom brings a cheap bottle of wine to our dinner party, I might let them know I'm not impressed or I might let it slide. Life's too short to be always taking offence.

But this was different. This was one step down from life and death. It seemed unlikely that both our marriage and my self-respect could come out of it intact. Something would have to give. And even if I ate shit, would that see us through? Maybe the condition was too serious to respond to a change of diet, however radical.

Then again the hard line didn't have much going for it either: starting over, living alone, being the only single at dinner parties, getting tagged as a social cripple or a closet queen ... The prospect of having my life turned upside down and shaken out was terrifying. If push came to shove, I could get by without my self-respect but I had precious little confidence in my ability to get by without Anne. Her fingerprints were all over my existence, from the flower arrangement in the hallway to the biennial lunch at our favourite restaurant in the 16th arrondissement. Was I tough enough to walk away from that?

As my pupils say, ad nauseam, I don't think so.

CHAPTER 2

It all started with Harry. If it hadn't been for him, I wouldn't have got to first base.

I'm going back seventeen years now. I was a junior housemaster at a boarding school in the southern highlands, teaching English to all comers and Latin to a handful of scholarly drones. The school had had its day. It was no longer the first or even second choice for farming folk wanting a coating of couth slapped on their feral sons or nouveau riche townies needing a place to warehouse their encumbrances while they got on with the good life. Each intake owed a little more to old boys who actually wanted their sons to turn out just like them.

Harry Carew was in my sixth form English class. I can't speak for the state system, thank christ, but at private schools, there's one like Harry in every class and any teacher with a rudimentary sense of self-preservation can identify him at a glance. He's bright, not that you'd know it from his marks; he made up his mind some time ago that book learning's no use where he's going. He's a bully but rarely in the physical sense. Pushing people around gets boring after a while and boredom is the real enemy. All his little routine acts of cruelty and sabotage are part of his war of resistance against the paralysing dullness of school life. He doesn't have to be a tough customer: he has brutes on call to do his scrapping for him. His weapons are wit – crude or sly depending on the target – a torturer's instinct for the sensitive spot, a stand-up comedian's ability to manipulate an audience, and a mastery of brinkmanship. He sits at the back of the class surrounded by courtiers and stooges, his cruel gaze sweeping the room for his next target. He has the power. He's number one. And if you can't handle him, you're in big trouble, brother.

When it comes to dealing with boys like Harry, I have an advantage over most of my colleagues: in some respects I was a boy like Harry myself. I know what's going on there; I know where he's vulnerable. He controls the mob – for now. But if he mismanages one of his campaigns of persecution, if he's bested in a verbal set-piece, beaten at his own game, the mob will round on him. Behind that puppet-master cockiness, he wonders when his turn will come.

It's really not that hard. The teacher, after all, is the adult in this head-to-head. He or she has authority on their side. Apart from genuine psychos – and you don't muck around with them, you get them expelled double-quick, you make them someone else's problem – most troublemakers understand that they can't beat the system so they go so far and no further. The only restraints on a teacher are professional ethics and squeamishness and I've never been over-burdened with either. Especially not squeamishness. Deformities, puppy fat, speech impediments, general spasticity, sporting ignominy, unruly acne, unsightly sisters, unstylish parents – as far as I was concerned, everything was on the table.

Don't get me wrong, I wasn't a monster. I operated by the golden rule, with one slight modification: if what was done unto me was unwelcome, I favoured – to use the computer-generated language of the Pentagon – the doctrine of massive retaliation as opposed to proportionate response.

And Harry and co soon realised that I wasn't a soft target like the bat-eared bumpkin cowering in the corner or the suicidally timid biology teacher with the cluster moles and the mongoloid child. I had no visible physical peculiarities, I didn't have an absurd foreign accent, I didn't have a name that lent itself to obscene word-play, and – most important of all – I wasn't homosexual. If they get an inkling of that, you're doomed. They'll come after you like a wolf-pack.

Harry, in fact, wasn't that malicious. He wasn't a hard-core anarchist, the sort who sets out to break teachers psychologically. As Thatcher said of Gorbachev, he was someone you could do business with. I generally avoid head-on confrontations with these princelings, preferring to draw them into nod and wink alliances. After some preliminary sparring, that was what I did with Harry. From then on, we rubbed along pretty well.

Walking down the main drive one visitors Sunday, I saw Harry approaching with a girl on his arm. Glib, handsome Harry, showing off again. As they got closer, I saw that not only was the girl pretty, she was a few years older than him. Well, well, Harry, I thought, you've got a big girl there. You'll be the envy of every grim masturbator in the school.

Harry grinned at me. I realised he was going to introduce his girlfriend, a bravura piece of one-upmanship. He nodded affably. 'Afternoon, sir.'

I nodded back. 'Harry.'

The girl stood there quite relaxed, still hanging onto his arm and smiling, at least with her mouth. She was a blonde but not in the tabloid sense. Her make-up was low-key – a little bronze foundation on the cheeks and pale pink lipstick. Her clothes were quietly chic. She looked *well-bred*. It was curious: everything about her emphasised the age difference. It was a look which said, I'm not a girl, I'm a woman. And how many women, I asked myself, go out with schoolboys, even ones as worldly as Harry Carew?

Harry said, 'Annie, this is Mr Souter. He does his best to teach me English.' Then to me, 'Anne's my sister but I guess you'd worked that out for yourself.'

'Well,' I said, 'there is a resemblance.' Which was true; they were both good-looking. 'Nice to meet you.'

She held out a slim, brown hand, looking at her brother. 'Teaches you English, does he?' she laughed. 'Lucky old him.'

During the banter that followed, I took the opportunity to get a good look at Anne Carew. And unless it was my imagination running away with me, she had a pretty good look at me.

After a few minutes, Anne said they'd better get back to their parents before hostilities resumed. Naturally, I glanced over my shoulder to get the all-important rear view. Anne Carew wore her tailored trousers well and without the aid of high heels which so often perform a cosmetic function on behalf of the low-slung bottom. There was indeed something in the way she moved. It wasn't a tarty wiggle or that catwalk sashay the models do, as if they're trying to tell us that they really are for sale. It was the graceful saunter of a woman who knew what she had down there and, when the time was right, would know what to do with it.

The next day, as the classroom emptied at the end of a period, Harry drifted up to my desk.

'Well, Harry,' I said, 'what can I do for you?'

He shrugged. 'Sir, I was just wondering what you thought of my sister.'

I stared, tempted to give it to him straight, just to see how he'd handle it. He displayed the half-formed, guileless smile which usually meant mischief was afoot. I said carefully, 'She seemed very nice.' After a pause and pointedly: 'Why do you ask?'

His still face and wide eyes were a parody of innocence. 'Well, she was . . . quite taken with you.'

This was a new one on me, a boy pimping his sister. 'Is that so?' I said even more carefully. 'I'm flattered.'

'And so you should be, sir,' said Harry breezily. 'She's spoilt for choice, that girl – an absolute man-magnet.'

'I can imagine.'

Harry studied me expectantly but I was on full alert now: he'd started this, he could finish it. After maybe half a minute and with the impatient air of someone who feels he's having to do more than his fair share, he said, 'Well, sir, do you want her phone number or not? She won't make the first move, you know.'

A responsible teacher would have sent Master Carew on his way with a shoe up the backside but I had an image to live up to. Harry and his cronies thought I was different; they thought I was 'on their wavelength'. Besides which, there was just a chance that he was on the level.

So I said, 'If you think it'd be a good idea.'

Harry scrawled a Sydney number on a sheet of pad-paper. 'I can't see that too much harm can come of it,' he said suavely. 'I'm sure you'll behave like a gentleman.'

And I was pretty sure it was a practical joke. Okay, Harry and I had an understanding but, as any teacher will tell you, teenagers are the most treacherous creatures on the planet. Theirs is a fickle, volatile society in which alliances are formed and abandoned at the drop of a hat and today's best friend can be tomorrow's arch-enemy.

I flip-flopped for a couple of days. If Anne really was 'taken with me', then a magnificent opportunity was going begging while I dithered. Sure, it was hard to believe but, then again, hadn't I seen interest stir in her eyes? Well, hadn't I? Without Harry's input, I wouldn't have even considered trying my luck. What would have been the point? Anne Carew had looks and her family was old money. Even if great-grand pop made his pile selling meths to the Aborigines, that double whammy instils high expectations.

I rang the number. A female voice said, 'Hello,' and I was off like an auctioneer: 'Anne, this is Nick Souter ...'

'Hang on, before you propose, you've got the wrong girl. Just a sec.'

She dumped the receiver on a hard surface, shrieking, 'Annie, there's a guy on the phone for you – he sounds *rilly* nervous. How come I don't have that effect on men?'

I timed Anne: it took her two minutes to come to the phone.

'Anne speaking.'

'Oh, Anne, this is Nick Souter, we met out at the college last Sunday ...' Silence. Dense, implacable silence. I ploughed on, dry-mouthed: 'I'm the lucky man who teaches your brother English ...'

That got no response either, not even a dismissive 'Oh, yes?' or an impatient throat clearance. That little swine, by christ he'd pay for this. I was close to blurting out some fantastically implausible professional reason for the call – 'Look, I'm a bit worried about Harry: matron found a disembowelled goat under his bed ...' – when she said, 'Sorry, my mind went blank for a moment there. I'm trying to write this English lit essay and it's driving me round the bend.'

Manna from heaven! I had an MA in English; I'd done some tutoring when I was finishing off my thesis. What I didn't know about writing an English lit essay wasn't worth knowing. 'Well, you've come to the right man,' I burbled, 'or rather, he's come to you.'

It transpired that Anne had a law degree but didn't want to be a lawyer. She was doing a few arts papers while she tried to work out what she did want to be. The essay topic was a trick question, designed to sort out the wheat from the chaff: 'Is this poetry? If so, why? If not, why not?' She had to apply the test to some Chaucer, an Elizabethan sonnet, *Reflections on Ice-breaking* by Ogden Nash, William Carlos Williams' *The Red Wheelbarrow*, *r-p-o-p-h-s-s-a-g-r* by e.e. cummings, a haiku, a verse of Bob Dylan's *Stuck Inside Of Mobile*, a toilet door limerick, and a splatter of subway graffiti. She'd made the mistake of taking it at face-value and had tied herself in knots trying to define poetry. When I asked her if she'd been to an art gallery lately, she cottoned on straightaway.

Her gratitude was so effusive, I didn't even have to psyche myself up to take the plunge: I was coming up to Sydney the weekend after next, would she like to go out for dinner? I could pass on some handy tips – there were plenty more where that came from ...

She said that sounded like a good idea. She sounded as if she meant it.

I figured there was no point in going upmarket. I couldn't afford it and it wouldn't impress her anyway. We went to a cheap Italian place in East Sydney where we ate spaghetti, drank rough red and talked about literature, politics and movies with the awesome arrogance which seizes moderately clever young people when they hold forth on these subjects. I experienced the blissful first date moment when you realise that conversation is going to be effortless and you won't have to spend the evening squeezing a few lifeless sentences out of the menu, the service, and whatever else is at hand. When I dropped her home, she didn't invite me in and she didn't kiss me goodnight but she did suggest going to the movies the next day.

It was a German film called *A Woman in Flames*, a sombre fable about a middle-class woman who walks out on her husband to become a prostitute. That's about all I remember. The cinema was near-empty and five minutes after the lights went down, Anne reached for my hand.

Later, when we were an item, I told her about Harry.

She frowned. 'You didn't believe him, did you?'

'That wasn't why I rang you, if that's what you mean,' I lied.

She shook her head, bemused. 'As if I'd tell him – him of all people.'

It wasn't long before I was driving to Sydney and back twice a week – eight solitary hours on the Hume Highway in a third-hand Toyota. It was like doing an extra day's work and paying for the privilege. And after six weeks of it, I still hadn't gone to bed with Anne Carew.

She spelt it out early on: she was fresh out of her first serious relationship and wary of the rebound syndrome. The sub-text was delayed gratification: just be patient, my lad, and, one day, all this will be yours. I went along with it, pretty meekly in hindsight. A more assertive beau would have insisted that she put a timeframe on it.

The ex-boyfriend was some kind of yuppie with a pad in Kirribilli. 'Stunning views,' she told me more than once. 'So romantic.' I didn't press her for further information but it dribbled out anyway. The yuppie, who was younger than me, had almost paid off his mortgage and, yes, since you ask, he did have a BMW.

I tried not to let this stuff bug me. We all have a past – some more eventful or just messier than others – and I've always thought it childish to smoulder over those who passed this way before. But there's a limit to how much unsolicited information about an ex-lover you can absorb before rough sarcasm tingles on the tip of the tongue: 'Well, that all sounds hunky-fucking-dory.' An alternative reaction is to ask what went wrong.

She found out that he'd been to a brothel. She didn't say how – I assumed she'd done something unsporting like run a stealthy eye over his credit card bill. He tried to excuse it as a boys' night out which went one round of drinks too far, spawning a dare he couldn't decline without losing face.

Did she regard it as cheating on her? I asked.

'What would you call it?'

'You could argue that getting a skinful and going to a hooker isn't on a par with ...'

'Jumping into bed with my best friend?'

I nodded. 'That kind of thing.'

She shrugged. 'I guess it depends on whether you think it's better or worse if there's feeling involved. If it was a case of two people being so attracted to each other that they ignore their obligations to a third person, I'm not saying I'd like it but I could understand it. But going to a hooker, it's like, what the hell, they're all pink in the dark.'

So she walked away from the Kirribilli pad and the BMW to a flat in Darling Point, sharing with a couple of fun-lovers who didn't let creaking beds or thin walls cramp their style. When they brought someone home, Anne heard everything – every giggle, every moan, even the soft, moist plop of discarded tissues. And in the morning, strange men peering down the front of her dressing-gown as she passed them in the corridor and fixed smiles and loose arrangements as the curtain fell on another one-night stand.

All in all, it didn't look as if I was going to see any action in her bedroom.

So there I was, cross-eyed with desire but having to settle for jaw-bending necking sessions in the front seat of my car. There was a night when I really thought she'd decided not to fight it any longer, to just let it happen. As I cuddled her more boldly than usual, her thighs eased apart and I swooped under the short skirt. Her bottom rose off the seat when I lifted the edge of her underpants and she lapped my neck. I squished away joyfully for perhaps a minute before she groaned – a heartfelt expression of pleasure and regret – and trapped my hand between her thighs, breathing apologies.

She composed herself and kissed me goodnight. I watched her walk up the path to the entrance to her apartment block. She blew me a kiss and disappeared inside and I sat there with her groan ringing in my ears. To this day, it remains the most erotic sound I've ever heard. I started the car, bleakly contemplating what lay ahead: another two-hour trundle down the white line, another abbreviated sleep, another short-fused, headachy day. I must admit I lay awake that night wondering if I'd fallen into the feathery clutches of an accomplished cock-teaser.

A couple of dates later, as she reached for the doorhandle, I asked, 'Don't you think this is a little bit ... unnatural?'

'What?'

'Healthy, open-minded adults having a romantic relationship which doesn't involve sex.'

'What would you call what we've been doing for the last half-hour?'

'I'd call it necking,' I said. 'I'd call it pashing. I'd call it foreplay except it doesn't lead to anything. I'd call it frustrating. What I wouldn't call it is sex.'

'Oh, I see: it's not sex unless you have an orgasm?'

'Or at least give yourself a chance of having one. I have to say, I don't think I'm in the minority on this one.'

She raised her eyebrows. 'Well, I don't know about you but, by that definition, I've got a reasonably active sex life. As a matter of fact, I don't see myself missing out tonight.'

'Well, yeah, but it's not the same, is it?'

'It's got a few things going for it.'

'Okay, it's sex with the one you love and you don't have to get dressed up. What else?'

She shifted position so that she was directly facing me. She wasn't taking this matter lightly. 'You do it when you feel like it and only when you feel like it. You do what you want, not what someone else wants. There's nothing to worry about and you can go straight to sleep afterwards.' She smiled. 'I'm sure others will occur to me before the night's out.'

'I thought only men worried about their performance.'

'You thought wrong.'

'What do women worry about?'

'The same as men – was it good for you?'

I nodded. 'So what do you think about?'

Her eyes narrowed. 'When?'

'When you're, you know, flying solo.'

'Uh-uh.'

'Come on,' I wheedled.

'Forget it.' She said it firmly and with several shakes of the head.

Talking dirty with a woman mightn't be the next best thing but it's up there and it can be useful groundwork. But even that, it seemed, was too much to ask. I shrugged sulkily and stared out the window.

Anne said disbelievingly, 'You're not pissed off, are you?'

'No, I'm not pissed off.' My tone made a liar of me.

'Don't push it, Nick.'

'What's that meant to mean?'

'If I was you, I'd drop the subject.'

You'd think I would have got the message, wouldn't you? She'd made it pretty clear that there was nothing in it for me.

I said, 'You're not me.'

Her face set grimly. 'You really want to know, do you?'

There was no turning back now. 'Yeah, I really want to know.'

'Okay,' she said, nodding slowly. 'I think about my ex-boyfriend. Happy now?'

I stared at her, too shocked by her ruthless honesty to see that I'd got what I sat up and begged for. Anne bent forward to dab an almost formal kiss on my cheek. 'Goodnight.'

I didn't move or say a word. She got out of the car and went inside, without looking back.

CHAPTER 3

The next week I stayed in the southern highlands. In fact, I stayed completely out of contact. I didn't want to fall in love with a woman who was still hot-wired to an ex-boyfriend. I didn't want to bleed for a lost cause. When the mopes wouldn't go away, I began to suspect I'd left it too late.

Anne rang late one night. It wasn't much of a conversation, all fits and starts and heavy silences. Eventually she said, 'Maybe this wasn't such a good idea.'

All I had to do was agree and that would have been the end of it. Coming that close, just a word away, made me realise that I didn't want to lose this woman. No, it was stronger than that: I couldn't bear to lose her. I said, 'I'm glad you called. I've missed you.'

She said softly, 'Missed you too.'

My heart picked up speed. 'You want to do something this weekend?'

'Actually, I was thinking it'd be good to get out of town. I don't know if I told you, we've got a place in the Blue Mountains.'

'You didn't tell me but I figured you'd have one somewhere.'

'Well, it's there so we might as well use it. If you want to, that is.'

Of course I did but there had to be a catch. Her parents for instance. A weekend under their supercilious gazes wasn't my idea of a relaxing break. I said tentatively, 'Who else will be there?'

'No-one.' After a pause, she added, 'In body or in spirit. It'll be just you and me.'

I think I can safely say it now: that weekend in the Blue Mountains was the best time I'll ever have.

Anne took the train from Sydney and got there before me. It was dark when I arrived and the stage was set: the table was laid, the champagne was chilling, the double bed was turned down. Our reunion was laconic, both of us pretending we were old hands at this sort of thing. She even gave me a brisk guided tour, as if I was a first-timer at her B & B.

We polished off the champagne in next to no time, trying to force the mood. Anne studied the label on the bottle of red wine I'd brought. I could have told her it was unremarkable.

She put it aside without comment and sent me down to the wine cellar.

In those days I was unsure of the etiquette of taking your pick of someone else's cellar. In fact, there's no such thing: it doesn't matter how you gained entry, once you're in, you're in, and you should make the most of it. After much dithering, I returned with a bottle which, I calculated, would do us nicely without antagonising the old man. It wasn't what Anne had in mind at all. She sent me back, this time with specific instructions: Grange Hermitage or Hill of Grace, at least ten years old. I could feel my old life receding, slowly but irrevocably, like a great ship going down the slipway.

We were pleasantly tipsy when we climbed the stairs to the mezzanine bedroom, loosely holding hands, a worldly couple just doing what came naturally. There's nothing natural about me – I am, after all, a pessimist with an active imagination. I entered that bedroom aflutter with anxiety. Anne wasn't the first or even the first I'd thought I was in love with. As a romantic young man, inclined to put women on a pedestal and lacking a practical, down-to-earth attitude to sex, I wasn't good at closing the deal, as it were, and therefore tended to fall in love with any moderately pretty girl who'd meet me halfway. But I was a grown-up now, suspicious of emotionalism and far less prone to agonising over the implications of a quiet sex life. What I felt for Anne wasn't an adolescent reflex or a flush of gratitude. It had seeped into me, taken me over and now it was so real, so deep, that I half-wished I'd saved myself for her.

There was also a physical dimension to my anxiety. Greed and nerves had caused me to eat too much, too quickly. The slab of sirloin I'd bolted felt as if it had reconstituted and was now reproducing itself like some sci-fi monstrosity in my already overcrowded stomach. Needless to say, I'd also drunk too much, too quickly. I hadn't yet suffered brewer's droop but the militant pessimist inside me was whispering, 'There's always a first time ...'

And on top of all that, there was the spectre of first-night fumbles. But Anne took care of it. She took care of everything. She was very good. I'm not talking about virtuosity or lasciviousness. Pornography divides women into fuck machines – 'Yessss, right there. Now make me come, damn you!' – and fuck dolls – 'Do anything you want with me.' Anne was eager all right but the onset of pleasure didn't unhinge her. She made it easy but not run-of-the-mill. Definitely not run-of-the-mill.

In the morning I brought her breakfast in bed. In those days, she liked soft-boiled eggs, buttered toast, and sugar in her tea. When I took the tray away, she asked if I was coming back to bed.

Later, after she'd showered, she made a provocative entrance wrapped in a towel, sweeping damp tendrils off her forehead. When I sat up in bed to get a better look, she said, 'I guess this means we're serious?'

'I always was.'

'How serious is serious?'

I hesitated, not wanting to spook her.

'Got to think about it, eh?'

I was concentrating now, intent on saying the right thing. 'No, it's not that. I just don't want to get ahead of myself. I wouldn't want you to think I'm rushing things.'

That made her smile. 'You could hardly be accused of that.'

I shrugged. 'It was worth the wait.'

'Glad to hear it,' she said, 'but you still haven't answered the question.'

I went for broke. 'As serious as you want it to be. I won't be the one dragging their feet.'

A month later we went out to Vaucluse to break the news.

It was late autumn, still quite warm. Roger and Fiona Carew were doing what the middle-aged rich do in Sydney on a sunny Sunday afternoon: sit in the loggia with their sunglasses on and the collars of their Lacoste polo shirts turned up, eating seafood and pasta, watching the sea change colour, and wondering what sort of capital gain they'd make if they sold the place tomorrow. There was an empty bottle of chardonnay upside down in an ice-bucket and a half-empty one on the table, exactly midway between them. I was to witness this scene many times and came to realise that this was as good as it got for them, sitting in that sun-dappled loggia, working their way through some fine wine, exchanging the odd clipped, disconnected remark. Alcohol can be a dangerous ingredient in a decaying marriage but they used it like a seltzer to dilute the animosity which frothed inside them.

I always felt there was something phoney about Roger Carew. It was partly his appearance, the baked-on tan and immaculate head of hair, going silver at the temples right on cue. From a distance he looked like a patriarch in some glossy American soap opera but any casting director worth their salt would have baulked at the meanness in his washed-out blue eyes. My childhood reading had implanted the notion that privilege bestowed generosity and expansiveness of spirit. It didn't take long for sour, edgy Roger to knock that nonsense out of me.

Fiona was in her mid-forties. Being almost twenty years younger and smitten with her daughter, it didn't really occur to me then that she was a fine-looking, indeed desirable, woman. It was perhaps five years into our marriage before I got a sudden pang of lust from an old photograph of my mother-in-law. Inspecting her closely next time I saw her in the flesh, I realised – uneasily – that the essentials hadn't changed a great deal. Appearances aside, she was, in her own way, almost as dislikeable as her husband. She was undemonstratively fond of her children but kept most others at arm's length with her bored, distant smile and languid indifference.

Roger's eyes narrowed, as if he'd sensed straightaway that this wasn't a routine visit. Seizing my hand in a grip which I couldn't have broken without resorting to an elaborate and brutal manoeuvre, Anne announced that we had something to tell them.

Roger stared at Fiona. 'Is this what I think it is?'

Fiona ignored him, watching Anne with a calm half-smile. 'We're all ears, dear,' she said.

'Nick and I have got engaged.'

Roger's head began to vibrate. 'I knew it,' he barked, glaring at his wife. 'The minute she walked in here, I knew what was coming.' He turned back to Anne. 'When are you planning to tie the knot?'

'Not for at least a year,' said Anne. She squeezed my hand. 'We're not in any rush.'

White teeth gleamed mirthlessly in Roger's mahogany face. 'No need to panic just yet then.' He stood up. 'I suppose this calls for champagne.'

On his way inside, he kissed Anne and patted me on the shoulder as if I'd done something useful, like unblock a toilet. We sat down. Fiona lit a cigarette, half-heartedly fanning away the smoke. 'Well, congratulations, you two,' she said. 'What is it they say? Don't think of it as losing a daughter, think of it as gaining a son.' She laughed quietly. 'I must remember to point that out to Roger.'

I said, 'I'm not sure he'll see it that way.'

'Perhaps not,' she said. 'Anne's his little darling – always was, always will be.' She paused. 'I don't think he's been all that keen on any of your boyfriends.'

'He got on okay with Alan,' said Anne. 'Better than I did.'

'Oh yes, Alan. How could I forget him?' Fiona laughed her quiet laugh again. 'There you are, Nick – there's hope for you yet.'

But when it finally dawned on Roger that Anne was going to go through with it, even the lordly pats on the back and the desultory banter dried up. To the extent that his wife and children allowed him to get away with it, he'd simply act as if I wasn't there. Fiona didn't take it so hard. To her, it was just a vaguely unpleasant fact of life, like bad weather or mass starvation in Africa.

Their attitude worried me much more than it worried their daughter. More than once she urged me, 'I don't give a stuff what they think so why should you?' I hadn't yet grasped how secure she was, how free from self-doubt. I still believed, as young men do, that I was the warrior and she was my rose. I still thought our life together would be powered by my achievements.

The reception was held at her father's club, an antique but charmless place with an art collection celebrating British feats of arms and grandfather clocks ticking ominously in the corridors. As he would make a habit of doing at family gatherings, young Harry got falling-down drunk.

Late in the evening, I came across him at the bar. He had a slack grin and a film of perspiration on his forehead. It seemed a good time and place to ask him what he'd been playing at when he'd slipped me Anne's phone number under false pretences.

The grin took shape. 'I could tell you had the hots for her,' he said. 'Stood out like dog's balls. But if I hadn't given you a push, you wouldn't have done anything about it, would you?' I shrugged. He shook his head, seemingly mystified by the way some men could make such heavy weather of their dealings with women. 'I just wanted to see what would happen,' he said. 'I never thought you'd fucking get married.'

'I take it you don't approve?'

He rolled his head wearily. 'No offence, Nick, but I don't give a shit. It's not my life.'

'I just realised,' I said. 'You take after your mother.'

Harry stared at me as if I'd said something profound. 'You think so? Who do you reckon Annie takes after?'

'Neither of them.'

He winked at me. 'You'd have to hope so, wouldn't you? Don't go away, I'm just going for a slash.' He took a few steps, then turned back. 'You know why Rog doesn't like you, don't you?'

It was my party and Harry had a robust sense of humour. 'Because he's a cunt?'

He raised an urbane eyebrow. Maybe he wasn't as drunk as I thought he was. 'Apart from that.'

'Because he thinks I'm not good enough for her?'

This time he rolled his eyes. 'Jesus christ, Nick, that goes without saying.'

'Okay, you tell me.'

'Because,' he said, 'Annie's in love with you. Fuck knows why but she is.'

'Yeah, but . . .'

'He's jealous, okay? It's that simple.'

Not long after that, Harry went off to California to make his fortune. On his flying visits home, usually at Christmas, he'd throw money around while deflecting all attempts to find out where it had come from. Whatever I accused him of, from drug pushing to peddling his arse, he'd jovially go along with. Eventually, he confided that he was in the movie industry, on the financing side. It seemed no more or less likely that my scurrilous speculations.

Harry suited himself, whether that meant getting stoned before breakfast or showing up for Christmas dinner with some nasty little scrubber he'd picked up the previous night. He was full of filthy Hollywood gossip, such as the claim that a certain megastar got a buzz – that's a direct quote – from having a tube full of wasps shoved up his arse. 'It's another world over there,' he'd say. 'They're sick fucks, the lot of them.'

Back then, we were all entranced at the prospect of this golden boy taking Hollywood by storm. But it was all a front. Harry thought that if he played the part with enough conviction, image would become reality. I dare say it's easy to drift into that state of mind over there. In fact, he was just another dodgy remittance man hanging around LA in the hope that, one day, he'd happen to be in the right place at the right time. By his late twenties, he was quibbling over unexceptional restaurant bills. His coming down to earth coincided with a swift physical decline. Almost overnight, it seemed, he became a tubby little gent with a pink, puffy face and sad hair.

I used to leave the finances to Anne but every now and again – say, after I'd had to listen to a colleague whine about how hard it is to make ends meet on a teacher's salary – I enjoyed gloating over our latest bank statement. I assumed the $25,000 withdrawal was some sort of tax minimisation wheeze but when I asked, Anne said she'd lent the money to Harry. Now she was the financial wizard but I had to challenge her choice of words: to say she'd lent it implied that she expected to get it back and she knew as well as I did that there was no chance of that.

'I earned it,' she said coldly. 'I'll do what I like with it.'

Like any couple, we'd had our share of rows over money but that was the first time she'd ever played that card.

The slap-down was as resounding as it was out of character but I let it go. It's hard to defend the indefensible without resorting to overkill and I took it to mean that she privately doubted the wisdom of tossing Harry that much play money.

All the same, it wasn't a pleasant memory and it jerked me back to reality. As my pupils would say, that stuff was history. Meaning it didn't matter any more, it had no relevance to the here and now. It could be worse, I thought. I could be a history teacher.

CHAPTER 4

I rang home, going through the motions right up until the moment the cocoon crumbled. Anne took her time coming to the phone.

'It's me,' I said. 'Am I interrupting something?'

'I was in the garden.'

'Sorry. Bad timing.'

'That's okay. Where are you?'

'At work,' I said. 'Didn't you get enough exercise playing tennis?'

'God, yes. I just went to get something from the herb garden and spotted a few weeds. You know me – two hours later ...'

I thought I knew you, my dear. I thought I knew you like the back of my hand. 'It's about time you learned how to do nothing.'

'I know,' she said. 'I want to be a slob but I lack the willpower.'

'I was just checking in to see if I should pick up something for dinner.'

'It's all under control.'

'What are we having?'

'Lamb.'

'I thought you didn't feel like meat?'

'That was before three sets of tennis. How long are you going to be?'

'About an hour.'

'Okay.' Her tone grew cosy. 'I'm looking forward to a nice, quiet evening at home.'

'Yeah,' I said, 'me too.'

So she was all for a nice, quiet evening at home, was she? Just the two of us. She was compartmentalising, putting me in one box, J in another. I was the reliable stand-by, the home cooking, and let's face it, who wants haute cuisine every night? You'd never have anything to look forward to.

Was that so bad? She'd still come home to me. We'd still have nice, quiet evenings together, sinking into one another's company like old armchairs. All I had to do was turn a blind eye.

Oh, it was seductive all right, the notion that the way out of this dilemma was via the path of least resistance. As long as I did nothing, everything would be all right. How often in history have leaders persuaded themselves that inaction was the soundest policy? But if you choose to do nothing, you must have the stoicism to live with the consequences and I feared my imagination too much for that.

I went to the college gym and whirred away on a bike till the sweat fell off me in fat, warm drops. The exercise high was short-lived. By the time I got out of the shower, I felt lumpy and lifeless again and pressure was rebuilding behind my eyes.

Anne was still in the garden when I got home. I stood at the French windows watching her apply manure to a flowerbed. She wore red gumboots and a baseball cap and there was a graze of dirt on her cheek. She worked steadily, absorbed in the task. That was her way: whether she was writing a public relations strategy for a billion-dollar corporation or spreading dung, her concentration was absolute.

It's interesting to observe people engaged in a solitary activity, unaware that they're being watched. I don't mean through a telescope trained on their bedroom although I suppose that has its own rewards. They tend to look younger. Perhaps our facial muscles relax when we're not putting on a public face. Anne's face was sweetly solemn and bore no evidence of a troubled mind.

When I tapped on the window, she gathered up her tools and put them in the shed. I opened the French windows as she stepped out of her gumboots.

'I decided to keep at it till you got home,' she said. As she came inside, she kissed me then stepped back, frowning. 'You okay?'

I nodded.

'I'm going to have a shower,' she said. 'Could you turn the oven on?'

'Anything else I can do?'

She smiled. 'Yes, cheer up.'

When her eyes narrowed, I realised I hadn't returned the smile. I forced one. It felt taut, pasted on, but it seemed to satisfy her. As she walked away, I put my hand in my pocket and rolled the note between my fingers like a bus ticket.

A little later, she crossed the corridor in her white towelling robe. I flashed back to her in the Blue Mountains, coming into the bedroom wrapped in a towel, pushing damp hair off her forehead, saying, 'I guess this means we're serious?' I made it to the spare bathroom in time, not that it mattered. I'd hardly eaten anything all day so a string of saliva was all there was to show for the convulsions over the toilet bowl. In the mirror I saw that my cheeks were wet. Dry retching can do that. It can make your eyes water.

I didn't have high expectations but the face in the mirror still shocked me. No wonder Anne had asked if I was okay. Wanting to stay out of sight until I'd got some colour back, I called out to her, offering to light a fire. She called back, 'Fine, but first things first: I'll have a G and T, thanks.'

My hand shook as I poured the gin. Anne was waiting for me in the kitchen with a wedge of lemon. 'Nick, are you sure you're okay?' she asked, her face tightening. 'You're so pale.'

My mouth started to quiver and I ducked behind the fridge door before my face wobbled out of control. It was a fine time to be reminded that only my mother cared about me as much as she did. When you're forty-three, though, your mother can't break your heart.

'It's this bloody cold,' I said thickly.

'Poor old thing. Maybe you should go to bed?'

'I'll be right once I get a couple of glasses of wine into me.'

When I pulled my head out of the fridge, she was carefully placing sprigs of rosemary on the leg of lamb. I left her drink on the bench and went to get firewood.

As I was filling the wood-basket, it occurred to me that there was a third way of approaching it, a compromise between tackling her head-on and looking the other way: I could introduce the subject of adultery in the context of an imaginary third party. That way, I could study her reaction and relieve some of the tension that was pounding my insides to jelly, while leaving both of us some room to manoeuvre.

We were sitting in front of the fire. Anne was on the sofa, stockinged feet tucked under her, speed-reading *The Economist*. I sat opposite, literally on the edge of my seat.

Heart-in-mouth, I ventured, 'You wouldn't believe what happened at school this afternoon.'

She looked up, registering cautious interest. My job had not, hitherto, been a mother-lode of sensation.

'Have I ever mentioned Keith Jennings, teaches chemistry?'

Anne shook her head. 'Doesn't ring a bell.' It was a safe enough fabrication; I rarely talked about work and she rarely asked.

'He's one of those clingy people, you know – if you're halfway civil to them, they treat you like a long-lost friend.'

'Sounds like a Labrador.'

'Well, he doesn't leave fur all over the place ...'

'What about lick his balls in public?'

It hadn't gone anything like this when I'd rehearsed it in my head. 'Not that I've noticed but who knows what goes on in those laboratories? Anyway, he poked his head into my office, wanting to have a word. Well, talk about the understatement of the year – he sat down and poured his heart out. The poor bastard's just found out his wife's having an affair.'

Anne put the magazine aside and adjusted her position. 'How did he find out?' Smooth as you like.

'Someone saw his wife smooching a guy in a bar when she was meant to be at her Italian cooking class,' I said. 'Jennings checked with the people who run the course – turned out they'd never set eyes on her.'

Her expression didn't change but amusement stirred in her eyes. 'Didn't he get suspicious when she kept dishing up macaroni cheese?'

Jesus christ, I thought, she thinks it's a joke. 'I suppose it is rather comical,' I said, 'but Jennings is having trouble seeing the funny side of it.'

'The fall-guy always does.'

'Your point being?'

'My darling, aren't you being ever so slightly pompous? I believe you've been known to get a chuckle out of other people's misfortunes.'

'The guy's a mess,' I said doggedly. 'He doesn't know what to do: forgive her, kick her out or pretend it never happened.'

'She might decide for him.'

'How do you mean?'

'He might get a Dear Keith e-mail. Apparently, it's the fashionable way to dump someone.'

I stared at her. She shrugged, raising her eyebrows. It seemed pretty clear that adultery wasn't a subject she could take too seriously.

'So what would you do if you were in his shoes? Have it out with her?'

She sighed as if I'd asked her to do something tedious. 'Well, that depends,' she said eventually. 'I mean, if it's just a fling and things are okay otherwise, you could argue why rock the boat? They might be able to discuss it like adults then put it behind them, but you wouldn't bet on it. On the other hand, if he doesn't raise it, how's he going to know whether it's serious or not?'

There was that word again. I nodded, still staring at her, thinking, when did you start making that distinction?

I think at that moment she realised I knew. Her eyes slid away and her face got very still. It was a pivotal moment, like the one in our phone conversation all those years ago when I could have killed off the relationship with a single word. But this time, there was no moment of clarity, no conscious decision. I've often wondered since whether I would have acted differently if she'd been less flippant, if she'd shown an ounce of sympathy for my stricken doppelganger.

I took the note out of my pocket, unfolded it and held it up for her to see. 'How about this, Anne?' I said. 'Would you call this serious?'

I'd covered a lot of territory since I'd found the note. I'd thought about the past and the future; I'd thought about truth and consequences. I hadn't got around to anticipating Anne's instant, unguarded reaction.

She wailed, 'Nooooo!' and *tried to snatch the note out of my hand.*

What was she going to do with it? Throw it in the fire and insist that it wasn't a billet doux congratulating her on being hot stuff in the sack, it was something else altogether? Something entirely innocent, ho-hum even? It was … a shopping list.

And when I begged to differ, what then? Was she going to tell me that I was hallucinating? Or that I couldn't *read*?

I whipped the note out of her reach. She stood over me, wild-eyed and blushing furiously. For a moment I thought she was going to wrestle me for it. Then she slowly backed away and lowered herself onto the sofa. She was breathing hard through the nose, almost snorting, and her cheeks were ablaze.

'Where did you get that?' she said huskily, pressing her palms to her cheeks.

'Does it really matter?'

She nodded, starting to look a little dazed. 'I'd like to know.'

I told her. She stared at me, frozen-faced, for a few seconds. Then she laughed. It was one of those abrupt, almost involuntary and hurriedly suppressed laughs that burst out when you know it's no laughing matter but you just can't help yourself. I was too taken aback to be outraged.

She clamped a hand over her mouth. In other circumstances, I would have found this childish gesture endearing. I waited for her to take the hand away and say something.

'Are you serious?'

I felt like going for her then. I felt like wiping the infuriating expression – arched eyebrows, half-formed quizzical grin – off her face. I didn't, of course; I just sat there, stony-faced.

'How ridiculous,' she said, in a brittle voice. 'How ... banal. Here I was thinking you must've hired a private detective or something.'

'Why the fuck would I do that? I trusted you.'

'I'm so sorry, Nick.'

She served it up with downcast eyes and a contrite expression but I wasn't that soft a touch. 'Yeah, I'm sure you are – sorry you got caught. Okay, let's hear it.'

She hesitated. 'What do you want to know?'

I stared at her. 'Oh, you know, what his star-sign is, what brand of aftershave he uses ...'

She opted for the near-empty tube of toothpaste strategy, making me squeeze the information out in dribs and drabs. 'His name's Jason.'

'Jason who?'

'Swann.'

'Who is he?'

'A client. I mean, he works for one of my clients.'

'And how many times have you fucked him?'

She blinked and her mouth shrank into a prim shape, as if she was about to complain that there was no need to be so crude. 'Only once.'

'Last night?'

Furrows of uncertainty appeared on her forehead. 'I didn't see him last night.'

'Is that the truth?'

'Yes.'

My heart was thumping now. I was on the verge of boiling over. 'The reason I ask,' I said with a shake in my voice, 'is that someone had been there before me last night. If it wasn't him, who was it?'

Anne turned away, averting eyes awash with guilt. Before I knew what I was doing, I was out of my chair, swinging wildly, like someone trying to swat a mosquito in the dark. My aim and timing were off and my open hand skidded off her cheekbone. It would have come as a shock, nonetheless. She would have assumed that flailing verbal violence was as far as I'd go.

She shrieked and fell sideways onto the sofa. The follow-up swipe was even further astray, catching her on the shoulder. She brought her knees up and wrapped her arms around her head, as victims do. I crouched over her, right arm drawn back, screaming, 'You fucking bitch, I should fucking kill you, I should smash your fucking head in!'

But the sight of her rolled into a foetal ball, braced for a beating, shamed me out of going on with it. I let my hand fall and straightened up, muttering, 'Jesus, you'll fucking pay for this.'

She sat up, rubbing her cheek and eyeing me warily. 'That's enough, Nick,' she said in a level voice. 'I don't altogether blame you but that's enough. Don't hit me again.'

'Fuck you,' I said without conviction, slumping back into the chair. 'You're in no position to tell me what to do.'

'Assault is assault, Nick, no matter what. Promise me you won't do it again.'

Now it was me who had to look away. I'd done what I'd vowed not to do. No, it was worse than that: I'd rampaged from the moral high ground all the way down to the back alley. The rage receded, replaced by a wave of self-pity. Without meeting her eye, I said, 'Why did you do it?'

She went slowly, feeling her way. 'Before you found that note, did it ever cross your mind that there might be something wrong?'

I looked at her then, thinking, here it comes; here comes the spin.

'Well, did it?'

'No,' I said. 'Which just goes to show what a stupid bastard I am.'

'No you're not,' she said. 'There isn't anything wrong with our relationship. This has got nothing to do with you and me. Do you understand what I'm saying?'

'No.'

'It's about me, Nick, it's not about us. My feelings about us haven't changed.'

'Oh, I see,' I said. 'So we're just going to carry on as if this never happened?'

She looked me straight in the eye. 'I know it's not that easy but I hope we can – carry on. I really do.'

'Call me old-fashioned but I always thought the basis of a successful marriage was that you didn't go around jumping into bed with other people.' The words straggled out, labouring under the weight of their bitterness.

'That's an ideal, Nick. Sometimes ideals are hard to live up to.'

'Speak for yourself.'

'I am.'

'What are you trying to say? That it was unreasonable of me to expect you to be faithful?'

'No, I'm not saying that.' She paused. 'Have you ever been unfaithful?'

'Is that the best you can do?' I sneered. 'You know bloody well I haven't.'

She was quite composed now. The rancour trickled off her like raindrops off an oilskin. 'Have you ever come close?'

'You'll find this difficult to believe, but no, I haven't even come close.'

'Have you ever thought about it?'

'Jesus fucking christ,' I yelled, 'why bring me into it? All I did was go looking for a fucking handkerchief.'

'I'm not trying to wriggle out of it,' she said, shaking her head. 'I'm just trying to explain something. Last question, I promise: do you ever find other women desirable?'

'Maybe I do,' I said, defensive in spite of myself, 'but there's a bloody big difference between thinking about it and doing it.'

'Of course there is,' she said soothingly. 'And there's also a big difference between you and me here: you don't have attractive women coming onto you at work.'

I said, 'I don't know what the hell you're talking about.' Which wasn't quite true.

'I spend three-quarters of my working life dealing with men. Quite a few of them flirt; some go further . . .'

'I think we've established that.'

'So if you were in my position, don't you think you might've been tempted once or twice?'

'Well, I suppose it's one way to keep the clients happy.'

That was better. Her head snapped up. I was enjoying the wounded look in her eyes and didn't see the counter-punch coming.

'As a matter of fact, it's not just clients and it's not just at work. All sorts of men try it on – even friends of yours.'

I felt my face go slack. 'What?'

'I'm not making this up, Nick. You don't see it because you're not like that but some men are always on the prowl. The fact that a woman's in a relationship or married – even to a friend of theirs – doesn't mean a thing.'

I was feeling nauseous again. 'Who?' I croaked.

She stood up. 'Can I make a suggestion: why don't you sleep on it? Tomorrow I'll tell you everything – if that's what you want.'

'Is that a warning? Is it so bad you don't think I'll be able to handle it?'

'I'm just worried that it'll make it more painful.' Her studied sincerity hung in the air, like fly-spray. 'And harder for you to forgive me.'

'How bad is it, Anne?'

Instead of answering the question, she came over and carefully laid a hand on my shoulder. 'I don't want to lose you, Nick.'

Perhaps she expected me to soften then – to reach out to her, tell her that it was okay, we'd work it out, maybe even join hands and shed some healing tears together.

'You should've thought of that before you opened your legs,' I said.

She took it without flinching. 'On that note, I think I'll go to bed.'

Numbness set in as I watched the fire burn down. I stirred up the embers and threw in the note. It went black around the edges, then disappeared in a ripple of flame.

When I eventually made a move, it resembled a geriatric groping his way to the toilet at four in the morning. Anne had her eyes closed and the covers pulled up her to chin but late-night jazz seeped from the bedside clock radio.

I asked, 'What are the sleeping arrangements?' She opened her eyes but otherwise gave no indication that she understood the question. 'I don't see why I should have to sleep in the spare room.'

'You want me to?'

'Well, one of us has to.'

'Couldn't you bear to sleep in the same bed as me?' She sounded genuinely curious.

'You set the precedent,' I said. 'I've been banished to the spare room for a hell of a lot less than infidelity.'

'And now the boot's on the other foot, you're going to make the most of it, right?' Anne threw back the covers, swung her legs off the bed and stood up in one smooth, gymnastic movement. She was naked. She put her hands on her hips, casually displaying her body. 'Throw me my bathrobe?'

It was on a hook on the back of the door. I tossed it to her. 'Since when did you sleep in the nude?'

She raised her eyebrows as if the question was impertinent. 'Since I got hot sitting in front of the fire. Is that okay?' She inched past me, taking exaggerated care to avoid the slightest contact, and lobbed an ironic 'Sleep tight' from the doorway.

'As if,' I replied. The fatuous catch-phrase seemed an appropriate last word.

Fatuous, perhaps, but prescient. During the night I got up for a glass of water. The door to the spare room was half-open. Anne was sleeping for both of us, breathing easily, her face as settled as if she was sitting for a portrait. And she'd changed her mind about sleeping in the nude.

I dozed in till mid-morning. I dreamed that Anne and I were at a party in a mansion of many rooms. We became separated. I went looking for her but she was nowhere to be found. I grew frantic, butting in on conversations and canoodles, demanding information. A pretty boy sniggered that he'd tell me where to find her if I made it worth his while but when I shoved him against the wall, he whimpered that he was only teasing. At the end of a long corridor, a fat thug stood guard in front of closed double doors. He leered when I asked if

Anne was in there. I heard her giddy laugh and suddenly there was a pistol in my hand. I ordered the thug to stand aside. He stayed put, his bloated jowls jiggling with amusement. I aimed at his chest and pulled the trigger. The bullet floated from the barrel and bounced at his feet. I woke up.

Anne was in the kitchen, skimming a Sunday paper. We exchanged guarded 'hellos'. I told her, 'Ready when you are.'

She folded the paper and went straight into it, making me wonder if she'd got up early to jot down a few bullet points. 'Last night you asked me how bad it was. Well, that's for you to decide but I want to make the point that it only happened once. I did meet a man the other night but nothing happened.'

The scowl was back on my face. It felt like it had never gone away. 'When you said you'd tell me everything, I assumed that meant the truth ...'

'That is the truth.'

I searched her face for evidence of deceit. She held my stare patiently. 'Well,' I said ungraciously, 'I feel better already.'

CHAPTER 5

Jason Swann was a marketing executive but was more rounded and less puffed-up than a lot of the men Anne dealt with. She'd prepared a product-launch campaign for him which meant thrice-daily phone conversations, twice-weekly meetings and regular working lunches. That level of contact inevitably puts life outside work on the agenda. Jason was freshly but irrevocably separated: he and his New Zealand wife had come to a fork in the road over whether to have kids and which side of the Tasman to live. Now he was easing his way back into the single life.

'How old is he?'

She hesitated. 'Younger than me.'

'That wasn't what I asked.'

'Thirty-four.'

Anne enjoyed being able to talk to someone who understood what running a business was all about. She couldn't do it at home – I gave up feigning interest long ago. Like, I suspect, a lot of people who have never worked in business and take for granted their moral and intellectual superiority to those who do, the thought of being at the mercy of those mysterious market forces terrified me. Sensible people play safe: they put their money in the bank and don't expose themselves to continual, beady-eyed assessment. They take the steady job and the guaranteed salary and let someone else worry about where the money's coming from. I remember the goose-pimpling chill I felt when Anne announced that she was chucking in what seemed to me a handsomely-paid job with a big PR firm to go it alone. Where I saw security, she saw exploitation; where I saw obstacles, she saw challenges. I argued that it would end in tears and a millstone of debt; she countered by asking how long I wanted to remain beholden to her parents. We know who was right and who was wrong.

When the campaign wrapped up, Jason clutched her hand and urged her to stay in touch. He'd fallen for her – no great surprise there. What was a surprise was how good it made her feel. It wasn't that she was unhappy or restless but she did have that vaguely depressing sense of being stuck in a routine – the days and weeks seemed to roll by like newspapers off the press, carbon copies of each other. Nothing a little harmless excitement couldn't fix. And that was the thing: Jason was tame. She could almost picture him squatting on his haunches, tongue hanging out, panting away, watching her every move with adoring eyes. All that was missing was a tail to wag ...

They started meeting for a drink after work. Pecks on the cheek gave way to lingering hugs. Each time they got together, Jason put a little more work into his pats and squeezes. All part of the game.

They had this running gag over the snail's pace renovation of his apartment. Everything that could go wrong had gone wrong; every tradesman atrocity story she'd ever heard, he could go one better. But all bad things come to an end and he invited her over to see what the angst had been in aid of.

She rationalised that it was a perfectly natural thing to do – she felt like she'd lived through the bloody renovation herself. She'd go along, have a glass of wine, and see if there was more to Jason than met the eye. She suspected not: her money was on the apartment having everything except taste. If she'd been honest with herself, she would have acknowledged that she was going because she couldn't resist seeing what would happen. It was like reading a whodunit: once you reach a certain point, you've got to keep going just to see how it ends.

Both Jason and his apartment turned out to be more sophisticated than she'd anticipated. He played it cool – got her a drink, showed her around, talked her though the design concept, all the while keeping a respectful distance. After half an hour she was beginning to feel short-changed, like, I waded through four hundred pages for *this*?

They were in the kitchen. Why the kitchen? she wondered as he took the glass out of her hand. Why do these things always happen in the kitchen? Jason now had the constipated expression of a perfect gentleman in the grip of extreme carnal desire. She thought of the old joke – 'this thing's bigger than both of us' – and would've giggled if he hadn't put his mouth on hers. She let him do all the work, still wanting to see where it would lead, still thinking she could hit the off-button at any time.

She stopped there. I said, 'And?'

'I made my second mistake,' she said flatly. 'I let it go too far.'

'That goes without saying, doesn't it?'

'What I mean is, I wasn't swept away. This is going to sound ridiculous but I let it get to a point where I was too embarrassed to stop it.'

'I'm not sure ridiculous is the term you want,' I said. 'Try completely fucking unbelievable.'

That drew an unruffled nod, Madam Chair politely ignoring another pea-brained outburst from the floor. 'It was my fault. I knew where he was coming from and I played along with it, most of all by going to his apartment. And when it came to the crunch, I didn't have the guts to tell him it was just a game and this is where it ends. So I took the coward's way out.'

They had what she described as 'brisk, unmemorable intercourse'. Jason, that hopeless romantic, must have put the note in her pocket while she was in the bathroom. As he saw her out, she turned away from his kiss. She told him the whole thing had been a mistake and she couldn't see him again.

'How did he take it?'

'Oh, he thought it was just an attack of the guilts and I'd soon get over it. He knows better now.'

'Why?'

'I don't take his calls, I don't reply to his e-mails . . . in fact, I don't read his e-mails. And I won't be renewing the contract when it runs out next month.'

'Why not?'

She shrugged. 'I'm compromised.'

'An expensive mistake.'

'Yes, well, I'll just have to go out and find some new business, won't I?'

Honest account or damage control? Silly woman or calculating cheat? I really couldn't tell.

We moved on to Friday night. She'd just sat down to dinner with some clients when she noticed the man at the next table staring at her. Which was kind of flattering because he was Hollywood handsome and his companion barely into her twenties. All through the meal, she could feel his gaze on her face, like an interrogation lamp. She didn't want to play up to it but it's impossible to resist the odd peek when you know someone's got his eye on you.

She went to the toilet. When she came out, Mr Handsome was smoking a cigarette in the corridor. He dropped the cigarette, stepped on it and told her, 'You're the most desirable woman I've seen for a long time and I see a lot of desirable women.' For some reason, it didn't sound preposterous.

Anne couldn't believe it was happening to her. She said the first thing that popped into her head: 'What about your date?'

He made a face and put up his hands. 'She's not a woman, she's a girl. And I'm not on a date – any more than you are. Once we've done our duty, perhaps we could have a drink?'

Anne showed him her wedding ring. 'You mean you didn't notice? I find that hard to believe.'

Mr Handsome's lopsided, collusive grin revealed perfect teeth. He was almost too good to be true. 'I can never remember which is the wedding ring finger.'

'It's really not that hard,' she said, returning the grin because she couldn't help it. 'I'll pass on the drink but thanks anyway . . .'

He offered her a card. 'The invitation stands.'

She took it, figuring it was the simplest way of extricating herself. 'So does my response,' she said, and went back into the restaurant.

When Mr Handsome returned to his table, Anne studiously avoided his eye. He left soon afterwards. Anne tore up the card without even glancing at it.

'I don't get it,' I said. 'So what got you in such a lather?'

'That was it. It was pure fantasy.'

'Sounds more like lust at first sight.'

She shook her head. 'No, I'll tell you what it was like. It was like going to the movies: there's some hunk up there on the screen and you think, god, isn't he gorgeous, but you're reacting to a fantasy figure, not a real person.'

'Except he was a real person.'

'That's why I walked away. Reality would've spoilt it.'

She had an answer for everything. 'Call it whatever you want,' I grumbled, 'but there's something going on with you. I mean, that's twice in a week.'

'No, Nick, it's once in fifteen years. In this day and age, I think most people would settle for that.' She paused. 'I know I would.'

CHAPTER 6

'I know I would.'

Yes, if Anne had been in my shoes, it would have been a breeze. I mean, she was a reasonable person and any reasonable person would have accepted her argument. Which went roughly as follows: okay, I made a mistake but let's put it in perspective. One lapse, one loss of control, in a decade and a half – how does that begin to stack up against what we've been through and what we've got? Besides, it's not as if it meant anything to me. On the contrary, an embarrassment, that's what it was; a silly self-indulgence that left me feeling cheap and weak, like the easiest pick-up in the bar. (Yes, I've suffered too, I have my cross to bear.) Is that worth splitting up over?

And Anne was a realist. The sub-text went roughly as follows: come on, Nick, look at me – what do you see? A successful, attractive woman of the world – the real world, that is, as opposed to your boys-only ivory tower. In my world, there are many men, some of whom make no secret of their desire. Do I encourage them? Do I respond? Once. Once in fifteen years. Frankly, Nick, if I were you, I'd be counting my blessings.

So what was a cuckold to do? Forgive and forget or burn down the house over a single, half-hearted indiscretion? Assuming Anne had told the truth, of course. That was where I had to make a leap of faith. Before I could eat shit, otherwise known as forgive and forget, I had to accept that it was an aberration. Once I got there, I could believe in anything, even happily ever after.

I haven't said much about love but I loved Anne. I'm not a believer; it just doesn't come naturally to me. Even now, when no-one could blame me for shopping around for a saviour or a shining path, I don't really believe in anything. But I believed in her and I believed in us. What I'd told her was true: since that day Harry introduced us on the college drive, I hadn't been with another woman, hadn't pursued another woman, hadn't seriously thought about another woman. Don't get me wrong – I'm no saint. I was as furtively occupied with other women as the next married man; I too was an early-morning fantasist with an angry bladder and a rubbery prong. But that's all. When you love someone, sex with anyone else should be all in the mind.

Pornography has two ideas, if you can call them that. One is that all women, whether they recognise it or not, just want to get fucked, the more the merrier. Deep down, not even bikies really believe that. The other is that sex has nothing to do with love. This is no longer a radical proposition. I don't believe it but I'm pretty sure I'm in the minority.

So I forgave her. In the end, she made it easy for me. When we turned the page and talked about the future, her gaze never wavered, her promises didn't peter out in a flurry of airy words and disconnected gestures, and there was no veil of cynicism at the back of her eyes. And when I asked her if she loved me, she smiled glowingly and touched my face and asked, 'Haven't you listened to a word I've said?'

We sealed it over a robust lunch – fish, meat, cheese, pudding; white wine, red wine, dessert wine, Armagnac – at a regular haunt in Paddington. The mood was upbeat – nothing generates optimism like a close shave – but I still had to ask about my lecherous friends.

'Are you planning to raise it with them?'

'I might.'

She provided a couple of names, triggering a flush of irrational, retrospective relief. Not that these guys were deformed or anything but they were dull. Jesus, were they dull.

'It wasn't direct,' she said. 'They left themselves wiggle room if I took offence or you turned up breathing fire. You know the sort of thing: "She didn't think I was serious, did she? It was just a bit of fun, for god's sake."'

'But you knew it wasn't?'

'We both knew it wasn't.'

'So what did you do?'

'Ignored it; carried on as if it hadn't happened.'

'And they got the message?'

'Well, they didn't pursue it.'

'It just goes to show,' I said. 'Of all of my so-called mates, the one I would've put money on is . . .'

'Jock? Oh, don't worry, you would've collected on that bet. Jock was the exception – he came right out with it.' She swirled the dessert wine, holding it up to the light. '"I'd love to get you into bed," I think were his exact words.'

'Not much wiggle room there.' I hadn't had a best friend since I was sixteen but of the current crop of acquaintances, Jock came as close as any. 'To which you replied?'

'I said, "Well, I suspect Nick might have a problem with that."' She watched me smoulder. 'It's the nature of the beast, Nick. Everyone knows what Jock's like – well, everyone except Debbie.'

'The long-suffering spouse – always the last to know.'

Anne leaned forward, resting her chin on the heel of her hand. 'Is that a general observation or are you lumping yourself in with Debbie – and, by implication, me in with Jock?'

'A general observation. Very general.'

She smiled faintly. 'As I said, everyone knows what Jock's like. You'd think his mates would be pretty wary of him by now. I mean, I obviously wasn't the first and won't be the last.'

You've got to take your hat off to her, don't you? The way she could turn things around. You can see what I was up against.

'So it's his mates' fault for not hauling him into line?'

'To an extent. By the way, I'm not including you in that, Nick – you're different, you're a romantic. But the rest of them – they don't have Jock's nerve but they think pretty much the same as him.'

'And what exactly does Jock think?'

'That he's irresistible.' She paused. 'And that all women are open to persuasion.'

She had a point: deep-down, I'd always known that Jock was a pornographer. 'Well, perhaps it's time someone did have him on.'

'You know what he'll say, don't you?'

'What?'

'That he doesn't remember, he must've been pissed.'

'Was he?'

'I can never really tell with Jock.'

'When it happened, were you thinking, he won't remember this tomorrow?'

She didn't have to think about it. 'No.'

'So let's say he did remember it: he must have wondered why you didn't tell me.'

'I didn't see any point.' She held my stare. 'If I'd thought for one minute that he'd do it again or if he had done it again, I would've told you. Same goes for the others. But you know what would've happened then: you would've had a go at Jock, he would've denied it, Debbie would've got in on the act convinced that it was really the other way around – I'd tried to get Jock into bed ... Next thing, people are either not speaking to each other or saying things which won't be forgotten in a hurry.'

'Well,' I said, forcing a smile, 'I guess everyone deserves a second chance.'

Back at home, Anne announced she was going to have a lie-down. She gave me a long look, full of sleepy irony. 'I don't have to use the spare room, do I?' When I went into the bedroom a few minutes later, she asked, 'What kept you?'

Afterwards, she murmured, 'Thank you, darling.'

'What for?' I said. 'You did most of the work.'

'For being strong enough to forgive me.'

We lay face-to-face, our moist and matted groins pressed together. Eventually, she rolled onto her back. I propped myself up on an elbow to brush the hair away from her face. I kissed her cheek and told her that I loved her. She was already asleep.

You know what's truly terrifying? The way life can change cataclysmically, turn upside down, in a day, an hour, in the time it takes to get a handkerchief.

The other day in a bookshop, I picked up a biography of Keith Moon. Remember him? The drummer in The Who, the original hotel room vandal, a maniac even by rock'n'roll standards. I must have spent five minutes staring at one particular photo: Keith sitting at a table with a mild, slightly detached expression, as if he's bored but doesn't want to make a song and dance about it. He might have been completely off his face but he doesn't look it. He looks okay. He looks as if he's got a grip on things. The caption says, here's Keith and his bird at such-and-such a do and – and this is the point, in case you're wondering – 'within twenty-four hours he was dead'.

When we're thirty-two, we take tomorrow for granted, just as when we're secure, we can't imagine things coming unstuck. But it's a thinner line than we think and nothing lasts forever.

CHAPTER 7

So domestic bliss returned to the Souter household. Anne sold her company to a US-based multinational and worked out a two-year management contract. I gave up teaching and wrote a novel about an apparently rock-solid marriage jeopardised by the husband's infidelity, switching the roles to throw nosey journalists off the scent. Blow me down if it wasn't a runaway bestseller, translated into thirty-eight languages including French and, by all accounts, those Frogs know a thing or two about adultery. We spread our wings, went boho in Greenwich Village and did the Tuscan villa thing. We paddled up the Orinoco and crossed the Mongolian steppes on horseback. After many adventures and some enlightenment, we settled down in a beachfront shack – well, that's what we liked to call it, anyway – on an unspoilt Pacific island and lived happily ever after.

Actually, it wasn't quite like that. Anne didn't sell the business and I didn't quit teaching or write a bestseller. And we didn't live happily ever after.

We didn't reinvent ourselves either although we made a few changes. Anne cut back her hours and we expanded our culinary horizons via celebrity chef cookbooks and cross-town shopping expeditions to ugly suburbs, ethnic strongholds where we queued behind fellow foodies in disorderly shops with bleached tourist posters wilting on the walls.

We communicated more if not better, making a point of talking to each other even when we had nothing much to say and there was a Clint Eastwood movie on TV. I made sure I didn't moan about work. It's a form of therapy, I suppose: we get home tired and churned-up with frustration and just have to let off steam – bleat about how hard we work, how lazy and/or incompetent our colleagues are, how everyone takes advantage of our good nature, what an ignorant arsehole the boss is, how we'd do a much better job if we ran the show ... All very well for us but not a pretty sight or sound for the person we go home to.

I used to do a lot of it. Teachers of a certain age are prone to self-pity, they just can't help themselves. Some may even be addicted to it. Anne would listen, not saying much, chewing away fatalistically, like a cow on a hillock watching the flood-waters rise. But it got to her in the end. I hadn't noticed the warning signs so I was shocked when she suddenly started yelling: if it's such a pain, don't do it. Do something else, stay in bed all day if you want to, but for christ's sake, stop digging yourself into this hole. It's your fucking life, take control of it.

Anne didn't moan about work. In fact, she could talk about it for hours without a furrow appearing on her forehead. Some of it I didn't mind – she could talk all she liked about new clients, fat retainers, success fees. I enjoyed hearing the busy rustle of money coming in the door.

The rest of it didn't do much for me, though. When she got onto strategies and outcomes and spin and perception or became starry-eyed over plutocrats and media demagogues, she lost her audience. I was irritated by her complacency and her shiny-faced enthusiasm for what was, at bottom, a tawdry occupation – professional bullshit-artistry. Take the money by all means, I'd think, but please, keep your distance. Show a little cynicism.

We even put children back on the agenda, albeit with the diffidence of a steeplechaser approaching a jump where he'd previously come a cropper. Having kids had always been just around the corner. Let's just get through the exam period or knock twenty grand off the mortgage or do up the kitchen; let's just take that European holiday we've been promising ourselves. Let's just give ourselves some breathing space, then we can sit down and talk about it. I mean, really talk about it: names, godparents, circumcision – the pros and cons.

We never got there. I left it to Anne to carry the weight but she couldn't do it on her own. At the end of the day, I'd tell her, it had to be her decision. No skin off my nose; I just had to keep pumping those little wrigglers up the pipe till one of them made contact. I wouldn't have to change my life, feel like shit, watch my body turn into a beanbag.

Then our friends started having families. For couples contemplating parenthood, exposure to other people's tots can be aversion therapy at its most basic. You enter a medieval world of bedlam, tyranny, squalor and martyrdom. You leave purged of the notion that happiness is other people, even those you create.

At least I did. Eventually, and with a lofty disinterest at odds with her fixed expression, Anne would raise it again. 'Thought any more about kids lately?'

I'd frown and blink, take a slow sip and swallow. 'Can't say I have,' I'd stall. 'How about you?'

'Not especially but ...' – and here there'd be a casual shrug – '...well, you know, the old biological clock's ticking.'

By now I'd have remembered my lines: it's got to be your decision, darling; life turned upside down, morning sickness, stretch marks, blah, blah, blah.

I came to believe, perhaps self-servingly, that it was just talk. Anne had too much to lose – too much time, too much freedom, too much career. Too much of her *prime*.

But every once in a while, during moments of ecstatic or tender interaction with Rosie's children, I could see her wondering if it was too late to override what had been decided by default.

My cold dried up leaving me with one of those maddening tickles in the throat which you hardly notice during the day, as long as you don't talk too much. The torment begins when the lights go out and you're horizontal. You feel a faint, pleasantly ticklish buzz at the back of your throat. It gradually intensifies. At some stage, it's going to trigger a cough, a gentle uh huh or two, nothing that should disturb your twitching, snuffling bedmate. Suddenly the cough arrives, like an anally punctual guest – here I am, ready or not. It settles in, kicks off its shoes, makes itself right at home. Your wife stirs; she sighs and re-positions herself with the hint of a flounce. Regretful as you are, there's nothing you can do about it. The cough is now relentless and jarring, like the bark of a home-alone dog with one thought in its mutty little head: if it stops barking, no-one will come. Ever.

And then the cough simply takes possession of you. You are no longer in control of yourself. You're coughing so hard that your head twangs like a speedball worked by a blur-fisted maestro. You thrash around the bed; a deaf person observing you would assume you're having an epileptic fit. In the fleeting moments of respite, you wonder if this is what it's like being in the wrong place at the wrong time when nature goes on the rampage, for instance when a freak wave explodes onto the deck or a twister howls through a one-horse town. You feel like flotsam and jetsam.

Everything comes to end, even these fiendish fucking coughs. You lie there panting, sniffing, watery-eyed. You might curse but with no great conviction because what you feel above all else is gratitude. You're actually grateful to that bug or virus or microbe for calling off the cough, for giving you a break. Only for the time being though, because it's not over: you know it, the bug knows it, and your wife certainly knows it. So you lie there, waiting for the inevitable snarled query: when are you going to get that fucking cough seen to? It's a rhetorical question, of course. There is only one answer: tomorrow.

My doctor was a chummy little Englishman with a pile of glossy black hair. Sometimes it was parted on the left, sometimes on the right; sometimes he wore it au naturel, cascading down his forehead, sometimes swept back and gelled into place. I doubt I was the only patient who found this teddy-boy narcissism unsettling. Perhaps that was why the walls of his surgery were covered with documentary proof of his wide-ranging expertise. I can't speak for the others but I drew little comfort from the fact that he was qualified to treat survivors of a plane crash.

As always, I was ushered into his surgery half an hour after the appointed time. As always, he began by checking my blood pressure. Like his routine, it never varied. He went behind a desk cluttered with drug companies' cheapjack giveaways and opened my file.

'Let's see, your last visit was February the seventeenth; you had a rash on the inner right thigh. I prescribed a cortisone-based anti-fungal cream.' He glanced up to make sure the rash hadn't spread. 'I assume it did the trick?'

'Yeah, it cleared up pretty quickly.'

'Yes. Fine product, that. Yes. Now then, what can I do for you today?'

I explained. He shone a light down my throat. The infection was viral rather than bacterial, he said, so antibiotics were no use. He prescribed cough mixture and extra-strength Panadol and suggested I spend a few nights in the spare bedroom.

Many doctors, having pocketed fifty dollars for a two-and-a-half minute diagnosis and treatment, would have hustled me out of there, next patient, please. Chummy always had time to look at the bigger picture. 'How are you otherwise?' he'd ask, eyebrows swooping over his half-moon spectacles. 'Anything else I can help you with?'

I guess GPs get quite a few patients whose trifling afflictions are a smokescreen and who have to be gently nudged into revealing what really is the matter. This was the moment to announce haltingly that the morning's stool-watch had detected traces of blood.

I gave him the usual, 'No, don't think so.'

He probed again; maybe he could see something behind my blank surface. 'Everything okay at work?' Then, after a meaningful pause: 'What about on the home front?'

'Yeah, fine.'

His head bobbed. I sensed scepticism. 'Well, good for you, Nick. You're in the minority, mind you. Not too many chaps in your age group could honestly say that.'

'Is that right?'

'Oh yes, I see it every day.' He peered at my file. 'How old are you?'

'Forty-three.'

'Yes, well, there you are. After forty, the chickens start coming home to roost.' He patted himself as if he were a dog. 'The body starts to play up and . . .' – drilling a finger into his temple – '. . . so does upstairs. Chaps start to fret because things haven't quite turned out as planned.' Another pause. 'And on top of all that, sex tends to rear its ugly head. The jolly old mid-life crisis: like being seventeen all over again but without the poke.'

'Can't get it up, eh?'

He nodded. 'Lot of that; lot of sniffing around for away games because the fun's gone out of it at home.'

'Well, I don't have either of those problems.'

'Lucky you. Not that these things can't be sorted out, of course. Amazing what a week's holiday without the offspring and a hundred milligrams of Viagra can do. Yes.'

I paid my fifty bucks and left. I didn't need his medicine and I definitely didn't need his sad stories.

Struggling to contain his bitterness, a colleague once told me that I'd married well. It runs in the family, I replied. You think I've cracked it, you should meet my sister. I wasn't kidding. Anne was a pretty good earner but not a patch on my brother-in-law. He worked in the slot-machine economy: you punch numbers into a computer and it spews out money.

They're pretty thick on the ground out east, the svelte corporate wives with their German cars and their master-race children. These women are lucky: they're sure of their place in the scheme of things. They've never wanted to be anything else or anywhere else; they never wonder why life has been so kind to them. The question simply doesn't arise. Rosie became one of them, identikit, interchangeable.

There's a vague resemblance but we weren't peas in a pod. Rosie was six years younger. In my experience, the younger or youngest child tends to do well on the genetic roulette wheel. They're usually more outgoing, more confident, less hung-up. Again in my experience, for what it's worth, when nature decides to make an exception to this rule, it doesn't muck around: some of the most dismal fuck-ups I've come across were the babies of the family – or after-thoughts or 'accidents' as they invariably put it. Rosie was in the blessed majority. She grew up with a smile on her face. Pretty but not a princess, lively but not manic, she was one of those children whom strangers want to handle, hug, briefly possess, just to feel the warmth of their radiant innocence. Later, her popularity was a thing to behold, a social phenomenon. Every circle she entered seemed to re-form and coalesce around her.

She breezed through a media and marketing degree then set off to see the world, or at least the parts with good snow, white sand and flushing toilets. She spent a year in the Bahamas, teaching tourists to windsurf and letting drug-runners buy her drinks. She crossed the Atlantic to do Europe but Europe did something to her. Instead of basing herself in London until she'd kicked the travel-bug, she got off the train in Berlin and moved into an anarchist squat. My parents were beside themselves. Courtesy of Hitler and *Cabaret*, they already had a dim view of Berlin. Add the squat and the anarchists and it's not hard to imagine their nightmarish visions: their little angel strung-out and naked on a filthy mattress as another freak shambles into frame unbuttoning his jeans ... I preferred to see her as Red Rosie, Urban Terrorist, Bonnie to some scraggly-bearded Clyde with a sociology degree and a submachine gun, leading the western intelligence services a merry dance before settling down in a revolutionary's retirement: a Libyan state pension, a two-room flat in suburban Tripoli, and as many dates as she could eat.

Then suddenly she was back home, not exactly transformed, just a little less luminous, less of an open book. Questions about Berlin were dodged, deflected and eventually stone-walled with an edgy, 'Look, it was an experience, that's about all I can say. I wouldn't want to repeat it and I don't particularly want to dwell on it so let's talk about something else, okay?' I sensed suppressed hysteria in her evasiveness and wondered – guiltily – whether it derived from shame or pain.

Her friends, who weren't the sort to look too closely, insisted she hadn't changed a bit. They reclaimed her with proprietorial assertiveness and set about ensuring that she stayed put. Enter Julian, a money market wizard. Julian had it all – the pad, the Porsche, the yacht, and three more decades of jackpotting rewards ahead of him. I had more reason than most to loathe yuppies but Julian was as likeable as they come. It wasn't his fault that he just couldn't help making money.

Everyone agreed that Julian and Rosie were made for each other. Well, everyone except Julian's fiancée. Breaking her heart was the hardest thing he'd ever done, he said, but he had no choice; he and Rosie were meant to be. It took some getting used to, hearing this nonchalant market-manipulator invoke destiny like an otherworldly poet.

You could say that was that. There followed in quick succession the splendid wedding, the splendid house, and the babies who were widely thought of as beautiful although to my – possibly jaundiced – eye they looked every bit as blotchy and prune-faced as everybody else's. Rosie came to resemble all the other millionaire-mile mothers, ferrying their kids around in plush cars, talking only of families and homes and holidays, worshipping their little gods and goddesses and their meal-ticket husbands until it was time to turn off the TV and go to bed.

Rosie liked to talk about our parents. More than I did.

'Have you noticed how Dad's really starting to show his age?'

'You think so?'

'When did you last see him?'

'I don't know, a month ago, maybe.'

'Well, we were down there last weekend and it really struck me: he's an old man, there's no getting away from it. It's not the white hair and wrinkles, it's what's in the tank – he's just run out of gas. All he wants to do is plonk himself in front of the TV.'

'As long as he doesn't watch cartoons. When he starts watching *The Flintstones*, that's when I'll get worried.'

'That could be sooner than you think. You know what he watches? Those old British comedies: *Dad's Army*, *It Ain't Half Hot, Mum*, even – wait for it – *Are You Being Served?* You thought they were pretty bad twenty-five years ago, you should try watching them now. Dad just laps them up – he literally can't get enough of them. He actually tapes them and watches them over and over again.'

'Shit, if he can work the video, that puts him ahead of seventy-five per cent of the adult population.'

'Well, that's another way of looking at it, I suppose.' She paused before opening a new line of inquiry: 'Who do you want to go first, Mum or Dad?'

'Gee, I don't know. I don't think I've actually got a preference.'

'You know what I mean – which of them do you think would cope best on their own?'

'Better.'

'What?'

'Which of the two would cope better.'

'Give it a rest, Nick. It's a perfectly valid question – which could have major implications for us.'

'Christ, how would I know? Here's a couple whose lives have revolved around each other for fifty-odd years so what happens when one of them croaks? Who knows? I certainly don't. They probably don't know themselves. You're taking it for granted that the one left over will be a lost soul but it's conceivable he or she will find it quite liberating.'

'Yeah, right, life begins at seventy-five. You know as well as I do, Dad would be hopeless if Mum went first. He's just not capable of looking after himself. And the flip-side of the coin is that Mum's role in life is looking after Dad – if he goes, what does she do with herself?'

'Well, maybe a suicide pact would be the best solution all round.'

'Honestly, Nick, there are times ...' She shook her head slowly, a gesture which always seems intended to speak louder than words but seldom does. 'They're still in love, you know; after all this time. How many of our generation will they be able to say that about?'

That was a good question and I knew what it was leading up to. 'Well, I guess their lot took the old till-death-us-do-part stuff seriously.'

'Exactly. You made a commitment and you stuck to it. These days, it's like, to hell with that, what am I missing out on?' She held the pause for as long as she could then lightened her tone, pretending to change the subject. 'So how are things with Anne?'

'Okay.'

'That wasn't the impression I got the other day ...'

'Forget about it,' I said. 'There was nothing to it.'

'Nick, I'm your sister . . .'

It was a little late in the day to play that card. I still didn't know what happened in Berlin.

'I got the wrong end of the stick,' I said, drawing a frown. 'I'm a pessimist, okay? We had a little misunderstanding and I jumped to the worst-case conclusion.'

'For god's sake, Nick, little misunderstandings happen every day. You must spend half your life thinking she's carrying on behind your back.'

'Okay, so it was a big misunderstanding. But it's been sorted out; everything's fine.'

She would have liked the details but could see that I wasn't going to volunteer them. 'Glad to hear it,' she said, nodding. 'We've got a lot invested in you two so let's keep it that way.'

CHAPTER 8

I caught up with Jock, dropping in on him unannounced one
Sunday morning. The house he shared with Debbie and
their sly, rangy sixteen year old, Mark, was like something
from a fairytale, a jumble of stairs and landings and lofts and
tiny, pointless rooms. Compounding the Brothers Grimm feel
was Debbie's taste in furniture which ran to reproduction
French provincial but on a baronial scale. For years she'd
planned sweeping renovations to make the Crooked House,
as it was known, more user-friendly but her proposals always
met opposition from one quarter or another, usually because
of some grotesque flourish contributed by Jock.

He seemed pleased to see me. 'Just the bloke I want to talk to,' he said. 'I was going to give you a ring. I need some advice.'

I wasn't Jock's confidant – far from it. He was well aware that I wasn't qualified to provide useful input on any of the things which exercised him: golf, cryptic crosswords, the St Kilda football club, and having sex with women other than his wife.

We had the Crooked House to ourselves. Debbie was at yoga and Mark had simply vanished. Jock took me up to his den, a cell-like space in the roof kitted out with a semi-eviscerated two-seater sofa, a mini-fridge and a television. He spent most of his spare time up there, smoking, drinking, watching sport, doing crosswords, and, I assume, masturbating.

He thrust a beer at me. We sat side by side, not the ideal arrangement for earnest dialogue. Sure, it was Sunday but Jock looked thoroughly disreputable, even to a fellow atheist. He was stubbly and puffy-eyed and his tired, middle-aged hair sprawled greasily across his scalp. His shirt collar was grimy and frayed and there were streaks of crusted paint and worse on his ancient corduroy trousers. I flinched when he bored in confidentially but his breath smelt of nothing worse than beer.

'It's about Mark,' he said.

'Problems at school?'

Jock shook his head. 'No, but you know the sort of shit these kids get up to.'

'I don't know about that,' I said cagily. 'What my lot do in their own time isn't my problem, thank christ.'

A fortnight earlier, Mark had knocked on the door of the den wanting a word. Father–son interface was erratic and then generally about money but Mark's tongue-tied stalling put Jock on alert. After a few false starts, Mark got it out: he and his buddy Ben had gone halves on a hooker.

Jock established that they'd practised safe sex before confronting the issue which really troubled him: 'Why are you telling me this?'

Because he had to. The hooker had made a house call but Ben's father had changed his mind about overnighting in Melbourne and caught the last flight home. He'd told Mark, if you don't tell your parents, I will.

Jock asked his son if that was it. Mark nodded. Jock told him, 'Well, I hope you got your money's worth.'

Jock was known for his cruel smile and it was pleasing to see it deployed at his own expense. 'Needless to say, that wasn't quite it.'

I nodded and sucked eagerly on my beer.

Jock knew Ben's father to say hello to. When they bumped into each other in the golf club car park, Ben's father went hi, how are you, I hear Mark told you what happened. Jock said yes, he did.

Ben's father cocked his head. 'And?'

'Well, you know,' said Jock, 'boys will be boys.'

Ben's father's eyebrows went up and down. 'If only. You mean to say it doesn't worry you?'

Jock shrugged. 'What aspect of it, exactly, should I be worried about?'

Ben's father nodded slowly, as if it was starting to make sense. 'Tell me, did Mark go into any detail?'

'Like what?'

'Like, for instance, did he mention the fact that the hooker was a transvestite? I didn't think so. You see, Jock, our sons had their dicks sucked by a man dressed up as a woman. How do you feel about that?'

Jock still wasn't sure what he felt or should feel about that. I told him to look on the bright side: at least Mark had been on the preferable end of the transaction.

Driving home, I realised that for once Jock hadn't greeted me with his standard line, 'Nickelarse: to what do we owe the pleasure?'

By the time I got home, I was beginning to wonder about Jock's little tale. As in, was it for real or was it a diversionary tactic? I'd arrived on his doorstep unannounced and with a fixated air. Say he'd assumed he had an outraged husband on his hands, what would he do? Improvise? Try to short-circuit me by enlisting my help to save his son from sodomy?

He was foxy enough. Those who saw him as a Mr Magoo figure shuffling through life oblivious to what was going on around him had bought an act. Jock liked to please himself and he understood that people will put up with a lot, even psychopathic selfishness, if they can classify it as eccentricity.

And at second blush the story seemed unlikely, just the sort of thing a sick-minded bullshit artist might concoct on the spur of the moment. As I've alluded to, teenage boys are rabidly homophobic, possibly because their sexuality is a work in progress and they secretly fear that they may be the one in four or one in ten, depending on who you believe, who'll end up riding the chocolate speedway. (Oh yeah, I've heard them all, every skid-marked metaphor.) Given the outlay, you'd have thought the boys would have wanted a show, would have insisted that the hooker stripped down to his/her mail-order underwear. Which raised the question: what had given the game away? Had Mark's father spotted a lumpy, bobbing Adam's apple or had he walked in as the trannie revealed his true self, announcing that, for his next trick, he'd need a volunteer?

Jock called a couple of days later. 'I've had it out with Mark.'

'And?'

'Well, put it his way, he hasn't shaved his legs yet.'

'Is he okay?'

'Yeah, he's just a bit embarrassed.'

'So it was embarrassment that stopped him telling you?'

'That and the fact he thought I'd go spare. Mind you, I'd have done the same in his shoes – don't admit to anything unless you absolutely have to, that's my motto. Start with indignant denial. If that won't wash, lie. If you can't lie your way out of it, tell them the bare minimum. Information management, son; need to know basis and all that. The fact is, most people prefer it that way – they don't want to know the truth, the whole truth, and nothing but. Which is eminently fucking sensible because nine times out of ten, the truth does more harm than good. Once the genie's out of the bottle, you can't get the fucker back in.'

A week or so later I drifted into the common room to find a couple of classicists blushing over a confiscated magazine. It was called *Asian She-Males* and certainly lived up to its tell-it-like-it-is title. I'd pretty well forgotten about the transvestite mini-drama. Mark took after his old man, all right; he would have got away with the air-brushed version if Jock hadn't run into Ben's father. What was the formula? If you can't get away with denying it outright, lie, and if that doesn't work, edit the truth down to a bare-bones version the injured party can live with. I wondered how many times Jock had practised what he preached on poor old Debbie.

Then I stopped thinking about them and started thinking about us.

Specifically, I considered the possibility that Anne had practised something similar on me. I'd expected worse than the single encounter she'd more or less sleepwalked into and the schoolgirl swoon in the restaurant. It hadn't taken long for my reflexive spasm of rage to give way to relief. After that, I couldn't forgive her fast enough.

Relief skews judgement. When something turns out to be not as bad as expected, we celebrate by persuading ourselves that what is, nonetheless, a negative situation is actually neutral. Not too bad at all. In fact, there are some things to be said for it: timely reminder, wake-up call, reality check ...

I'd ended up feeling that, all things considered, I'd got off pretty lightly. But what if Anne had decided I was too fragile to cope with the truth? Let's face it, she knew all about information management. She did it for a living.

Anne had said Jason Swann – that's *Jxxx* to you and me – was head of marketing at Trigon Insurance. Trigon operated out of a new office block at the north end of Clarence Street. I went there after school. I didn't have a plan as such; I just wanted to know more about Jason than his snazzy apartment and his failed marriage.

In the foyer a receptionist sat behind a slab of marble, as if she was waiting for the world to beat a path to her. I asked her if Trigon had a corporate brochure or information pack. This wasn't quite a fishing expedition: I remembered Anne saying that one of her underlings was preparing something of the sort. The receptionist handed over a fat folder. On the front, in embossed silver, it said, TRIGON: A MORE SECURE TOMORROW.

I sat in the foyer and leafed through it. In amongst the scaremongering hard sell was a brochure entitled *Our People, Our Edge*. I wondered if Anne and Jason had dreamed that up between them during a brainstorming session over a bottle of chardonnay. The Trigon management team each got a two-line biography, space for a wet and woolly personal mission statement, and a head and shoulders photo. Whatever else he was, there was no getting away from the fact that Jason Swann was good-looking.

By now, it was after five, rush hour in the elevator shaft. I sat there, idly people-watching. Some noisy young women piled out of a lift, rummaging in their handbags for cigarettes and eyeing up the gentleman who held the doors at bay. It was Jason. If anything, the photo didn't do him justice.

He strode past me, swinging a pilot's jumbo briefcase. He had the air of a man who'd done an honest day's work and was looking forward to unwinding over a cold one. I got up and followed him outside. He turned into the first side-street and opened the passenger door of a Saab convertible. The driver was a huge young guy wearing a City Gym singlet. Jason leaned over and gave him a long, chewy kiss. As the driver went to start the car, he noticed me watching them from the opposite footpath.

He lowered the window. 'What the fuck are you staring at?'

'Nothing,' I shrugged. 'Just admiring the car.'

That didn't wash with Jason. He leaned across his boyfriend and gave me the finger. Which, I was beginning to think, was probably more than he'd given Anne.

Jock justified his Liar's Charter on the grounds that people don't want to know the truth. The truth was detached: it didn't get involved, it didn't stick around for a cuddle. Not like illusions. Say what you like about illusions, they're always there for you.

Well, I liked having something to cling onto at four in the morning too but a couple of awkward questions kept coming between us: could Jason, last seen in a tongue-tangle with Muscle Mary, really be *J*? And if he wasn't, who was?

Anne was putting together a salad; I was timing the pasta. I said, 'I saw something pretty weird this afternoon.'

She didn't look up. 'What was that?'

'Well, I was having a wander around town and I found myself outside the Trigon building . . .'

Anne's head jerked up. She clamped a hand down on the salad spinner to stop it whirring. Without taking her eyes off me, she reached for her wine glass.

'...so I went in.'

'Why would you do that?'

'Curiosity. That's understandable, isn't it?'

'What else did you need to know?'

'I wouldn't say "need" but I was kind of interested to see what he looks like.'

Her face collapsed into an expression of weary exasperation. Our respective roles had been established: I upset the apple-cart, she picked up the apples. 'So what did you do – make an appointment?'

'No, I just picked up the corporate brochure – there's a photo of him in there.' Anne nodded carefully. 'You didn't tell me he was that good-looking.'

She shrugged. 'Would it have helped?'

I shrugged back. 'Probably not.'

'So what was weird about it?' She smiled coolly. 'That a man like that could find me attractive?'

'Come on, you know better than that. Apart from maybe that guy in the restaurant, I'm your greatest admirer. Anyway, as I was sitting there looking at the photo, guess who stepped out of the lift?'

She sighed and her smile faded away. 'Nick, is this a good idea?'

'Hang on, I'm just getting to the weird bit. I was going anyway so I followed him outside. He walked round the corner, got in a car, and stuck his tongue down the driver's throat ...'

'Who was a guy, right?' The smile was back, this time with more than a hint of mockery. She'd enjoyed beating me to the punchline.

'Oh, so you knew he was gay? I thought it might've come as something of a surprise.'

Anne shook her head. 'Nick, this is asking for trouble, not because you've somehow caught me out – you haven't – but I thought we'd agreed to put this behind us. Spying on Jason isn't my idea of ...'

'I wasn't fucking spying on him.' There I was again, back on the back foot. 'I didn't know he was going to appear, let alone stage a public love scene. I saw the Trigon building, I remembered you talking about the corporate brochure, I thought why not just pop in and see if there's a photo of him – curiosity, pure and simple ...'

'Make that morbid.'

'Call it what you like, it's beside the point – which is that the Jason I observed bears no resemblance to the guy you described. Or have you forgotten the sob-story about his marriage breaking up?'

'Okay, I changed his ex-partner's gender. Apart from that, it happened just as I told you. In case the penny hasn't dropped yet, Jason's bisexual.'

Over dinner, I got the uncut version.

At Trigon it was taken for granted that Jason was gay all the way although that didn't stop some of the women fluttering around him. It was a game, them pretending to be wild things, him pretending to be open to persuasion. And seeing there was no physical contact, no-one got hurt.

Anne didn't join in but it was nice nevertheless to be cheerfully pleasant to a corporate male without him interpreting it as an indication of interest. It was nice not to realise halfway through a meeting that she wasn't being taken seriously, not because she was under-prepared or not up to it, but because the guy's mind wasn't on the job. It was nice not to have to ignore innuendo or ration eye contact. Men are always saying how much they like doing business with a bloke who looks them in the eye. Apparently it's a sign of integrity. When a woman looks them in the eye, they think it means her pants are on fire.

Jason also had a malicious sense of humour which made him much more fun to be around than the chest-beaters. She suspected he picked her apart behind her back too but better that than being the object of a verbal group grope around the coffee machine. And when her instincts told her he was responding to her man to woman, she told herself, don't be ridiculous – even if you wanted to, you don't have what it takes to turn him on.

Jason confided in her that he was getting over a broken relationship. With a fella as it happened although he was actually bi. In theory anyway: it had been a while since his straight side had seen any action. In fact, until Anne came along, he was starting to think his straight side had given up the ghost ...

'Why didn't you just tell me at the time?' I asked.

'I was afraid it would make it worse.' She sounded slightly aggrieved that this good turn should now be held against her.

'Why would it have made it worse?'

'Well, I suppose there's the paranoia factor ... He did use a condom, by the way – not that he's HIV-positive.'

'I guess we'll have to take his word for that.'

'As a matter of fact, he'd just been tested,' she said equably. 'I suppose what it really boiled down to, I was worried that it'd be the straw which broke the camel's back. I'm not saying you're homophobic but ...'

'But what?'

'Well, let's face it, Nick, you're in the ballpark.'

'I'm sorry, I didn't realise my unenlightened attitudes – if that's what they are – were the issue here. And for what it's worth, I'm not homophobic. I'm just not interested in their sub-culture – any more than they're interested in mine.'

'That's an interesting distinction.' She pushed her plate aside, clearing the decks. 'Look, Nick, I'm sorry I wasn't completely honest with you but it was done with the best of intentions. I just thought it would complicate an already difficult situation. Is there anything else about this that still bothers you? Because if there is, now's the time to raise it. I'd like to think that by the time we go to bed tonight, this thing will be dealt with and out of the way, once and for all.'

And I'd like to think that I'll never wake up with a hangover again. I tried to replicate her cool smile. 'I have no further questions.'

She brought out the smile again. She did it much better than me. 'I take it then that the prosecution rests?'

Anne had butched up Jason in the retelling but I was still left wondering whether his straight side was really up to the job. It wasn't that I didn't believe her – at a push, I could get my head around the concept of bisexuality – but when I replayed the love scene with a woman in the driver's seat, it just didn't have the same zing. Then there was the attitude: Jason didn't come across as a bob-each-way man.

The City Gym lived up to expectations: hard-core muscle pump for hard-core narcissists, a temple for self-worship. When these freaks locked eyes with their reflections, the air crackled with electricity. Jason's boyfriend was in a corner, sitting on a bench doing slow-motion curls. He had on the same singlet, lycra bicycle shorts, weight-lifting gloves, a red bandana and earphones.

His biceps billowed as he hoisted and lowered the stacked dumbbell. I could almost hear the creak of stretched skin and the high-pressure surge of blood through the ropey veins. Eight this side, eight that side, rest. After a set, he lay back on the bench, pipeline thighs jiggling to the beat. I saw myself in the ceiling to floor mirror: an ordinary Joe. We looked like different species, he and I, and no Darwinian would have held out much hope for mine.

He sat up, his eyes popping open as if he'd been given smelling salts. When he noticed me hovering, he slid off the earphones. 'Yeah?'

There wasn't a hint of recognition. I said, 'I believe you're a friend of Jason Swann?'

'Who wants to know?' His voice contained no trace of that trill you hear in every café from Potts Point to Oxford

Street. He sounded like he looked, like some new strain of beast bred for pure, unadulterated muscle mass – Neanderthal Man crossed with a pit-bull terrier.

'I'm a friend of a friend of Jason's.'

'Could've fooled me.'

'One of his female friends. You got a moment?'

'Make it quick.'

'Well,' I said, 'this woman's pretty keen on Jason but if she's wasting her time, she'd prefer to know now – before she embarrasses them both.'

The manicured eyebrows bobbled. 'What the fuck are you talking about?'

'There seem to be two schools of thought: one, that Jason's exclusively gay, the other, that he's bisexual …'

The Beast grunted, heaving his meaty shoulders. 'Yeah, right,' he said, 'Jason's bi. And I'm Richard Gere's hamster.'

'I thought that was an urban myth.'

He nodded. 'You've got to ask yourself: a big movie star wants to get off, what's he going to do? Go to a fucking pet shop?'

'My brother-in-law works in Hollywood,' I said. 'He reckons it's another world.'

'Yeah? What does he do there?' The Beast seemed genuinely interested. Perhaps he saw himself in LA. A lot of people in this town do.

'He's on the financing side.'

'Oh.' He leaned down to scoop up a dumbbell. My time was up.

'So Jason's definitely not bi?'

The Beast gave his wrists a workout, rotating the dumb-bell as if he was stirring a cup of coffee. 'That's fucking official, man – you can tell the bitch to give it up. Jason's one of those queens who gets a kick out of messing with women's heads but he's never going to be anyone's boyfriend, you know what I'm saying?' I thought I did but he saw no harm in labouring the point. 'This friend of yours, is she hot? I mean, does she like dick?'

I shrugged. 'No more than the next woman, I wouldn't have thought.'

'Well, I can tell you this: I haven't met a chick yet who likes dick half as much as Jason. Does that solve your little problem?'

Well, yes and no.

Maybe Jason led a secret life and the Beast, like so many saps before him, was the last to know. You could see how it could happen: narcissists don't get a lot of use out of their powers of observation.

Maybe. It was within the realms of possibility but then so are most things. The smart money, though, was picking that Jason just wasn't wired that way. The smart money was on the favourite. Her form justified it.

Anne's first lie could be put down to panic and the odd notion that, for a man like me, it was somehow worse to be cuckolded by a bisexual. But to lie a second time smacked of premeditation, cover-up. Which in turn implied that the truth was dangerous.

It was her word against the Beast's. He was vehement but he was a stranger with no apparent redeeming features. She was my wife, the person I loved. And I was afraid.

CHAPTER 9

When Anne went out on her own, she vowed to keep her professional and personal lives separate. Apparently there were PRs who measured their success by the number of journalists' home phone numbers in their filofax. Others preferred to cosy up to their clients, on the theory that if you became friends, if the wives met for coffee and the kids had each other over to play, you'd have to screw up pretty badly before they'd fire you.

As they say, that was then ...

Our dinner party guests were: Geoff, the editor of *High Finance* magazine, his partner Kate, a food photographer;

Joel, who was setting up an Australian operation for an LA-based movie company, and his date Ellie, who worked in the hospitality industry and aspired to be an actor. Joel was the latest addition to Anne's client-list. She was thrilled to get the business; I believe the term 'potential gold mine' was used. As I understood it, Joel's idea was that Australian investors would put up the money and he and his people would do the rest: develop projects, source talent, oversee production, and distribute the finished product. But it was all talk until they got their hands on the money, which was where PR came in. Which was where Geoff came in. Which was why there were four strangers at our table that Saturday night.

Joel and Ellie arrived first. Joel was a boyish little thing which must have made his receding hairline doubly galling. His most distinctive feature, though, was his voice which was effortlessly huge, way out of proportion to his compact frame. It really belonged to one of those steroid-crazed ogres on the TV wrestling shows or the pre-fight hypester at Caesar's Palace. In fact, given what the night held, Joel could have kicked things off with 'ARE YOU READY TO RUUUUUMBLE!!!!???' He brought a half-bottle of notable dessert wine and three bottles of still mineral water all the way from Snowdonia, North Wales. Just as well. We had plenty of mineral water but it was carbonated and came from Victoria in plastic bottles. Joel drank his Welsh mineral water before and during dinner. I imagine he would have drunk it after dinner too if he'd stuck around that long.

He hadn't exercised such self-denial in his choice of companion: Ellie looked like a sack-artist from way back. She'd slithered into a little black dress, climbed up onto a pair of fuck-me shoes, and daubed on Promise of Fellatio lipstick. After a few minutes of her mutely decorative company, I decided that her riding instructions were to remain within fondling distance of Joel, keep her mouth shut – especially when he wanted to say something, which was most of the time – and then, at a pre-arranged signal, fuck the daylights out of him. If anything, she seemed over-qualified for the assignment.

At least she took a drink, a vodka martini no less. Anne joined me in the kitchen as I was adding the twists of lemon.

She took a tiny sip of mine. 'Good grief, that's pure alcohol.'

'Ellie likes them dry.'

'It's not her I'm worried about. Just take it easy, okay? Remember what happened last time you had too many of these.'

She was referring to the Christmas lunch before last at her parents' place, a less-than-joyous occasion.

I shrugged. 'Whatever gets you through the night.'

'For god's sake, Nick, give them a chance,' she said. 'They're perfectly good company – so are Geoff and Kate – and it's only for a few hours. You don't have to write yourself off.'

'No, but it helps.'

She left with a plate of antipasto and a warning look, nothing too heavy, just putting me on notice: be supportive, don't rock the boat, don't make a prick of yourself.

Joel was taking us through the Who's Fucked Who of Hollywood, an ambitious undertaking, and I was on my third martini when our other guests arrived. Geoff, also forty-odd, was good-looking in a rubbery, anonymous sort of way and didn't get dressed up for anyone: he wore washed-out black jeans, sneakers, and a T-shirt under a blue denim jacket. There was a touch of the spoilt child about him, as if he was used to being fussed over. Kate was fleshy, darkly attractive and down-to-earth.

Women 2, Men 0.

The first course was a chilled soup which earned the chef high praise. Personally, I couldn't get to the bottom of it. Joel was still telling Hollywood tales which at least meant there was something for everyone. I asked him about Richard Gere and the hamster.

He chuckled. 'Hey, if you believe that, you'll believe anything.'

That made Anne titter. Perhaps I was being over-sensitive but it felt like, 'You'll have to excuse my husband – he's a teacher.'

'Anne's brother works in Hollywood,' I said. 'Maybe you've come across him – Harry Carew?'

Joel didn't know the name but felt obliged to show interest. I left it to Anne to put a gloss on Harry's fringe dweller existence.

We were well into the main course – $45 a kilo wild barramundi; Joel, of course, didn't eat meat – when it all went bad. Mutual admiration society to seconds out in two messy minutes.

We extras had endured Joel's dissertation on the film industry's murky accountancy procedures and Geoff's address-in-reply, an overview of Australian investment trends.

Anne facilitated unobtrusively. Eventually they ran out of puff. We all chewed thoughtfully, waiting for someone else to fill the vacuum. It fell to me, as co-host, to head off an awkward silence. I remarked lightly – or so I thought – that dinner party conversations weren't what they used to be during the Clinton-Lewinsky circus.

I suppose I should have expected the leads to take it personally. 'Well, I'm sorry,' huffed Joel, 'I didn't realise we were the cabaret.'

Geoff followed up with, 'Jesus, you must go to some pretty dire dinner parties.' He helped himself to more wine; he and I were going glass for glass.

'What makes you say that?' I asked.

'Just that I can't remember the subject coming up at any dinner party we were at,' he said. 'Probably because no-one gave a shit. But then we make it a rule to avoid rednecks and bible bashers.'

Support came from an unlikely source. 'Well, I'm a non-practising Jew from LA,' said Joel, 'and I gave a shit about it. I thought Clinton had a lot to answer for.'

'Like being human?' said Geoff. 'The first decent president since Kennedy and they try to run him out of office because some groupie sucked his dick. Only in America. Still, I suppose he's lucky they didn't fucking shoot him.'

'Let me tell you something,' rumbled Joel. 'Any way you cut it, Ronald Reagan was twice the president JFK was – so where does that leave Clinton?'

At this point, Anne let it be known that she felt there was something to be said for the rule about excluding politics and religion from dinner-party conversation but her intervention was already too late.

Geoff said to Joel, 'Excuse me?' His loose grin was a provocation in its own right.

'I think you heard me just fine,' said Joel.

'Ronald fucking Reagan?' scoffed Geoff. 'Shit, he was a better actor than a president and we all know what a shithouse actor he was.'

'You know, people like you really make me laugh,' said Joel, although his expression didn't bear this out. 'You think you're such a goddamn expert but you don't know shit.'

Anne's face fell. The horse had well and truly bolted now. Kate put a restraining hand on Geoff's forearm but that was too late too. Ellie excused herself and retreated to the bathroom.

I've probably seen – and participated in – nastier dinner-party arguments but none spring to mind. As they traded sneers, I powered through the red wine and chuckled at the more florid insults. Between them, Anne and Kate had several stabs at brokering a cease-fire, including pointing out to the combatants that they were ruining things for the rest of us. As if they gave a shit.

They'd covered the deficit and the Contras and were onto *Bedtime for Bonzo* when Ellie returned from her prolonged comfort break. Joel bounced up and grabbed her arm. 'Come on, honey, we're out of here,' he said, grinding out the words. 'I've had it up to here with this fucking jerk.' He switched his glare to Anne who was scrambling, red-faced, to her feet. 'Thanks a bunch, Anne – it's been a real blast.'

An exchange of business cards had taken place earlier. Now Joel took Geoff's card out of his breast pocket. 'I sure as shit won't be needing this,' he said, flicking it across the table. It veered off course to land in front of me.

I don't know about you but I have this thing with names: I always assume it's Geoff with a G, Catherine with a C, Stephen as opposed to Steven, Graeme as opposed to Graham, and so on. Obviously, it puts me wrong from time to time.

I glanced at the card. He was Jeff with a J.

Anne and I saw them out. Ellie seemed distracted. Perhaps she was already thinking about what it would take to salvage the evening. Joel's last words were, 'I guess it seemed like a good idea at the time, huh?' Meanwhile, back in the dining room, Kate glowed with embarrassment while Jeff was insouciance itself. He slouched in his chair, rolling a joint.

I raised my glass. 'God bless America.'

Jeff joined in the toast. 'Amen to that, brother.'

'So,' I said, 'what do you think of the pope?'

'Fuck the pope.' He inhaled heavily and passed the joint on. 'Anne, I hope this won't affect our professional relationship. I mean, I'd hate to think you'll never buy me lunch again.'

Anne produced one of her cool smiles. 'As long as there's a client to charge it to, Jeff, I promise to buy you lunch.'

'You don't seriously think little Jojo will take his business elsewhere, do you?'

'I don't know,' she said. 'I don't know him well enough to have any idea how he'll feel when he cools down.'

'If he cools down,' said Kate.

'Well, as I always say,' said Jeff, 'fuck 'em if they can't take a joke.'

He thought that was frightfully amusing. Less predictably, so did Anne.

I'm not an alcoholic although I take it for granted that some snake-eyed social engineer has come up with a definition which says otherwise. I happen to enjoy half a bottle of wine with my dinner; most civilised people do. Sometimes, though, half a bottle just isn't enough and that's when it can get away from you. There's only one stop between Not Enough and Too Much, a quiet little zone called Just Right. You've got to look out for it, though: it's the sort of place, blink and you've missed it.

There are aspects of the drinking process which I don't really understand. Why, for instance, does an identical quantity of alcohol wash gently over us one night and slam-dunk us next time around? (Assuming obvious factors like fatigue and food intake are equal.) Sometimes it happens nice and slow, sometimes it hits us like a sucker punch, and there doesn't seem to be much we can do to influence it. The booze and our chemical make-up on the day work it out between them. And why does our behaviour under the influence so often take us by surprise? What will we be tonight – mellow or domineering, maudlin or mean, tiresome or amusing?

I was actually feeling pretty good as we ploughed into the liqueurs and chocolates; it was shaping up as one of those nights when the system has everything under control. I went through the check-list. Mind: clear; nerves: steady; mood: calm. Status report: as normal as could be expected. Cleared to proceed.

I mainly talked to Kate. It was just burble, neither of us making much of an effort. We both knew it was a one-off. Anne and Jeff, on the other hand, were sparking off each other. Their rapport was exclusionary and Kate looked relieved when Jeff finally agreed it was time to call a cab.

Here's another one: those mood swings – what the fuck? The moment the front door closed, Anne's party smile shrivelled. 'I suppose you thought that was funny?' she said.

'Well, it had its moments.'

She brushed past me. 'Typical.'

I followed her down the corridor to the dining room where she collected the brandy balloons.

'Did I miss something?' I said.

She didn't bother looking at me. 'You must be feeling pleased with yourself – mission accomplished and all that. It'll certainly be a bloody long time before I try that again.'

We moved into the kitchen. I could feel the temperature rising. 'Call me paranoid,' I said, 'but I'm getting the distinct impression you blame me for what happened.'

Anne leaned against the bench, arms folded, raking me with a spiky gaze. 'Everything was going fine until you got bored. Never mind that the whole point of the exercise was to get Joel and Jeff talking to each other; you weren't having a good time so you decided to stir things up. And don't try to deny it – I was watching you, I could see what was going through your mind.'

I decided we could both do with another drink. Anne accepted her cognac with a 'Why not?' shrug.

I said, 'Okay, well, seeing you're a mind-reader, why don't you tell me what Jeff was thinking?'

'I don't have to be a mind-reader to see what you're up to.'

'Let's stick with Jeff: it didn't occur to you that he was winding Joel up?'

'I suppose there was an element of that.'

'Thank you. So how come I get the blame and he gets your undivided attention?'

'What?'

'From the moment Joel buggered off, you two started carrying on like long-lost friends. You'd still be at it if Kate hadn't practically begged him to go home.'

Anne sighed as people do when it's late and they're having to explain the obvious. 'Jeff's not my husband, he's a business contact. At the end of the day, it's no skin off his nose if I lose a client.'

'Well, now I know what they mean by journalistic licence. He picks a fight with the guy you want him to hit it off with, probably loses you an important account, manifestly doesn't give a fuck about it, and what do you do? Fawn all over him. And don't deny it – I was watching *you*.'

'It's called cutting your losses; it's something you have to do in business from time to time. Sure, I could've torn a strip off him but what would that have achieved apart from pissing him off? So I get in to work on Monday and another client wants to get their story into *High Finance*. Trouble is, I'm no bloody use to them because I've fallen out with the editor.

That'd be really good, wouldn't it?' She rushed down her cognac, impatient with me and impatient with the conversation. 'Don't worry about it, Nick; leave that to me. You just enjoy the benefits.'

A man can only take so much, right? 'It wouldn't have anything to do with the way he spells his name, would it?' She had her back to me, putting something away. 'Jeff with a J. I was just thinking about the signature on your love note.' She turned around. 'You know – J kiss, kiss, kiss. I mean, we both know it's not J for Jason.'

'I don't fucking believe this,' she said slowly and, I couldn't help thinking, a touch theatrically. 'God, how many times do we have to go through it?'

'I know it's a bit late to ask you not to insult my intelligence,' I said, 'but Jason's not bisexual. He's gay and that's that.'

'Well, of course he is. I don't know what on earth possessed me to think I could pull the wool over your eyes, you being such an expert on the subject.' The clunking sarcasm was a prelude to icy formality. 'Perhaps we could continue this conversation another time – I'm going to bed. Goodnight.'

'Oh, I know I'm no expert,' I said. 'That's why I consulted one.'

'Really? And who might that be?'

'Jason's boyfriend. I figured he ought to know.'

Her eyes widened. I think she thought I was joking and was astounded that I could cavort on such dangerous ground. 'His boyfriend?'

'Yeah.'

'The guy you saw him with?'

I nodded.

'How did you get hold of him?'

I told her about the Beast's singlet.

'So you went to his gym and asked him if Jason was bisexual?' She needed to know how I'd got there before she could believe it.

I nodded.

'And what did he say?'

'He said that if Jason's bisexual, he's Richard Gere's hamster.'

She smiled then, an unnerving, bitter half-smile which I hadn't seen before. 'Well, you heard what Joel said about that.'

'Call it striving for effect. It worked for me.'

'So you believed him?'

'On balance, yes.'

'Which obviously means you don't believe me?'

'On balance, no.'

'Why are you doing this, Nick?' She looked and sounded genuinely baffled. 'Why are you driving me away?'

'I'm not trying to drive you away,' I said. 'I just want to know the truth.'

'I just want to know the truth.' Her mimicry reduced it to a childish, egomaniacal slogan – We Want The World And We Want It Now! 'You want to know what I think? I don't think you really give a shit about the truth. This is some kind of sick game. What are you, Nick – a masochist or a sadist? Is the idea to punish me or torment yourself?'

'You're the one who's kept it going,' I said. 'If you'd told the truth at the outset . . .'

'Why can't you just leave it? It happened. I'm sorry it happened but I can't undo it. All I can do is make sure it doesn't happen again. Can't you simply accept the situation for what it is and move on so we can get on with life?'

'That's exactly what I want to do,' I said. 'But I can't get over it until I know what it was.'

She shook her head. 'This is pointless – we're just going around in circles.' She walked past me. 'You can use the spare room. Tomorrow we'll have to sort out a more permanent arrangement.'

'What do you mean by that?'

There was only sadness in her eyes. 'I can't take much more of this, Nick. Isn't that what you wanted to hear?'

I woke up with a brutal hangover. Anne was at the kitchen table, drinking coffee and manhandling a Sunday tabloid. Her face was scrubbed but her eyes were pink and puffy and she had her ugly face on. We've all got one. It's that face we wear when we're sick or tired or angry or hung-over. It's all relative, of course. Many women would have settled for Anne's ugly face.

I asked, 'How do you feel?'

'How do you think?'

I poured orange juice and put bread in the toaster. 'Yeah, well, if it's any consolation, I feel like shit.'

'Oh, that's your penance, is it? The fact that you've got a hangover is somehow supposed to make up for last night?'

In the ten minutes or so between waking up and getting out of bed, I'd remembered the sadness in Anne's eyes and regretted my part in the flare-up. I'd made up my mind not to carry on from where we left off. We needed to get back to being friends. This newborn sentiment, though, was too frail to withstand the chill of Anne's hair-trigger self-righteousness.

'A number of things happened last night,' I said challengingly. 'Which one are you referring to?'

She looked at me as if she couldn't believe I had to ask. 'You called me a liar.'

'No, I didn't.'

'You said you didn't believe me,' she said, her voice rising to the challenge. 'What the hell does that mean if it doesn't mean you think I'm a liar?'

'I'm not falling for this old trick, Anne,' I said. 'The issue here isn't that I don't believe you; it's the fact that your explanation was unbelievable.'

We stared at each other, the ticking of the kitchen clock measuring the impasse. Anne's face was stiff, locked into an offended expression, and she breathed heavily through her nose. Eventually she said, 'Well, if nothing else, that sums up where we've got to – we can't even agree what the problem is.' She paused, steadying herself. 'We've reached a dead end: one of us has got to go and it's not going to be me.'

'Go where?'

'That's up to you.'

Suddenly I was hot and damp all over. 'What are you saying – you want me to move out?'

'Well, we can't go on like this, can we? And seeing you've brought us to this point, it seems only fair that you should be the one to go.'

'Just like that?'

'What did you expect?'

'I thought we could start with the truth ...'

'You don't get it, do you? We're way past that. What matters now is that you don't trust my word and I don't trust yours. Which means we're stuffed.'

'How did you get to this position of moral equivalence, as a matter of interest?'

'You promised to forgive and forget; you've done the exact opposite.'

'What happened to "I don't want to lose you"?'

'That was the old you.'

'Is that so? Well, I can tell you the old me didn't like being lied to either. You resent the fact that I won't take your word for it? There's an easy way to fix that: just look me in the eye and tell me that Jason Swann wrote that note.'

She did look me in the eye but what she said was, 'You're not listening, Nick – it's all academic now.'

Then she turned away from me.

I didn't go quietly. I followed her up the stairs, telling her she was being self-serving and arbitrary. When it became apparent that nothing I could say would make a jot of difference, I added dishonest. She went remorselessly about her business.

'Why are you so hostile?' I asked.

'That's your view – I don't feel hostile. But if I seem a little offhand, it's probably because you keep calling me a liar. Touchy of me, I know.'

'So what are we talking about – a trial separation?'

'If that's what you want to call it,' she said.

'Well, what are you going to call it? Or aren't you going to tell anyone?'

She opened and closed her mouth. I suspected she'd been about to say that she'd just tell them the truth. Instead, she fell back on, 'I'll cross that bridge when I come to it.' She gathered up her handbag and satchel. 'I'm going into the office. I'll be there most of the day, then I'm having dinner with my parents ...'

'Going solo already, eh?'

She ignored me. 'I've got to tell them sometime so I might as well get it over with.'

'How do you think they'll feel about it?'

'I imagine they'll be concerned for both of us.'

'You really think so? I predict they'll say, "We told you so," then Roger will break out the champagne.'

'Well, I certainly won't be having any.'

At the time I took it to mean that she wouldn't be party to any celebrations. Later I realised that she'd been referring to her hangover.

'What exactly are you going to tell them? I mean you wouldn't lie to Mummy and Daddy, would you?'

'You just can't help yourself, can you?'

I'd trailed her throughout the house and now we were at the front door. 'Well,' I said, 'I know one thing for sure.'

She was impatient to be gone but she waited on the door-step, humouring me while she rummaged for her carkeys.

'There was more to you and J – whoever he is – than you let on,' I said. 'Maybe there still is. Once you look at it that way, it all starts to make sense.'

She let out a long breath and her eyelids drooped. 'If you get bored with doing nothing,' she said, 'perhaps you could start packing.'

I didn't hear Anne come in that night and by the time I woke up, she'd already left.

CHAPTER 10

I couldn't come to terms with the change in her. It was as if she'd jettisoned a whole chunk of her personality and installed something cold and hard in its place. Unless it was an over-reaction or a bluff to teach me a lesson. I checked my voice-mail regularly, just in case. At 3.23, she left a message asking me to call. I rang and was put on hold. Nine minutes went by. Even before she picked up the phone and I overheard her promise someone she'd be with them in two ticks, I had a feeling it wasn't going to be a let's-kiss-and-make-up conversation.

'You there, Nick?'

'Yeah.'

'Sorry about that, it's a madhouse here today.'

'You heard from Joel?' I asked, as if this was just another manic Monday.

'I have – he'd had a call from Jeff. Not exactly contrite, by the sound of it, but at least he made the right noises.'

'So he bloody well should have.'

'Well, you can rest assured he wouldn't have done it if I'd given him a blast. Anyway, the reason I rang: you know Sarah?'

Sarah was a librarian, a sucker for a politically correct cause, and a confirmed spinster. According to Anne, she was asexual, albeit coolly disposed towards males on ideological grounds. As kids they'd lived in the same street and gone to the same school, establishing a bond strong enough to survive Sarah's father's bankruptcy and her periodic flirtations with the lunatic fringe.

'She's off to India for a couple of months and she's happy for you to stay in her flat. We'd actually be doing her a favour – typical Sarah, it hadn't occurred to her to try sub-letting it.' There was a pause. 'You can move in tonight.'

'Tonight? Christ, anyone would think you've had this planned all along.'

'Well, they'd be wrong. She's not going for a week or so but I'll put her up in a serviced apartment, save you having to make two moves.'

'You really can't wait to get rid of me, can you?'

'I'm just trying to be constructive. Whether you choose to recognise it or not, the way we were going, another week under the same roof and it would've been lawyers at ten paces.'

'So this is about saving our marriage, is it? Short-term pain for long-term gain?'

'Let's just say it's for the best. We've both got a lot of thinking to do.'

Just as well I'd given up expecting a straight answer to a straight question.

Four hours later, Sarah was giving me a user's guide to her flat. It was a dump – threadbare and grimy with garage sale furniture and Heath-Robinson appliances. There was a bedroom, a toilet/bathroom, a kitchenette, a dining/living room, and a spare bedroom containing a fold-up bed, a PC, and all the junk she couldn't put away or throw away.

I'd lived in worse places but that was half a lifetime ago; since then I'd got used to the good life. Sarah must have sensed my gloom. Why else would she have mentioned that, unlike some, she couldn't afford a cleaning lady?

'It'll do me fine,' I said woodenly.

She handed me the keys. 'Okay, well, I'll leave you to it. I'm around for another week so any problems, give me a yell. After that, you're on your own.'

An insensitive remark under the circumstances but I let it go. I felt sorry for her, the poor, sad, silly bitch, stuck in that shit-hole with only the *Guardian Weekly* for company.

I offered to give her a hand with her bags but she said she had to get used to humping them around. As I held the door open for her, she peered at me through her goofy specs. 'Look, I know you and I haven't had much to do with each other and, to be absolutely honest, I had my doubts about you and Anne from the word go but, for what it's worth, I'm sorry.'

Touché. 'These things happen,' I shrugged. 'As a matter of interest, what caused the doubts?'

'Well, I suppose your different backgrounds, really. Just between you and me, I wouldn't wish your parents-in-law on my worst enemy – which you're not, I hasten to add.'

'Pleased to hear it. Anyway, let's not give up hope just yet. I think we've got a reasonable show of working it out.' She was no actor and it was obvious that she had a different impression. 'Does that surprise you?'

'No, not at all. I suppose it's just that, you know, when people separate after fifteen years ...' – she gesticulated like a music-hall Frenchman – '...well, you assume they wouldn't do that lightly.'

'What did Anne say?'

'Just that you'd separated. You know Anne – if she doesn't want to talk about something, you get the message loud and clear.' She stuck out her hand. 'Well, good luck.'

I watched her lug her bags to the lift. 'Have a good trip,' I called. 'Send me a postcard – you can't use the old excuse of forgetting the address.'

She smiled and waved and went to India.

Yeah, she'd lied to me but at least it bothered her. That made it a little easier to take.

I made myself at home: opened a bottle of wine, emptied my suitcase, put stuff away, stuck my toothbrush in the holder above the hand-basin. That took less than half an hour. It was 8.35.

You can learn a lot about a person from what's on their bookshelves. I learned that Sarah was a crossword nut. She had the Shorter Oxford, the Concise Oxford, the Collins, and the Macquarie, as well as dictionaries of mythology, quotations, and world history. I learned that she'd become a food faddist. There were some sound cookbooks in the spare room, including most of Elizabeth David, but the cookbooks which get used are the ones in the kitchen. They were the culinary equivalent of twelve-step self-improvement plans: *Vegetarians Can Be Gourmets Too, Wholesome Wholefood, Quick Meals For Busy People, Eat Your Way To Good Health.*

I learned that she wasn't just another sentimental pinko, she was one of the last unreconstructed reds in the western world. There they were on the bedroom bookshelf, the pin-up boys of the revolution, the landlords of the Gulag – Marx, Engels, Lenin, Trotsky, Uncle Joe Stalin, Mao, Castro, Ho Ho Ho Chi Minh.

On the floor beside the bed was a pile of paperbacks, mostly crime, all by women, plus a few oddities: *Cultivating Female Sexual Energy, The Best of Banjo Paterson* – a bigger book than you'd expect, and *Intimacy and Solitude*. I wondered if she'd left that one out for me.

I grilled a chicken breast, sliced it up with Spanish onion and pesto, and had it with pasta and a salad. I cleared up and did the dishes. It was 10.07. I put the TV on. I'd been living alone for just over two hours.

Within days I'd become a compulsive checker of the TV listings. At home, I'd had thirty-five channels at my fingertips but could hardly be bothered turning on the TV. Now the battiest conspiracy theory documentary or an action movie written by a committee and cranked out on an assembly line could make my night. Elizabeth David notwithstanding, I soon adjusted to the reality of cooking for one, stocking up on tinned salmon and reheat and serve pasta sauces.

Anne seemed intent on paring our contact back to the bare minimum. I'd anticipated regular phone conversations, café breakfasts, the odd meal out. What I got was coffee once a week with one eye on the time. Anything more would just defeat the purpose, she said: we needed time apart to clear our heads and reassess things. She wasn't adversarial but she'd withdrawn from me. She could be relaxed to the point of reviving an old private joke but gave no indication that she looked forward to these meetings or regretted having to hurry away. I began to feel like a needy old friend whom she'd outgrown but felt obliged to keep in touch with for old times sake.

I didn't tell anyone I'd moved out. I was in no hurry to send my parents into a panic and I rationalised that the bigger the drama, the more risk of the situation spinning out of our control. Last but not least, I didn't want to talk about it or be talked about. Anne went along with it reluctantly, agreeing to take messages as if I was still in residence. I didn't think it was too much to ask given that I wasn't in huge demand and we weren't a family who lived in each other's pockets.

I held the first vigil on the eighteenth night of my banishment. I'd fled a parent-teacher evening stupefied, as always, by their ability to disregard the most emphatic evidence of their sons' mediocrity. I tried a new and slightly roundabout route back to the flat which took me down our street.

I crawled past the house. There was a handy park and I had nothing to hurry home to so I pulled in. The curtains were drawn but I knew she was there. I could feel it. I wondered what she was doing and whether she was alone.

I sat there wondering for two hours, then drove on to Darlinghurst, tired, hungry and none the wiser.

So I went back the next night. Strictly speaking, I shouldn't have driven but I can drive well enough when I'm drunk as defined by the breathalyser. I realise many of the killers who end up on the wrong side of the road were thinking exactly that as they slid behind the wheel. The difference is, I don't disconnect when I'm drunk, I don't lose self-awareness, I can still see myself as others see me. I know only too well that there are things I shouldn't attempt when I'm drunk. I'm no good at pool, for instance. I'm no good at sex.

But the sorry truth was, I didn't care – about my blood-alcohol level or anything else.

The curtains were open but the lights weren't on. Sometimes Anne put on drinks for her staff on a Friday night; if she'd had a good month, she might take them out to dinner. I tilted the seat back and put the CD player on random play.

And fell asleep. That tends to happen when I stretch out to listen to music after a few drinks. I woke up after midnight with a dry mouth and a head full of static. The curtains still weren't drawn. I turned the car around and – sober now – steered myself back to Sarah's flat where I spent a slow, sweaty night trying to turn back the images of Anne giving herself away which kept crowding into my mind. I got up at half-past five and sat in the bath with the shower on, like an animal too dumb to come in out of the rain. Then I drove back to our place. Nothing had changed. It seemed reasonable to conclude that Anne had spent the night elsewhere.

It didn't shatter me because it didn't surprise me. For weeks now, my dark side had been whispering in my ear like Iago.

The answer-phone was on when I rang Anne three hours later. I got her at midday, on my sixth try. You must have been up bright and early, I said, prompting more autobiographical detail than such a banality deserved: she'd been for a walk on Bondi Beach, done forty lengths of the gym pool, had a massage, had her legs waxed, and met a business contact for brunch.

I wanted to inspect her, to see if the night had left its mark. 'So what are you up to now?'

'Well, actually, I'm throwing a few things in a bag as we speak,' she said. 'I'm about to head up to the beach.'

A few years earlier, her parents had swapped their weekender in the Blue Mountains for something bigger and better at Palm Beach. Anne had called it keeping up with the Joneses and she was probably right: the Joneses of Vaucluse probably did have million-dollar holiday homes.

'Are your parents going?'

It was a natural assumption – our separation seemed to have given her a renewed appetite for their company – but she was slow to answer. 'No, they're still dithering. They'll probably leave it till tomorrow.'

'When do you think you'll be back?'

'I don't know, it depends a bit on the weather. If it's like this tomorrow, I'll probably stay up there most of the day. Why?'

'I was just going to suggest a coffee but ... maybe next weekend.'

She didn't say yes but, then again, she didn't say no.

Latish that night, drunk by any definition, I rang the beach house. Anne's hello was more of a challenge than a greeting. I hung up without a word. Thinking is another thing I'm not much good at when I'm drunk.

We met for coffee the following Wednesday. I'd had to arrange it with her secretary which seemed to be rubbing it in on a couple of counts. Anne arrived late but made up for it by skipping the pleasantries. 'Did you ring me at the beach house the other night?'

I could have denied it but I was supposed to be marching under the banner of truth. 'Yeah, sorry about that. I just wanted to talk but as soon as you picked up the phone, I realised it was a bad idea.'

'It was late and you knew I was up there on my own.' She watched me closely as she said this. 'A creep call was the last thing I needed. Did you think about that or are you so wrapped up in yourself it didn't enter your mind?'

'I'll say it again, I'm sorry.'

She accepted the apology but without softening. And she was so pushed for time that she didn't ask what I'd wanted to talk about. Maybe she didn't believe me; maybe she thought I'd been checking up on her.

Another lonely, loopy vigil. I was surprised to see a pizza delivery van pull up; Anne wasn't a fan of the real thing, let alone the dial-up, dog's vomit variety. She came to the door in leggings and a sweatshirt and had to wait while the delivery boy patted himself down for change. I was parked directly across the road so I had a good view of her. Of course, that worked both ways – especially as I was right under a street light.

The delivery van drove off. Anne stalked across the road holding the pizza carton out in front of her as if she was going to offer me a slice.

I wound down the window. 'It'll get cold.'

She dumped the carton on the car roof and glared down at me, hands on hips. 'What the hell do you think you're playing at?'

'Nothing at all,' I said. 'I was in the neighbourhood and feeling nostalgic so I thought I'd check out the old homestead. No harm in that, is there?' So much for being truth's soldier.

'Yes, there bloody well is. You're intruding on my space . . .'

'You seem to have forgotten something: I don't have to go along with this. That house is as much mine as yours and legally there's nothing to stop me moving back in tomorrow.'

'Oh, been consulting a lawyer, have we?'

I shook my head. 'I didn't have to. I'm hardly the first guy to find myself in this situation.'

It was a strident exchange in a quiet street. Not wanting the neighbours to talk, Anne put her hands on her knees and bent down to my level. 'You've got to get a grip, Nick,' she said earnestly. 'You're making this much harder than it needs to be.'

'What would you like me to do, Anne – just disappear?'

'I don't expect you to disappear but I do expect you to give me some space. I feel like you're spying on me.'

'Well, I'm not so don't let it cramp your style.'

She sighed and looked away. 'Think about it, okay? This isn't doing us any good at all.'

Anne's tit-for-tat was to let the cat out of the bag next time she spoke to Rosie, triggering an urgent summons to the mansion. Not surprisingly, Anne had been cryptic so I was able to waffle about 'time out' and 'breathing space'.

The moment Julian retired to his study to check in with his informants and co-conspirators in New York, London, Hong Kong and wherever else in the world there was money to be made, Rosie asked, 'Does this have anything to do with ... what we talked about?'

'The affair? I told you, I got the wrong end of the stick.'

'Yes, you did.' Her gaze bored in on me; now it was my turn to be harried over a lie of convenience. 'So this is just an unhappy coincidence?'

'Let me put it this way,' I said. 'We're not living apart because Anne had an affair.'

'Why then?'

'We've got ourselves into a stand-off over an issue of trust and we can't seem to find a way out,' I said, choosing my words carefully. 'It's the old story: I think it's all her fault; she thinks it's all mine. We're hoping a bit of space and time to reflect will do the trick.'

She didn't pursue it. I guess she felt she could join the dots herself.

I managed to stay away for a couple of weeks. I found reasons to hang around after school, often ending up in the staff bar with all the others who didn't have a proper home to go to. A couple of them were flatting in my new neck of the woods and usually kicked on at a local pub which gave me an alternative to sitting in front of the TV with a tray on my lap.

But even on the better nights, I never thought it was over. I still had the symptoms – yearning, jealousy, prurient curiosity, self-pity. The fever hadn't gone away: it was burning a little lower but it was only a matter of time before it raged again.

This time the lights were on behind the curtains. Playing safe, I parked down the street and approached on foot, angry at Anne for putting me through this and ashamed of myself for collaborating in my humiliation. It was cold. I stood in the shadows on the other side of the road, collar turned up, hands balled deep in my pockets, seeing nothing, learning nothing, achieving nothing. Anne was right: I had to get a grip. Go home, sweat out the fever, wake up well, make a new start. Now that I'm here, though, I might as well have one last look. A close-up.

I slunk through the gate and went down the side of the house, through another gate – which should have been locked – to the back. The kitchen lights were on but the blinds were up. Security had gone to hell since I'd been sent packing. I sidled up to the window and peeped in. Unwashed dishes were stacked any old how on the bench. There were two of everything but only one of the champagne flutes had lipstick around the rim.

The door opened and Anne came in, patting her hair with a preoccupied little smile. I didn't move and she didn't look out the window. The top three buttons on her shirt were undone and when she bent over to put something in the dishwasher, I could see her breasts overflow her new black bra.

She started grinding coffee beans; it seemed like a good time to go. But I backed into some outdoor furniture – that white cast-iron stuff; I never liked it – and a chair hit the paving with a hideous clang. I ran for it. I thought I heard the front door open but I didn't look back.

Next morning there was an ultimatum on my voice-mail: 'Two things, Nick: one, you should get help; two, stay away from me. Or else.'

The 'or else' was spelt out, with some style, that afternoon. The headmaster's secretary rang to say that there was a gentleman waiting to see me in the Ridley Room, which was where HM received visitors who warranted grander surroundings than his study.

'Does he have a name?'

'Charles White.'

I didn't know a Charles White personally but, like most people, I knew of *the* Charles White – former state treasurer and federal attorney-general, now lawyer of choice of

Sydney's big money set. I couldn't imagine any circumstances in which our paths would cross. On the other hand, I could easily imagine the headmaster, all aquiver, placing the Ridley Room at his disposal.

'*The* Charles White?'

'Yes, Mr Souter, *the* Charles White.'

The Charles White was a tanned, craggy, silver-haired giant – two metres tall and at least 120 kilograms. He occupied the Ridley Room like a conquering general – feet planted, hands behind his back, warming his horsey arse in front of the fire.

He didn't smile, say hello or offer to shake hands. 'You know who I am?'

I nodded.

'I'm here to impress upon you the folly of your recent conduct towards your wife.'

'What?'

'You know what I'm talking about. It's called harassment – or perhaps you prefer stalking?'

This was surreal. Five minutes earlier I'd been on euphemism detail, as we called writing reports; now I was being heavied by a two thousand dollar an hour standover man in a Savile Row suit. 'You mean to tell me Anne hired you to come here and threaten me with legal action?'

'I've never met or spoken to your wife. She confided in a mutual acquaintance who asked me to intervene – in a private capacity. I believe the most effective contribution I can make is to point out that it would be highly undesirable, both for you personally and for St Bartholomew's, for this matter to be referred to the police. That's not a threat, Mr Souter; it's a statement of fact.'

'You could've fooled me. Did the mutual acquaintance suggest that you bring my boss into it – or was that your idea?'

That drew a glimmer of a smile. 'I did nothing of the kind. I merely asked the headmaster if he could provide us with a suitable venue.'

'Oh, very subtle. Well, as far as I'm concerned, you and your mutual acquaintance can go fuck yourselves.'

As I reached the door, White said, 'Not a terribly constructive suggestion, Mr Souter, but I trust it gave you some satisfaction. Let's get back to reality: I strongly advise you to give your wife a wide berth. If you don't, you stand to lose most of the things you value.'

I rang Anne. She was making a habit of getting others to do her dirty work. Her secretary said, 'I'm sorry, Mr Souter,' – previously I'd been Nick whether I liked it or not – 'but Anne doesn't wish to speak to you. You're welcome to leave a message on her voice-mail.'

I told the little cow where to go and left a snarled fuck-you on Anne's voice-mail. Later, I tried her at home. The number had been disconnected.

I couldn't see her or talk to her but I could still spend her money. The next day, Friday, was end of term. On the way home I filled the boot with some of the finer things in life, then settled in for the weekend.

Saturday morning arrived with a punchy middleweight of a hangover. I'd never been a hair-of-the-dog man, never had the level of intent to want to get straight back into drinking fettle after a big night. But I was alone and on holiday. I was also full of apathy and self-pity, the ideal state of mind for experimental substance abuse. Two crisp Heinekens with my bacon and eggs engendered a fuzzy sense of well-being which I nursed through till lunchtime. I started on the red then and peaked physically and temperamentally as it started to get dark. It was all downhill from there but I was prepared for that eventuality. I switched to cognac.

I didn't go out. I didn't talk to anyone. I just ate and drank and watched TV and slept. Mainly on the couch.

The knocking woke me from an unhealthy dream. I was on the couch, half-dressed. Watery light trickled in the window. I looked at my watch: 9.05. It took a little longer to establish what day it was. It was Monday.

The knocking started again, louder than before. Intrusive noise was unusual in that building: all I ever heard was the occasional heavy footfall in the flat above or greetings and goodbyes echoing in the stairwell. I never passed anyone in the foyer or had to share the lift. Sometimes I imagined that I was the only person there, like Rudolf Hess in Spandau prison, and that those snatches of laughter and conversation were my jailers bantering over their endless card games.

The knocker got a third wind. What was it with that fucker? What did it take to convince him that there was no-one home next door? There never was. I was about to bawl a complaint when a man said loudly, 'If you're in there, Mr Souter, please answer the door. This is the police.'

The police? The fucking bitch had gone and laid a complaint. I rolled off the couch into a pocket of rank body odour which reminded me that I hadn't washed for three days. I stumbled down the corridor and put an eye to the peephole. There were two of them, a bruiser in a leather jacket and an older man in a cheap grey suit.

I said, 'What do you want?'

The older man glanced at his sidekick. 'Nick Souter?'

'Yeah. Who are you?'

They held up ID. 'We're police officers, Mr Souter. I'm detective inspector Sutton and this is detective sergeant Muir. We'd like to talk to you.'

'So talk.'

There was another exchange of glances. 'If you wouldn't mind letting us in,' said Sutton, 'I'd prefer to do this in private.'

I tried the door. It wasn't locked. Sutton advanced, scrutinising me. 'Are you all right, Mr Souter? You don't look too good.'

'What are you – a doctor?' They came in, shutting the door behind them. 'I don't fucking believe this,' I said. 'If I'd been burgled, I'd be lucky to get a constable here within a week. But with this crap, which is no-one else's fucking business, I get you two pounding on my door first thing on Monday morning. Still, I suppose that's what you hire the Charles Whites of this world for.'

Sutton frowned. He had grey eyes to go with his hair, clothes and skin. 'So you know why we're here?'

'Of course I fucking do.'

His grey eyes locked onto mine. 'Well, that's very interesting, Mr Souter, seeing as your wife's body was only discovered an hour ago.'

CHAPTER 11

In this world, nothing can be said to be certain except death and taxes. Benjamin Franklin's bleak summary of the fragility of human arrangements – at least that's how I read it – has stood the test of time: often misquoted, seldom disputed.

Everyone dies but we still think of death as something that happens to other people. It seems to happen a hell of a lot in Africa, for instance, but not around here.

So when Sutton said my wife's body had been discovered, I didn't take that to mean Anne was dead. She couldn't be dead. She wasn't a number – 'Road toll soars after holiday weekend carnage' – she wasn't in a high-risk category, she wasn't one of nature's victims. Most of all, she wasn't other people.

I said, 'What do you mean?'

He reached inside his jacket and brought out a photograph: Anne and me on Pont Neuf, holding hands and glowing, the way lovers do. I studied the photo, focusing, as always, on the zesty sparkle in her eyes and the perfect curve of her smile. An intense young Frenchwoman
with cropped hair and nicotined fingers took it for us and Anne liked it so much she gave it pride of place on the bedside table, in a silver frame from an antiques shop on the Left Bank.

He pointed to her. 'Is this your wife?'

'Where did you get that?'

'From the main bedroom at 17 Washbrook Avenue, Woollahra.' Realising that I wasn't going to make it easy for him, Sutton dragged a hand across his mouth. 'I'm very sorry to have to tell you this, Mr Souter, but your wife is dead.' I stared at him; it was all I could do. 'It's early days but I'm afraid it looks as if she was murdered.'

From time to time, in my strange way, I'd wondered how I'd react to the death of a loved one. (You may think this contradicts what I was saying about death being something that happens to other people, but I'm a pessimist and pessimist superstition holds that disaster imagined is disaster forestalled or, putting it another way, to disregard the possibility of disaster is to tempt fate.) The policemen were wondering too. And waiting. Perhaps it was their expectant presence that caused me to seize up and my impassivity was the emotional equivalent of piss-shyness.

Farmers are a tough breed and my father was no exception. Life on the land is hard; there's a lot of blood and sweat but very few tears. They don't let it get to them, they don't let it show. My father had a kelpie called Roy who loved him as only a working dog can love his master. Roy was off his food so Dad took him to the vet; the diagnosis was that the rest of Roy's life wouldn't be worth living. Dad brought him home, got a spade and his .22 rifle and walked over the hill with Roy, as ever, by his side. The next day he went out and got himself another dog.

He fell off the roof onto a metal railing along the path up to the back door. For two months he was black from his armpit to his knee. He didn't complain or go to the doctor. Instead, he drank a couple of bottles of Guinness every day because one of his mates reckoned it was good for you.

Never let it show. That's the mark of a man. I'm not half the man my father was but I'd always tried not to let it show and maybe I'd forgotten how to. But I felt that stab they talk about. I felt like I'd been cut in two.

I said, 'When?'

'Too early to say,' said Sutton. 'Look, I know this must be terribly hard for you ...'

'What happened?'

'The forensic people have only just got there,' he said.
'We'll have a better idea in twenty-four hours. Listen, why
don't you sit down and we'll make you a cup of tea?'

I stared at him. 'I don't drink tea.'

They made coffee instead. Muir had to go without: he
wasn't a coffee drinker and, being on duty, chose not to
experiment with the aromatic leaves in the unmarked tin at
the back of the cupboard. Sutton lapped up the plunger
coffee like a man used to instant. I sat there, head hung,
wondering what was wrong with me.

'Mr Souter, I have to ask you this,' said Sutton gently.
'Purely routine. Can you account for your movements over
the weekend?'

'Nothing to account for,' I said. 'I was stuck in this dump
all weekend.'

Muir glanced around, as if he couldn't see the problem.
'You mean you didn't go out at all?' he asked.

'No.'

'You have any visitors?'

'No.'

'Any phone calls?'

I shook my head.

They raised eyebrows at each other. 'So what have you
been doing with yourself?' asked Muir.

I shrugged. 'Nothing much.'

Sutton's patient gaze tracked away over my shoulder.
There was a line-up of bottles on the bench. Some were
empty; none were full.

'You called this place a dump,' he said. 'Does that mean you're not here by choice?'

'Anne and I ...' – one of her lines popped into my head – '... were having some time apart.'

'Since when?'

'A couple of months.'

'When did you last see her?'

I assumed the eyeful through the kitchen window didn't count. 'I don't know, a couple of weeks ago, I suppose. We had coffee ...'

Sutton's mobile phone rang. He stood up, turning his back on me. His side of the conversation consisted of 'Okay,' 'Yeah, do that,' and 'Righto.' He put the phone back on his belt and waited for me to meet his eye. 'Your wife's parents have just formally identified the body. I'm sorry.'

Her parents had moved swiftly to reclaim their wilful child but now she'd been taken away from them too. My insides heaved and I began to weep, noisily and profusely. I hadn't wept like that since I was a child but heartache is never far away in a child's fraught world. I'd put away childish things; what mattered to me was a handful of people, one in particular. Now she was gone, ripped out of my life while I snored on the couch like a deadbeat.

After a while Sutton asked me if I was going to be all right. I wanted to say, 'How the fuck would I know?' but I couldn't get the words out.

I remember feverish daydreams interspersed with moments of aching clarity. For fifteen years, I'd worked on the basis that Anne and I were forever. After that conversation with Rosie, I'd found myself thinking that I didn't want to be the leftover. I didn't want to be a slack-bellied phantom shuffling through dusty rooms, seeing her touch everywhere. And I sure as hell didn't want to end up in an old folks' home, surrounded by zombies in dressing-gowns, withering slowly, like a neglected plant.

Lately, I'd had to contemplate the prospect of life without Anne but even though I could sense her being sucked away into another orbit, she still had a place in my scenarios. In the worst case, I saw us staying in touch, just good friends to the outside world but linked by intimate, unsullied memories. I wanted to believe in a bond impervious to time, change, and other people. I thought I'd always know where to find her.

I rang my parents but they were out. I rang Rosie. In the background I heard Arabella ask, 'Mummy, what's wrong? Why are you crying?' That set me off. Neither of us could complete a sentence so I hung up.

When Rosie rang me back, she wanted more information than I could provide. 'Watch the news,' I said. 'They've probably told the media more than they told me.'

She wanted me to come and stay. That held some attraction but I was wary of becoming the focus of their grief. I felt enough of a victim as it was.

'Nick, that conversation we had about Anne . . .'

'Jesus, Rosie, not now . . .'

'Believe me, I hate this as much as you do but there's a reason for it: did you talk about it to anyone else?'

'No. Why?'

'I was just thinking, they'll start with you, Nick. The police, I mean. They always do. You've seen the statistics. I know it's the last thing you want to be thinking about but you can't afford not to.'

'They didn't act as if they thought I had anything to do with it. In fact, they went pretty easy on me.'

'Whatever, you should get yourself a lawyer. I'll talk to Julian – he knows some good ones.'

'My wife is murdered and the first thing I do is get myself a lawyer: how's that going to look?'

'For god's sake, Nick, this is no time to be worrying about what other people think.'

I'd lived on cassoulet for three days and had the wind to prove it. Fart, mustiness, body odour – I was breathing slum air. I opened another jar and another bottle and later cried myself to sleep on the couch.

It was dark when the phone woke me. My father-in-law, who sounded drunker than I was, called me vile names and hoped I'd rot in hell.

'I didn't kill her, Roger.'

'Don't think you can lie your way out of it. I've fixed you, don't you worry; I've told the police all about you. They know what sort of scum they're dealing with.'

'Roger, I swear to god I didn't kill her. Why would I do that? I loved her.'

He snarled like a rogue dog. 'You're nothing but trash, you know that? Annie didn't love you. She never did.'

I resisted the temptation to share Harry's wedding day analysis with him. 'We were pretty happy for fifteen years, Roger. You can't deny that.'

'Fifteen years knowing that marrying you was the biggest mistake of her life.'

'If you say so.'

'You know why she stuck it out? Because she didn't want to hurt you. Jesus fucking christ. She finally realised what a waste it was and was starting a new life, the life she deserved. But you couldn't stand that, could you? So you killed her, you murdering piece of shit.'

'Look, Roger, I know how you must feel . . .'

'Don't say that.' His voice dissolved into a bubbling moan. 'Don't you dare say that – you don't have any fucking idea how I feel. You'll pay for this, you evil little cunt. I'll make sure of that if it's the last fucking thing I do.'

I hung up on him and rang Rosie to find out who was on Julian's short list.

The cops came back the next morning. I was still in bed, on the theory that if I stayed there long enough, oblivion would eventually sneak up on me.

This time it was Muir and a detective constable called Anderson who had bleached blond hair and sunglasses perched on top of his head. Muir looked me over, making a face. 'Mate, it's time you cleaned yourself up,' he said, steering me into the bathroom. 'Give it the full monty: shower, shampoo, shave, shit and shoeshine. On second thoughts, skip the shit and shoeshine – we're running late.'

'What for?'

'Sutton wants to talk to you and he doesn't like being kept waiting.'

'Is that my problem?'

Muir smiled thinly. 'It could be.'

I was nervous but I was also curious, in a spaced-out sort of way, about what came next. Anything was better than being holed up in Sarah's flat, grieving, crying over spilt milk, wondering what would become of me. They bunged me in the back seat of an unmarked Ford. Muir took the wheel. It wasn't much of a day: a concrete-coloured sky sagged low over the city and drizzle drifted silently across the rooftops. Muir turned the radio on and we sat in silence listening to ratbag talk-back all the way to Police Headquarters City East.

Sutton stood up and came out from behind his desk when I was shown into his office. He thanked me for coming in. I asked if I'd had any choice.

'Look, I know this must be hard for you but the fact is, we need your help. You're our best source of information.' He sat me down in front of the desk. 'How are you bearing up?'

'So so.'

'Do you have a support network? People in your situation usually need a bit of looking after.'

'I've got my parents.'

'Where are they?'

'Goulburn.'

He frowned. 'What about here?'

'Why, don't you want me to leave town?'

'Not particularly,' he said. 'As I said, we need your help. Today, for instance, I'd like you to take us over the crime scene.'

'You mean our house?'

'To us, it's the crime scene.'

'As a matter of interest, when will I be able to move back in?'

He swivelled unhurriedly in his executive chair. 'Oh, not for a wee while yet. So that's what you're going to do, is it? I thought you might want to get rid of the place.'

'I don't follow the property market but I wouldn't have thought there was a huge demand for crime scenes.'

'You never know,' said Sutton. 'You can't underestimate the ghoul factor.'

We locked eyes like schoolboys trying to stare each other out. I was aware of behaving oddly, saying things without knowing why. My life had been ransacked, stripped of all certainty, all normality, and I no longer had a natural sense of what was appropriate.

When he'd found whatever he was looking for, Sutton lowered his gaze to the open folder on his desk. 'We now have a clearer picture of what happened,' he said.

'Before we go any further,' I said, 'should I have a lawyer?'

'What, right here and now?'

I shrugged.

'Well, it's entirely up to you. I mean, if you feel you need one, you'd better have one. But let me just tell you what's happening: I'll update you on the facts of the case and what's come up from the lab; we'll take a set of your fingerprints for the purposes of elimination; then we'll visit the crime scene. That's it.' He pushed the phone across his desk. 'If you think you need a lawyer for that, go ahead.'

He waited. I said, 'Well, if that's all . . .'

'You're sure? Okay.' He bent his head again. 'Your wife was suffocated. It appears the perpetrator used a pillow from her bed, which was then removed from the scene. Estimated time of death was between 11.00 pm Sunday and 2.00 am Monday. There are no signs of forced entry and none of the nearby residents report hearing or seeing anything untoward. The cleaning woman let herself in at 7.30 am Monday and discovered the body in the main bedroom – on, as opposed to in, the bed.' He paused and flicked me a warning glance from under his eyebrows. Watch out, it said. This might hurt. 'The pathologist doesn't think your wife was sexually assaulted; he does think, though, that she'd engaged in some consensual sexual activity.'

The idea had been oozing around my head for so long that confirmation – and confirmation doesn't come much more official than that – was almost superfluous. I needed it in plain language though: the antiseptic officialese gave my mind too much room to move.

I said, 'You mean she'd had a fuck?'

'Not according to the pathologist,' said Sutton. 'Incidentally, there were no traces of ejaculate. Anywhere,' he added helpfully.

'I'm running out of ideas here.'

His mouth compressed to a thin, fastidious line, as if such fleshly detail wasn't to his taste. 'There were indications that the genital area had been stimulated, to the point of penetration.'

'Maybe she ...'

'On the basis of his examination, the pathologist doesn't think your wife manually stimulated herself and we didn't find a ... an aid. Would you happen to know if she had anything of the kind?'

'No, I wouldn't happen to know.'

'Well, even if she did, it didn't walk out of there.'

Sutton sat with his legs crossed and his hands in his lap, waiting for me to share our secrets. I said, 'So what does all that tell you, Inspector?'

'It tells me that your wife probably knew her killer.'

Once again Muir drove. Sutton sat in the back with me, chatting away like a stranger on a train. Did I enjoy teaching? Was St Bart's really worth it? And, by the way, what sort of money were we talking about? He whistled when I told him the fees. He didn't have much time for the local high school – your typical state-run zoo, by the sound of it – but it would have to do. Putting four kids through private school wasn't an option on a cop's salary. I wondered if it was a roundabout way of letting me know he wasn't on the take.

The uniformed constable at the gate was the only sign that the plague had spread to Washbrook Avenue. The middle class believes, as an article of faith, that there is an epidemic of violent crime out there. We live in fear of it breaking out of the wastelands where the battlers and the immigrants jostle and surging into our manicured suburbs.

As we went inside, Sutton said, 'Sure you can handle this?'

'Now he asks me. So what am I meant to be looking for?'

'Anything that doesn't look right or doesn't belong. We'll be wanting to check out everyone who's been through here lately so keep an eye open for anything that would've been delivered or would've required a tradesman. A lot of them operate on cash so we can't rely on finding the paperwork.'

'Did you ask the cleaning lady? We've had her for years.'

'Not yet. She's in a bit of a state.'

I was following Sutton down the corridor. 'That makes two of us,' I said but he gave no indication that he'd heard me.

I went from room to room seeing only signs of a life in progress: flowers on the sideboard, a stack of weekend papers on the ottoman, a bowl of oranges awaiting the juicer. After a while, I began to make out the curving wake of a life changing course. Some furniture had been rearranged and a couple of pictures I liked had given way to seething abstracts. There were new towels in the bathroom, new clothes in the wardrobe, new music in the CD rack, new books on the bedside table. Not all these acquisitions were entirely in character – the books were grimly high-brow while the CDs were the purchases of a woman who'd begun to lie about her age. I didn't mention them to Sutton; I didn't think that was what he had in mind.

The sense of loss was overpowering. What were we doing, the pair of us? How had we ever let it come to this, me on the skids in Sarah's flat and Anne here surrounded by presents to herself, trying to cobble together a new identity?

The clothes I'd left behind were in the spare room, along with bits and pieces to which I had first claim or in which she had nothing invested. I'd been reduced to the status of a possession which no longer fulfilled a purpose or provided pleasure: first you shove it away out of sight, then you get rid of it. Before she could start the new life her father talked about, she'd had to dismantle the old one. If she'd had visitors, they'd left without trace and, apart from the summer clothes in the spare room, so had I. There was precious little else to show that this was my home too.

I asked Sutton if they'd really found the Pont Neuf photo in the main bedroom.

'No, the cleaning lady dug it out for us.'

'Sparing my feelings, eh?'

'And mine. Sometimes it's the little things that get to you – whether you're hearing the news or breaking it. The time apart wasn't your idea, was it?'

His tone was sympathetic rather than interrogatory. I realised that talking about it to him wouldn't be the ordeal others would make it. He was detached, informed – he'd already had my father-in-law funnelling malice into his ear – and he hadn't known Anne. To Sutton, our home was a crime scene and my wife's murder was the latest in a long line.

I shook my head. 'No, it wasn't my idea.'

I told him as dispassionately as I could and without leaving out anything that seemed pertinent. He agreed that Jason didn't fit the bill and asked me who might. I referred him to the editor of *High Finance*.

'Why him?'

'Gut feeling.' He wanted more than that so I added, 'He was here for dinner not so long ago. I'd been led to believe that their relationship was purely professional but it didn't look that way.'

He nodded as if that was good enough for him. 'So how were you and your wife getting along?'

'Up and down.'

'You can't have been too thrilled when White showed up.'

'No,' I said. 'That seemed over the top. Whose idea was it?'

'I'm surprised you haven't worked it out.'

The penny dropped. 'Her father?' Sutton nodded. 'Did he tell you about White before or after he told you I killed his daughter?'

'What makes you think he did that?'

'He rang last night, got a few things off his chest. He seems to think it's an open-and-shut case.'

'Christ spare us from relatives.' Sutton's flash of irritation took me aback; I'd got used to his equanimity. 'Don't take it personally, it's pretty much par for the course.'

'Try telling him that. So does he know who J is?'

'The subject of his daughter's part in all this didn't come up,' he said thoughtfully. 'Funny that.'

That afternoon I made the front page. In living colour.

Rosie rang to say that the *Telegraph* had a photo of me and Sutton at the house with a caption identifying me as the victim's husband. There was a story too; she didn't elaborate so I assumed it wasn't one for the scrapbook.

I passed on what I'd told Sutton, apologising for my previous equivocation. She shushed me and pitied me for what I'd been through and what I still had to endure. She had many questions – What did Sutton tell you? What did he ask you? What does he think? – and grew gently exasperated with my lifeless responses. I told her I was tired, because I didn't want to say that I felt bereft and isolated and my body ached as if I'd spent a year in chains. That set off a welter of self-reproach and apology. Next time, she insisted, I should just tell her to shut up.

Her other news was that our parents were on their way up from Goulburn for a family conference. That promised to be a barrel of laughs, I said clumsily, and was reminded that it probably wasn't their idea of fun either. I grunted my way through the rest of the conversation and went out for a paper.

The photographer must have been down the street with a zoom lens, probably hiding behind a tree. That's the trouble with living in an avenue – plenty of cover for the paparazzi. I remembered the moment: Sutton had just asked me if I was sure I was up to the guided tour. I had a quizzical expression which I tend to think is my best look. All things considered, I didn't look too bad. Just as well Muir hadn't wanted me stinking out his car.

The caption read, *Murder victim Anne Souter's husband Nick (left) and Detective Inspector Sutton entering the family home in Woollahra where her body was discovered.*

A picture is supposedly worth ten thousand words. Call me a bookworm but that seems a little high to me. Take this picture: it didn't tell you anything about the state of our marriage. You had to read the story for that:

The estranged husband of murdered public relations high-flier Anne Souter today visited the marital home accompanied by the officer heading the investigation, Detective Inspector Garry Sutton.

Ms Souter (38), who ran her own CBD-based PR company, was found dead in the main bedroom of her Woollahra home yesterday morning. Police immediately launched a murder investigation. Although detectives are remaining tight-lipped on the cause of death, the Telegraph *has learned that she was suffocated.*

At the time of her death, Ms Souter was living apart from her husband Nick, an English teacher at an exclusive eastern suburbs private school. Mr Souter is understood to have moved out of their $1.5 million home two months ago.

A police spokesperson told the Telegraph *that the visit was 'standard procedure'. He said Mr Souter had provided useful assistance, particularly in helping detectives gain a clearer picture of his wife's routine and lifestyle. There were no suspects as yet, said the spokesperson, but the investigating team had already gathered a considerable amount of information from a variety of sources and was following up some strong leads.*

Anne Souter's PR expertise and dynamic personality had made her a well-known figure on the Sydney corporate scene and propelled her company into the upper tier of this intensely competitive industry. She and her husband had been married for fifteen years but did not have children.

Love that 'but'.

So these were my fifteen minutes. Our fifteen minutes.

My other caller that afternoon was the administrator at St Bart's, an ex-British Army man.

'Nick, Toby Jenner here. Dreadfully sorry about what happened. Absolutely appalling business. How are you coping?'

'I'm okay.'

'Well, our thoughts are with you. Anything we can do, don't hesitate. On that subject, I was on the blower to HM this morning – as you may know, he's in the UK – and he feels, as I do, that our absolute priority is to ensure you get through this in one piece. We're putting you on indefinite paid leave. You just take your time, do whatever you have to do. There'll be no pressure from this end.'

'That's nice to know. I wouldn't be much good to anyone at the moment but how I'll feel in a couple of weeks, I just don't know. I might be better off getting back to work rather than sitting around feeling sorry for myself.'

'Ah, well, you see, Nick,' – his tone shifted like a ham-fisted gear change – 'there are a couple of issues here. In the first place, there's a process involved. As of now, you're officially on unpaid leave and we're making arrangements to cover for your absence so you'd need to notify us in advance as opposed to just turning up. Secondly, and I say this with all the sympathy in the world, we can't have a situation where staff are using their jobs as a sort of therapy. As I'm sure you'd appreciate, we have an obligation to the lads and the parents not to send you back into the fray without the all-clear, as it were.'

'Toby, this paid leave: it hasn't got anything to do with what's on the front page of the *Telegraph*, has it?'

'You have the advantage of me there, old man – I'm afraid I don't take the *Telegraph*.'

CHAPTER 12

That night was the first and only time I saw my father cry. It was a deeply morose occasion although, just for the record, there was a dry eye in the house. I wasn't comfortable being the odd one out, the cold fish in a school of mammals, but I'd done my crying in solitary, where you can really let yourself go, and I couldn't muster a single tear, even for appearances' sake.

My parents retired early, solemnly watched over by Rosie as they stiffly negotiated the stairs down to the guest apartment. It occurred to me that if their health was to take a sudden turn for the worse, she'd find it hard not to attach some blame to me.

Rosie soon followed. I hadn't had enough to drink. More surprisingly, neither had Julian who'd looked red-eyed and washed-out at dinner, drained by emotional overload and punishing hours. The rewards were there for all to see but money never sleeps. Julian wasn't much of a drinker but he was a suave host who could watch his guests soak up a three-hundred-dollar bottle of cognac without a twitch. That night he brought out a twenty-year-old single malt.

In vino veritas. It began with, 'I don't know if I should tell you this . . .'

I sat up straighter. 'What?'

'It's about Anne – something I didn't tell you at the time and probably shouldn't tell you now. I can't see it doing any good.'

Julian's hesitancy was intended as a warning. I wasn't going to enjoy what he had to say so he needed my blessing before he went any further. As if I was going to withhold it.

'Well, it can't do any harm,' I said. 'I'm beyond that.'

'Are you absolutely sure?'

'Yes.'

'Okay,' he said. 'This happened last summer, just after the Metropolis opened.'

The Metropolis was a hotel. Or, as they put it in the lifestyle sections, the Metropolis was *the* hotel.

'They were offering pretty good deals then, trying to get word-of-mouth going, so we put on a lunch in the private dining room. I was meeting and greeting in the lobby when I noticed this woman. It was the shades that caught my eye. Have I ever told you that people wearing dark glasses inside is one of my pet hates?'

'It rings a bell.'

'Anyway she walked through the lobby with her head down ...'

'Let's call her Anne, shall we?' I was being a spoilsport but this wasn't a shaggy dog story to go with the sipping whisky.

Julian nodded. 'Okay. She was obviously in a big hurry so I didn't want to hold her up. She walked through the lobby and got straight into a lift. I assumed she was having a room service working lunch with someone staying in the hotel and didn't think anything more of it.' He poured himself another shot; I realised he couldn't have done this sober. 'That was the night the four of us had dinner at that little place in Bondi, remember?'

'Vaguely.'

'I got there late, as usual. You were talking to someone at another table and Anne was in the loo. As soon as I sat down, Rosie asked me what the Metropolis was like. When Anne came back – and bear in mind I hadn't mentioned the fact that I'd seen her there – Rosie asked her if she'd checked out the Metropolis yet. She said no, she hadn't got around to it. So while I'm sitting there wondering which part of the question didn't she understand, Rosie's telling her that I'd had lunch there that day and reckoned it lived up to all the hype. I'm not exaggerating, Nicky, Anne absolutely froze. I tried not to let on that I'd seen her, which wasn't easy the way she was staring at me. After thirty seconds or so, she snapped out of it and carried on as if nothing had happened. It was one of those situations, you know, five minutes later you're thinking, did I really see that or did I imagine it?'

I remembered talking to Rosie after I'd found the note and sensing misgivings behind her sweeping reassurances. 'You told Rosie?'

Julian nodded.

'But neither of you told me.'

'We talked about it. I said it was like having a jumper with a little pull in it: no-one else would notice but it bugs the hell out of you. When you look in the mirror, you don't see that the jumper looks good on you, all you see is this little bit of wool sticking out. So you fiddle around with it trying to fix it but you just make it worse. In the end, you shove the fucking thing in a plastic bag and give it to the Smith Family.'

I said, 'And the moral of the story is ...?'

'We didn't tell you because we didn't want to risk fucking a good thing up.' Suddenly the tears were back in Julian's eyes. 'We know a lot of couples, Nicky,' he said huskily, 'and you guys were up there with the best of them. You had something special. Okay, maybe it wasn't perfect but show me a relationship that is.'

He stood up unsteadily. So did I. He rubbed his eyes with the heels of his hands and embraced me. 'Oh, fuck, Nicky,' he whispered. 'What will you do without her?'

Julian described the lawyer he'd picked out for me as a street-fighter *and* a pit-bull. Fine, I said; next time I went drinking in Redfern, I'd give him a call. But I went to see him anyway. As the others kept saying, it couldn't do any harm.

We met at a sidewalk café in Double Bay. Tony Kiernan was one of those flat-faced, beetle-browed Irishmen who, even when they're sober, give the impression they're looking for a fight. But he wore cufflinks – always, I think, evidence of social aspirations – and expensive eau de toilette so he obviously saw himself as more than a bovver boy.

After we'd ordered and he'd carefully arranged his mobile, cigarettes and lighter on the table in front of him, he asked how I was doing. I'd come to realise that people now meant this question literally – they really wanted to know. What could I say? That I felt crushed under the weight of grief and the desolation which overtook me whenever I contemplated my derailed life? But there were also moments when I felt – guiltily – like a racing car driver limping away from his obliterated machine, surprised that I wasn't feeling more pain.

I said, 'I'm okay.'

Kiernan's eyebrows twitched indifferently. He was the exception; he'd said it just for something to say. Our espressos arrived. He tested the temperature and downed it in one gulp, then lit a cigarette, which he consumed with similar gusto. What next? I wondered. An invitation to arm-wrestle?

'I just want to make sure you understand what we're dealing with here,' he said. 'You do realise the cops take it for granted that you killed your wife?'

'No, I wasn't aware of that.'

His eyes lit up, like a stand-up comedian interrupted by a kamikaze heckler. 'Shit, you really do need a lawyer.'

'How do you know that? I mean, did they actually tell you?'

'They didn't have to. Listen, mate, I've got a line into City East; I can get it from the horse's mouth if you want. One phone call, that's all it'll take.'

'I'd just like to know what that statement's based on.'

He leaned forward, his blunt face parting the haze of smoke. 'It's based on the fact that there are no Sherlock Holmes in the New South Wales Police Service. They're not super-sleuths because they don't have to be – ninety per cent of the time, what it looks like at first glance is what it is. When a woman gets murdered, they start with the man in her life. And if she gave the man in her life the broom a couple of months ago and he didn't like it, they probably won't go any further. You've got to understand how the cops operate: they don't approach it with an open mind and see where the evidence leads them. What they do is, they walk into a crime scene, look around, and have déjà vu. "Remember the nurse in Marrickville?" "Doesn't this remind you of that housewife in Randwick?" Same old, same old. Every other time it's been the husband or the boyfriend or the de facto so why should this one be any different? You see what I'm saying? It's not a matter of figuring out who did it – they've already decided that – it's a matter of gathering the evidence and putting together a case that'll stand up in court.' I started to say something but he talked over me, numbering the points with his fingers. 'Your brother-in-law said the following: your wife had an affair; your relationship deteriorated; she told you to piss off; she wasn't receptive to your attempts to maintain contact; she called in Charles White to make sure you got the message; you don't have an alibi. True or false?'

'True.'

'All of it?'

'Yeah.'

He held out his hands, palms upward, inviting me to concede. 'You fucking did it – why would they think otherwise?' When I didn't respond, he slapped his hands down on the table. 'You still don't believe me, do you?'

I shrugged. It made a certain amount of sense but surely even the most ponderous policeman, the proverbial PC Plod – which Sutton certainly wasn't – could have seen that Anne and I didn't fit the formula.

He said, 'I presume you saw yesterday's *Telegraph*? The only thing missing was a seventy-two point screamer headline: *This Scumbag Killed His Wife*. You were set up, mate. I mean, didn't you wonder how come a photographer just happened to be there?'

'I assumed he was staking the place out.'

Kiernan rolled his eyes, looking pained. He seemed determined to go through his entire repertoire of theatrics. 'Yeah, that's right, they mounted a round-the-clock operation just on the off-chance you'd turn up. No, mate, the photographer was there because the cops tipped them off. And they returned the favour by running that particular photo.'

'What was wrong with it?'

'Nothing wrong with it but you don't look exactly grief-stricken, do you? As for that crap about the cops not revealing the cause of death, then telling us in the next sentence she was suffocated, jesus, give me a break ... That story should've had Sutton's by-line on it.'

'Why would he do that?'

'Just turning up the heat. You didn't get it because, right now, you don't know which way is up but plenty of other people would've read between the lines. Mate, you're about to find out who your real friends are.' I thought of the call from Toby Jenner; the comprehension in my eyes made Kiernan grin. 'That's always a chastening experience.'

Whether he was showing off or trying to make me feel stupid or both, he couldn't have asked for a more compliant straight man. And I came back for more. 'Sutton certainly doesn't give the impression that he thinks I did it,' I said.

'He's Mr Nice Guy, right? Tea and sympathy? He understands what you're going through and just wants to help? Like fuck. He wants you to feel that you can confide in him; he'll sit there listening to you pour your heart out, making all the right noises, filing it away, letting you talk yourself into a life sentence. It's a variation on the Stockholm Syndrome: I've heard of guys confessing to do a detective a favour – they wanted to make sure he got the credit or save him the trouble of an investigation. I've heard of guys confessing because they felt guilty about lying to such a nice bloke. It's just a means to an end. Repeat after me: Sutton is not my friend.'

'Well, anyway, it won't work because I didn't kill her.'

That really tickled him. 'Whoa, slow down, tiger – I don't go all the way on first date. Well, if the softly, softly approach doesn't work, they'll go to Plan B.'

'Which is?'

'They'll get nasty. As I said, we're not dealing with sophisticated people here.'

'It's hard to imagine Sutton doing that.'

'Maybe not him personally. That's what he's got Muir for.'

When Muir had nursemaided me into the shower, I'd seen it as an act of gruff kindness. Looked at through Kiernan's wide-open eyes, it was a way of keeping me occupied while they searched the flat.

Kiernan stubbed out his third cigarette and stood up.

I said, 'What happens now?'

'You sit tight. Next time they turn up, say nothing and call me.'

It seemed I had a lawyer whether I liked him or not. I said, 'Should I be worried?'

'Let's not shit our pants just yet but I have to tell you, they've already got a pretty strong circumstantial case. By the way, are you the beneficiary?'

'I don't know,' I said. 'We never talked about it. I'm not even sure Anne had a will.'

'Which would make you the beneficiary by default.' He shook his head. 'They've got motive coming out of their arse.'

'The circumstantial stuff wouldn't be enough for a conviction though, would it?'

'Mate, people go down on circumstantial evidence every day. Bear in mind beyond reasonable doubt means different things to different people. Shit, guys have been convicted of murder when the cops haven't even produced a body – in other words, the prosecution was able to prove beyond reasonable doubt that the defendant committed murder without being able to prove beyond a shadow of doubt that murder actually took place.' I was still digesting that when he thought of something else for me to worry about. 'Your other problem is that they're putting all their eggs in one basket. It's

Catch 22: the more they focus on you, the less they focus on other possibilities, the less likely they are to turn up information which would cause them to question whether they're on the right track. And as each day goes by, the real killer gets a little further away.' The wise-guy grin reappeared. 'Assuming you didn't do it, of course.'

Later that day, Rosie and I took our parents to Central. They were going home. Even with their son's life in mystifying flux, twenty-four hours in the raucous city was as much as they could handle.

Country folk are comfortable with the Old Testament; it speaks their language. In their fierce heart of hearts, they believe the city is damned. All they see is dog eat dog and money for nothing and the cult of self-gratification and they know the day will come when God's had it up to here. Then look out: remember what He did to Sodom and Gomorrah?

Not for the first time I'd sensed that staying with Julian and Rosie reinforced my parents' feeling of displacement. They were unsettled by the domestic comings and goings, the parade of strangers who seemed to have the run of the place – the cleaning ladies, the gardener, the nanny, the pool cleaner, the prole tradesmen with their beer guts and bad teeth. And they disapproved of the lack of restraint as exemplified by the sheer sprawl of the house and the shelves of redundant toys, like a mothballed air force.

On the platform, my father and I shook hands. Then he put me in a headlock and pressed his sandpapery cheek against mine – another first. 'Look after yourself, son,' he implored. My mother hugged me. 'Poor Nick,' she sobbed into my chest. 'My poor, poor Nick.'

On the way home, Rosie asked if my meeting with Kiernan was really as ho-hum as I'd made it out to be. Her face sagged as I told her what I'd kept from my parents.

'Shit, Nick, that's scary.'

I shrugged. 'I didn't kill Anne so the way I see it, as long as the system works, I've got nothing to worry about.'

That made her even gloomier. 'It sounds like you've got a lot more faith in the system than Kiernan has.'

'Of course I have,' I said. 'Most of his clients get off.'

I was glad when she changed the subject. 'So what did you and Julian get up to last night? I just about had to dynamite him out of bed this morning.'

'We drank a little whisky,' I said. 'Had a little chat.'

'He told you about seeing Anne at the Metropolis, didn't he?'

I nodded.

'What did you make of it?'

'Well, it's a bit like my situation, isn't it? If you're looking at it from the outside, the bare facts all seem to point one way.'

Her face sagged again but this time in disbelief. 'In other words, there could be a perfectly innocent explanation?'

'It's possible. You obviously don't think so?'

She wiped the disbelief off her face. 'I don't think it matters a damn any more, Nick. You've got to forget about it – all of it. You've got the rest of your life to worry about.'

Today is the first day of the rest of your life. Just do it. Make it happen. Live like there's no tomorrow. Love like you've never been hurt.

I'm too old to fall for these sales pitches and their mindless, Madison Avenue optimism. Life's harder than that. Life's anything but a pushover.

Sarah's flat wasn't conducive to looking on the bright side. It cornered me and hammered me down like a prison cell. In a minimum-security prison, admittedly; a prison where I could come and go as I pleased and which I had all to myself. A far cry from the barbarous ghettoes to which wife-killers are consigned.

I went for a walk in the squally dusk. On Oxford Street the salesgirls and boys slouched, the cruisers cruised and the posers posed. After dark, Oxford Street is the demimonde's turf. I might not have looked the part but I had the credentials: alienated, notorious, despised by the bourgeoisie.

The pubs looked boisterous but I wasn't tempted. I've always thought that people who go to pubs on their own have a problem, whether it's loneliness or an aversion to their own company or simply alcoholism. Besides, I didn't want to run into the guys from work. They probably would have made their excuses and left but I couldn't depend on it.

I wouldn't have looked twice at the car parked opposite the apartment building if it hadn't been for the brief, radioactive glow when a headlight beam splashed across the windscreen. I guess that's the whole point of bleached blond hair: you want to be noticed.

I crossed the road, tapped on the driver's window, and asked Anderson if I was officially under surveillance.

'I wouldn't say that.'

'Then what are you doing here?'

'I'm just doing my job, all right?'

It was like trying to have a conversation with a parrot: the fact that it can say a few words only gets you so far. As I went up the steps to the apartment building, a car door opened and closed behind me. I turned around, quite looking forward to telling Anderson to fuck off. Jock stood at the bottom of the steps with a bottle in a brown paper bag and the death's head grin of a man making a long overdue visit to a terminally ill friend.

'Nickelarse. How's it hanging?'

'Hello, Jock. How did you find me?'

'I asked your sister. Are we going to stand out here freezing our nuts off or are you going to invite me into your hide-out?'

'Some hide-out,' I said. 'There's a cop parked right over there.'

Jock glanced over his shoulder. 'He's a cop, is he? What's he doing here?'

'Keeping an eye on me. They seem to think I killed Anne.'

'Jesus wept.' He shook his head. 'Who's running this case – Inspector Clouseau?'

We sat at the table drinking wine. Naturally, Jock wanted the full story but he had to settle for the bare bones – which didn't include J.

'What makes them think you did it?'

'They're programmed that way. And there's a certain amount of circumstantial evidence. And I don't have an alibi. Just for the record though, I didn't do it.'

'For fuck's sake, you don't need to tell me that. You couldn't kill a fly.'

'If you're going to be a character witness, you'll have to do better than that. I've killed many a fly. I derive a certain amount of grim satisfaction from it.'

'Well, all right, a butterfly then.'

'Why would anyone want to kill a butterfly?'

'Why would you of all people want to kill Anne?'

I shrugged. 'Anger, jealousy, greed – if you're looking for motives, I've got the full set.'

'Why jealousy?'

I didn't feel any obligation to tell Jock the truth. 'They think I'd got it into my head that Anne was seeing someone.'

He lunged for his cigarettes. 'Was she?'

It was the unashamed curiosity that decided me. That and the fact his name began with J. 'You know what Anne told me a few weeks ago?'

'No, Nick,' he said, irked that I'd changed the subject, 'I haven't got a clue.'

'Okay, I'll give you a clue: it involved her, a close personal friend of mine, and an improper suggestion.'

He actually blushed, which I had to see to believe, and looked away. 'Jesus christ, Nick,' he mumbled. 'This is a hell of a time to bring that up.'

'So it's true?'

His eyes darted. He didn't want to meet my eye but he was anxious to know how much trouble he was in. 'What exactly did she say?'

'That you propositioned her and she declined.'

He nodded glumly. 'Yeah. You know what a shocker I can be when I've had a few.'

'That's it? No excuses? You're not going to claim she gave you the come-on?'

'She didn't give me the come-on.' He said it slowly, reflectively, with a faint but unmistakable ring of qualification.

'You know what that sounded like, Jock?' I said. 'It sounded like, "She didn't give me the come-on but ... "'

'It was a spur-of-the-moment thing,' he said. 'It wasn't like I planned it, I just got a bit pissed and thought, you know, nothing ventured, nothing gained.' He paused. 'No way did Anne egg me on; I wouldn't pretend that for one minute.' He was in a holding pattern now, awaiting permission to proceed to his destination. I kept my face blank and said nothing. 'But with Anne ... it's hard to explain but there was something about her ...'

'What?'

'As I say, it's hard to put it into words.'

'Have a go.'

He held up his hands, a gesture of self-absolution. Whatever happened now was on my head. 'Anne had class – everyone said so. I was always hearing about what a class act she was. Well, I had a slightly different view: I thought she was a bit too good to be true. Don't get me wrong, I'm not suggesting it was all an act but my gut feeling – and that's all it was; there was nothing I could put my finger on – was that underneath that immaculate surface, she was ... well, not quite so immaculate.'

'Come on, Jock, spit it out.'

'Okay, but I've got to warn you, there's no polite way to say this. My instinct was that she had a dirty streak. There you are.'

'And you're renowned for your unerring instinct when it comes to women, isn't that so?'

He shrugged, both to deflect my irony and to downplay the slur on my dead wife. It's no big deal, was the message. You thought Anne was different but she wasn't; she was just like all the rest.

You see, Jock was a pornographer and pornographers think all women have a dirty streak.

CHAPTER 13

The grungy pile in the corner of the bedroom reminded me that I was down to my last pair of clean underpants. I crammed it all into an overnight bag and went off to see the sweating Korean in the laundromat at the end of the street. I hadn't gone ten metres before Sutton got out of a car parked on the other side of the road. I didn't stop so he had to break into a gentle jog to catch up.

'Going somewhere?'

'It's a free country, isn't it?'

'Sure, but as I said the other day, I'd prefer you didn't leave town.'

'Oh, that's right,' I said. 'You need my help to crack the case.'

Sutton half-smiled as if I'd said something half-witty. 'Exactly. So where can we get in touch with you?'

'You could always try the friendly neighbourhood laundromat.'

He chuckled. 'Oh, just off to do the washing, are you? Mind if I tag along? I need to stretch my legs.'

I thought about calling Kiernan but hollering for a lawyer to ride shotgun to the end of the street and back seemed a little excitable. Five minutes each way: I could manage that without him holding my hand.

I could have asked Sutton what was going on but Kiernan had spelt it out for me: Anderson's role was to ensure that there was no peace for the wicked, and now Father Sutton had come to hear my confession.

He began with a eulogy: Anne was obviously a remarkable person – no-one had a bad word to say about her; everyone seemed devastated by her death. And we must have had a pretty solid marriage – most of the people they'd talked to had been stunned by the separation. This was all leading up to: 'It's a funny thing with relationships – good relationships can have really bad break-ups. Was that how it was with you?'

'No, not at all.'

'Some people seem to have that impression.'

'You've been talking to my father-in-law again.'

'Well, sure, that's his view but I'd have to say, what we're hearing from other people – people your wife worked with, for instance – is closer to his version than yours.'

It was time to call a halt and ring Kiernan but I couldn't wait – I wanted to hear what they were saying about me. 'What do they say?'

'In a nutshell, that your wife felt threatened by you.'

'That's fucking ridiculous.'

'Which, them saying it or her feeling it?'

'Either. Both. She had no reason to feel threatened by me.'

'She told people you were on a short fuse; she seemed to think you were capable of violence.'

'Oh, bullshit. I don't believe she said anything of the kind.'

'I can assure you, I'm not making this up.'

'If she said it, which I don't believe, it would've been meant as a joke. Anne was big on irony.'

'Strange subject to joke about, wouldn't you say?'

'Look, I don't know what she said or who she said it to or what got lost in the translation but that's just ludicrous. Christ almighty, we were together for nearly seventeen years and I never laid a finger on her.'

We'd reached the laundromat. Sutton stepped in front of me, blocking the entrance. Whether he meant me to see it or not, there was a predatory hardness in his grey eyes which hadn't been there before.

'The last time your wife went to her doctor, he noticed a bruise on her face. She didn't want to talk about it which he says is a deadset sign of domestic violence. When he put it on her that you'd done it, she nodded.'

Semantics. When we say never, we really mean hardly ever. And that nosey fucking doctor must have had eyes like a hawk because I didn't remember any bruise. Now I had Sutton thinking he'd caught me out in a lie. It was only a little lie, the difference between never, ever and just the once, but by the time the prosecutor had finished with it, it would seem like a whopper.

I said, 'I think it's time my lawyer got involved.'

Sutton nodded, as if he'd been expecting that. 'Anyone I know?'

'Tony Kiernan.'

He raised his eyebrows. 'Well, well. Still, I suppose this is no time for half-measures.' He got out of my way. 'I'll let you get on with it, Mr Souter. You've obviously got a lot of dirty laundry.'

Kiernan's take was that next time I saw Sutton, he'd be reading me my rights.

'Then what?'

'Then they'll interrogate you,' he said. 'Then they'll charge you. They're setting you up as the classic bitter male loser – wife kicked you out, your life turned to shit, you smouldered for a while, then one day you erupted. What I need from you is a list of everyone who can tell a different story, specifically that you didn't evince violent feelings towards your wife.' He paused. 'I presume such people exist?'

'I'm not so sure they do. I haven't exactly been a social butterfly lately.'

'No, but you haven't been a hermit either. Come on, mate, I need names. Don't send me naked into the conference chamber.'

'Aneurin Bevan, I believe.'

'Well, bugger me,' said Kiernan. 'You know, I've been using that line for years: plenty of people suspected it wasn't original but no-one knew who I'd pinched it from. I can see I'm going to have to get you out of this – an intellectual like you wouldn't last ten minutes in the clink.'

'I could've worked that out all by myself. When will they do it?'

'Pretty soon, I'd say. Sutton probably just wants to get the funeral out of the way.' Kiernan interpreted my silence correctly. 'You don't know about the funeral, do you?'

'I know I haven't done anything about it.'

'Your father-in-law has. It's at St Andrew's Cathedral, eleven o'clock tomorrow morning. You're not welcome but I guess that's something else you could've worked out all by yourself.'

'They can't stop me going.'

'You obviously like having your photo in the paper.'

I drank at lunchtime and spent the afternoon on the couch.

Dream One: Anne and I are on a cruise. It's late and we're hurrying back to the cabin, hand-in-hand; we can't wait to lock ourselves in. But when we get there, we can't find the key – we must have left it in the restaurant. I go back for it but get lost in a maze of identical corridors. For all I know, I could be going around in circles. Meanwhile,

Anne's down below, marking time in another empty corridor. Frustration turns to anxiety; soon I'm feeling sick with helplessness. Thank christ, here comes someone in uniform: it's the purser and he's got a master-key. He guides me back to the cabin but Anne's not there. She must have got tired of waiting and gone to see what was going on. The purser's disappeared so I set off blind again – and get lost again. I'm back in the maze, going around in circles, getting frustrated, anxious, nauseous . . . I wake up.

Dream Two: I'm sitting in the loggia with Roger Carew. We're smoking cigars – big, fat Cubans. That usually means it's Christmas but where's the rest of the gang? Hello, here's Fiona looking tanned and leggy in snug white shorts. It's amazing, she doesn't look a day older than when I first met her. Roger, on the other hand, is really starting to show his age. Oh, the old prick's leaving us, is he? He's due on the first tee in twenty minutes but he's sure Fiona will keep me entertained. Fiona watches him go, then turns to me with a tantalising smile: 'I trust that works both ways.' She holds the smile, lowering her eyelids. Is it my imagination or are those what they call bedroom eyes? Is she thinking what I think she's thinking? Fiona comes to my side of the table, sits on the arm of my chair, slips a hand inside my shirt. Her touch is warm, smooth, precise, practised. 'Why don't we find somewhere a little more private?' she whispers, her hot breath and flickering tongue transforming my ear into a raging erogenous zone. I'm thinking, I'm going to fuck my mother-in-law. I know I shouldn't, I know it's wrong, but I don't care. I wake up.

Dream Three: My lungs are straining. A great force is pressing down on me, smothering me, snuffing me out. Jesus fuck, someone's trying to suffocate me. Someone is going to suffocate me because I'm running out of breath and I can't budge this implacable weight. I wake up.

Dream Four: I'm climbing a sand dune. It's so hot the air seems to throb. I can feel the sun burning my bare shoulders and the sand burning my bare feet. The only cool thing is this gun in my hand. I reach the crest of the dune and look down on a crescent of white sand and a flat, iridescent sea. The beach is deserted except for a single sunbather who lies on his stomach with his face in the crook of his arm and a floppy hat shading his head. I wouldn't have picked Jeff as a sun-worshipper. Down on the beach the sand is moist beneath the crust. Jeff doesn't stir; he can't hear me over the rinse and rumble of the sea. Wakey, wakey, Jeff – time to die. I thumb back the hammer and he lifts his head, blinking sweat out of his eyes. But it's not Jeff, it's Jock. I wake up.

The phone rang.

'Hello.'

'Nick?' It was almost a whisper.

'Who's this?'

'Harry.'

'Harry?'

'Your brother-in-law, dipshit. Remember me?'

'Where are you?'

'At my parents' place. Why the fuck do you think I'm keeping my voice down? Roger's been frothing at the mouth ever since I got off the plane – man, has he got a hard-on for you. You know what he said when I told him I found it a little hard to believe you killed Annie? This is at the airport, okay? Like, I'd been back in the country for all of half an hour. He said, "If that's the way you feel, you can fuck off back to where you came from." No place like home, eh?'

'I think it's safe to say there's no place quite like your home. What does Fiona think?'

'Fiona? To be honest, I don't think it makes much fucking difference to her. Far as she's concerned, with Annie gone, you might as well not exist.'

'She must have an opinion though.'

Harry sighed. 'The state Roger's in, no-one in their right mind is going to argue with him but I'd be surprised if Fiona buys it. Say what you like about her, she's not stupid.'

I met Harry in a Kings Cross dive, three murky connecting rooms with a bar and sagging sofas against the walls. It was the wrong side of midnight for that sort of place so there was just us and a couple of pimps gloating in a corner. Harry's face still had a lightly poached look but it helped that the blowaway dandelion hair was suppressed by a baseball cap with the inscription, 'Too Sick To Pray'.

'I like this place,' he said. 'I feel at home here.' He looked it too, wedged into the corner of a sofa with a drink in one hand and a cigarette in the other. 'So should you.'

We talked about Anne. He asked if I knew what was in her will.

I shook my head. 'I didn't even know she had one.'

'She didn't.' He grinned merrily. 'Trick question. Which means, of course, it's all yours.'

'I expect Roger might have something to say about that.'

'Tell me about it. It's like he's on a fucking loop. I suppose you didn't know about the life insurance either?'

'I knew she had some.'

'You call it some, I call it five hundred large. You're fucking loaded, man – all you've got to do now is hang onto it.'

I outlined my attitude towards money which is basically that enough is enough.

'What is this – economics for the retarded? That's fine if you've got plenty and nothing much to spend it on but some of us ain't in that happy position. You see, buddy, I made the mistake of becoming a coke fiend before I got rich. It's much more manageable if you do it the other way around.'

'Are you serious?'

'Well, that depends,' he said with a throaty chuckle. 'If your benchmark is those dead men walking out there who need the spike every few hours, then no, I'm not. If it's someone who, at a push, can get by without their favourite pick-me-up but chooses not to because they enjoy it too much, then I guess I am. I see it as the difference between being a dependent and being a fan.'

'You know where the word "fan" comes from? Fanatic.'

'Whatever. The point is, if you regard that as being hooked, then my parents are hooked on alcohol. And you, Professor Asswipe, you must be in the ballpark.'

'You can leave me out of this. I would've thought the point is that your parents can afford it.'

'Can they? Roger keeps changing doctors because they tell him to lay off the booze.'

'We were talking about money and you used the word manageable. If you can't afford it and won't – or can't – give it up, how do you manage?'

He put his drink aside and gestured vaguely. 'I had help.'

I finally understood what we were talking about. 'Anne?'

Harry nodded. 'She told me you'd spotted a withdrawal from your joint account. It usually came out of the company but things must've been a bit tight that month.'

'So how much help did she give you?'

'All up? A hundred grand, maybe more – that's spread over a few years.'

'US I presume?'

'I'm afraid so. The folks I deal with insist on it.'

'And she knew where it was going?'

'Well, yes and no. The deal was she'd keep me solvent providing I put myself into rehab. Which I did – several times. It never quite worked for me though.'

'Why not?'

'As they always tell you: unless you really, truly, sincerely want to quit, you're wasting our time and your money.'

'Except it wasn't your money.'

'I know what you're thinking: if she hadn't blown it on her fucked-up kid brother, it'd be your money now.'

I shrugged: easy come, easy go. 'Anne's view was she'd earned it, she could do what she liked with it, and I didn't necessarily disagree. But it's all over now – without her, there is no company.' He nodded sadly but it was impossible to tell who he was feeling sorry for. 'What'll you do now?'

'The way I see it, I've got three choices: quit, turn to a life of crime, or suck dick.'

'That's a lot of dick.'

'Yeah, and I'm not the youngest or prettiest boy in LA.'

'Not any more, anyway.'

That made him smile but it was the rueful smile of someone who'd had to make some hard choices a long way from home. I realised then just how far Harry had fallen. To change the subject, I asked him why he was so sure I hadn't killed his sister.

'Shit, man, that's a no-brainer – I know how you felt about Annie. And, besides, you don't have it in you.'

'I bet you say that to all the suspects. I don't want to seem ungrateful but, you know, some guy's got twenty-five headless corpses in his basement freezer, there's always someone who'll say, "Oh, he couldn't possibly have done it, he's too nice a chap."'

'So what are you saying – you do have it in you?'

'No, I'm just pointing out that you and Roger are flip-sides of the same coin.'

'The fuck we are. I always had an open mind about you and Annie; his was closed tight from the start. Second of all, Annie told me stuff; she told Roger squat.'

'What did she say?' It came out in a rush, like a smitten teenager fishing for a second-hand compliment.

'That she was happy with you.'

The unspoken qualification hung in the air, mingling with the cigarette smoke.

'Up to a point, right?'

'Everything's up to a point, amigo; that's the bitch of it.' He drew on his cigarette, watching me closely. 'Whatever it was happened towards the end of last year. She told me she'd gotten involved in something that had the potential to fuck everything up but she was finding it real hard to walk away.'

'What did you think it was?'

'There didn't seem any reason to go past the obvious. Last time I talked to her, she went on about how much she hated the way she'd lost control of herself and the situation. She also said you couldn't see it yet but maybe you'd be better off without her.'

'Harry, I need you to do me a favour: I need you to tell this stuff to the police.'

He sighed and looked away. 'Sorry, man, I can't do that.'

'Why the fuck not? Listen, they're going to charge me any day now – I need all the help I can get.'

Harry kept his eyes fixed on the opposite wall. 'If I did that, Roger would disown me on the spot. Then where would I be?'

'I see your problem,' I said. 'There's a lot at stake – especially now you won't have to share it with your sister.'

'Every cloud has a silver lining, Nick,' he said with an unembarrassed half-smile. 'You ought to know that.'

There was no point in getting angry and no reason to stay. As I walked away, Harry called out, 'See you in church.'

CHAPTER 14

I'm no Johnny-come-lately to atheism. I came in from the fold when I was twelve, alienated, as much as anything, by all the grovelling: *We do not presume to come to this thy Table, O merciful Lord, trusting in our own righteousness, but in thy manifold and great mercies. We are not worthy so much as to gather up the crumbs under thy Table ...*

Watching the grown-ups in church, I'd think, if only they could see themselves; if only they knew how ridiculous they seem, with their moony expressions and their supplicants' wheedle: *Almighty and most merciful father, We have erred and strayed from thy ways like lost sheep, We have followed too much the devices and desires of our own hearts, We have offended against thy Holy laws, We have left undone those things which we ought to have done, And we have done those things which we ought not to have done, And there is no health in us* ... It all floated off into a void, like radio signals beamed into deep space on the off-chance that a little green man will hear us calling.

Did they really believe it? I wondered. Did they really believe there was such a place as heaven? Sitting at God's right hand for eternity isn't quite the hook it used to be – these days people literally want to live forever. If they had souls to sell, they'd happily offload them for a guarantee that, this time next century, they could be working out, having affairs, *water-skiing*. That's science's Big Project and if it comes off, the game's well and truly up.

Not that the future's all that rosy anyway. Take weddings: these days people only get married in churches for the location – it makes for a better home video. Thank God for death, the priests must think as the cameras zoom in on their blackheads and burst veins. At least people still take that seriously.

I left it late, slipping into the rear pew. It took less than a minute for heads to start turning. A buzz arose, subdued but insistent, like white noise. Is that him? You're kidding. God, what did she see in him? I heard she was having an affair ... I heard he lost the plot ... I heard she was insured up to the eyeballs ... I heard it's an open-and-shut case ...

I scanned the congregation for familiar faces. There weren't that many. As a newspaper reported the next day, the who's who of PR turned out to pay their respects. Rosie and Julian and their brood were with my parents a few rows away. I wondered what Mum and Dad made of it. When you get to their age, funerals come thick and fast but this was different. There'd be no tea and scones and wry reminiscences after this one.

Rosie beckoned but I stayed put. I wasn't keen on drawing more attention to myself. My parents smiled wanly and Arabella gave me a solemn little wave, as if she didn't expect to see me again for some time. There was a flurry of movement as Julian squeezed past several pairs of knees. He came and sat beside me, emphasising his solidarity with a fraternal hug. Would the image makers be impressed, I wondered, or would they be thinking, now there's a man who needs some sound PR advice? No doubt they knew the account was up for grabs: Julian's firm had been one of Anne's longest-standing clients.

I spotted Joel but no Ellie which was understandable. No matter what she wore, Ellie couldn't have disguised the fact that she represented sex and sex was sitting this one out. Kate and Jeff – defiantly open-necked – were there, so too Jock and family. Jock tapped his watch and mimicked tilting back a glass. A few drinks afterwards seemed like a good idea; I was already regretting not having had a few beforehand. Sutton and Muir were there. Sutton acknowledged me with a noncommittal nod, then lowered his head prayerfully. For some reason, that didn't come as a surprise. Muir, I was pretty sure, was one of nature's nihilists. I couldn't see the Carews. Doubtless they were in the front row, slump-shouldered and sombre-suited.

The priest, a doughty old performer with fine white hair which swayed from his scalp like sea-bed plant-life, surged through the service, projecting heroically. We give thee hearty thanks, he hollered as if he really meant it, for that it hath pleased thee to deliver this our sister out of the miseries of this sinful world.

Being a newcomer to the funeral circuit, I hadn't realised how much of the Order for the Burial of the Dead has entered the vernacular and been ground into cliché: O *death, where is thy sting? We brought nothing into this world, and it is certain we can carry nothing out. The Lord gave and the Lord hath taken away. In the midst of life, we are in death. Let us eat and drink for tomorrow we die. Earth to earth, ashes to ashes, dust to dust.*

This was a new one on me: *Lord, let me know mine end, and the number of my days; that I may be certified how long I have to live.* Fine for those who are granted a good innings and peg out without fuss. Not so good for those who cometh up and are cut down, like flowers; who fleeth as they were shadows, and never continueth in one stay.

The first eulogy was delivered by a PR woman, a self-styled personal friend and professional rival. I'd met several of these queen bees and couldn't tell them apart – they all seemed to stand a little too close and try a little too hard. Despite the tragedienne's tricks of the trade – long pauses gazing into the middle distance, audible swallows, gnawing on the lower lip – she was, I felt, a little too on message. I wasn't surprised, for instance, to be told that Anne had 'awesome' PR skills.

She was followed by Mary, a former best friend who'd married a geek and gone off to live in Silicon Valley. Mary's eulogy was the treacle tart rounding off her predecessor's Big Mac with fries and a shake. Her Anne was a montage of the female icons of our time – slap together some Jackie O and Princess Di, throw in a flash of Madonna, a splash of Hillary Clinton, and a dash of Mother Teresa *et voila*. I wasn't surprised to be told that the world was Anne's oyster.

Our marriage wasn't mentioned. It was obviously an aberration, like shoulder pads. I drew consolation from the knowledge that I wasn't the only ghost in the cathedral. These one-track sketches revealed as much of Anne as her passport photo.

Mary returned to her pew, smiling through her tears like a newly-crowned Miss World. There was a pause which stretched into a hiatus. The priest nodded encouragingly to someone in the front row but the prompt went unheeded. The mourners signalled their restlessness with shuffling feet and a flurry of whispers. Then Fiona was advancing to the pulpit. *Fiona* delivering a eulogy? No doubt she grieved in her own way but sharing it with strangers wasn't her style.

She surveyed the congregation, clear-eyed and unhurried. 'Anne's father was to have spoken now,' she said, 'but he's afraid he wouldn't be able to get through it. This has been an agonising time for us. We loved Anne deeply and we miss her terribly. I fear it will take us quite some time to recover – if indeed we ever do. Right now it's impossible for us to imagine getting back to anything approaching normality. I expect that applies to some of you too. That's really all I have to say. Thank you for coming.'

I was standing outside the cathedral, waiting for the others. My body tingled, as if an anaesthetic was wearing off, and middle-aged pain probed my joints. I half-heard rushing footsteps and a shout of alarm and turned my head to meet Roger's haymaker. Roger had pianist's hands – fine-boned and long-fingered – so it might have hurt him more than it hurt me. His momentum propelled him into me. I lost my footing and fell backwards, banging my head. Roger threw himself on top of me, hissing and spitting as he scrabbled at my throat. Dazed and disembodied, I observed this attempt on my life – to take Roger at his word – as if it was happening to someone else.

Who said the police are never there when you need them? Muir dragged Roger off me; Sutton helped me up, wanting to know if I was all right. He had a knack of popping these questions when I wasn't sure of the answer.

Muir was restraining – or perhaps supporting – Roger who looked as if he was taking a standing count. There was blood in his eyes and wedges of spittle in the corners of his stretched, gasping mouth. The jet-set perma-tan had turned an autumnal yellow and his cheeks were withered, like fallen leaves.

I heard Julian tell Roger he ought to be locked up and Sutton ask me if I wanted to press charges. I noticed photographers circle, lenses jutting from their faces like cartoon noses. I heard Fiona tell Roger that Anne would be really proud of him. She turned her cool, hazel gaze on me for a few seconds, then lowered her eyes and walked away. Shrugging helplessly and struggling to keep a straight face, Harry took her arm.

Sutton asked me again if I wanted to press charges. I shook my head.

He nodded. 'Nothing to be gained from it. Where will you be for the next forty-eight hours?'

'Why?'

His mouth flexed in an elusive smile. Nice try, it seemed to say, but you know that as well as I do.

Unannounced and ungracious, Muir came for me at 7.15 the next morning. I rang Kiernan who wasn't fazed by the hour or the situation. He told me to take my time, have a hearty breakfast, and he'd see me at Police Headquarters City East. I made Muir wait in the corridor while I got ready.

Despite the dawn raid, Sutton kept us waiting. I thought that would rattle Kiernan – time is money and all that – but he'd come prepared with a fat hardback. He told me: stick to the point, answer yes or no whenever possible, don't volunteer information, don't hypothesise, and, above all, don't lie about mundane matters of fact. Even though we'd be lost without them, lies are grist to the crime and punishment mill: seeing you lied about how many glasses of wine you had, we obviously can't believe anything you say.

We got started just before ten. Sutton sat opposite me; Kiernan was on my right, at the end of the table, with his tape recorder and foolscap pad; Muir leant against the wall, his psych-out stare as unblinking as the video camera in the corner. As Kiernan had pointed out, we weren't dealing with sophisticated people.

After cautioning me that anything I said could be taken down and used as evidence against me, Sutton began at the beginning: How and where did I meet Anne? How did our relationship develop? How did her family and friends react? How did our different backgrounds affect the relationship? One lollipop after another for me to pat back to the bowler, to get me thinking this isn't so hard after all. Why didn't we have children? We talked about it from time to time, I said, but it wasn't a priority for either of us.

Sutton browsed through the folder in front of him. 'Several of your wife's friends thought otherwise,' he said, raising his eyes. 'They had the impression it was a priority for her.'

'Really? Strange she should raise it with them rather than me.'

'Assuming she wanted to have your children.'

'I wouldn't bother responding to that,' said Kiernan.

Sutton's eyes slid over to Kiernan. When they were resting comfortably on me again, he said, 'Your wife gave quite a few people the impression that she wanted more out of life.'

'Who doesn't?' said Kiernan. 'Christ, they were living apart – that kind of implies not everything was rosy in the garden, doesn't it?'

'Are you pressed for time, Mr Kiernan?' asked Sutton. 'Because if you are, I should warn you this could take a while.'

Kiernan sat back in his chair. 'Oh, don't you worry about me – I'm here for the long haul.'

'Good,' said Sutton. 'Then we can take our time. Well, Mr Souter: were you aware your wife felt that way?'

'She had an affair,' I said, taking my cue from Kiernan. 'Doesn't that speak for itself?'

'Oh, yes, the mysterious J – who seems to have vanished without trace.'

'You mean you can't find him?'

'I mean we can't find any evidence that he exists.'

'You think I made it up?'

Sutton just looked at me.

'Did you talk to Jason Swann and his friend?'

He dabbed the tip of his index finger on his tongue and turned over a few pages. 'We did. They'd like to know what you're on – they were completely bemused by the whole business.'

'I don't blame them – they weren't in on it. Anne had to put a name to J so she plucked Jason out of the air. The question is, why didn't she simply tell the truth?'

'Hmmmm.' Sutton stroked his nose. 'We've been through your wife's existence with a fine toothcomb. We checked her movements, her phone records, her electronic organiser, her credit card and bank statements. We talked to her staff, her family, her friends – we must've talked to damn near every second person in the eastern suburbs and you know what? We haven't come across a single thing to back up your claim that she was having an affair.'

'Did you talk to her brother?'

Sutton looked surprised. 'Of course.'

'And?'

'You heard what I said.'

'So you don't believe in J?'

Sutton shook his head slowly, decisively, as if that was the end of the matter. 'Let's talk about money.' He finger-licked further into the folder. 'As you know, your wife didn't leave a will . . .'

'I didn't know – one way or the other.'

'What have we got here?' He ran his finger down the inventory. 'As the sole beneficiary of your wife's estate, you become the outright owner of a one and a half a million dollar house . . .'

'Did you get that figure out of the *Telegraph*?'

A smile tugged at the corner of his mouth. 'No, but we might've used the same valuer. Less the mortgage, it's worth one point two five million. Then there's half a million dollars worth of life insurance . . .'

'Which I also didn't know about.'

He nodded. 'You really didn't have much of a handle on your financial situation, did you?'

I shrugged. 'Anne looked after the finances. She said we were doing all right, I took her word for it. Why wouldn't I?'

Sutton carried on as if he hadn't heard me: 'Then there's the other bits and pieces: contents of the various bank accounts, superannuation, stocks and bonds, goods and chattels – all up, over two million dollars worth.'

'So I stood to be a millionaire anyway?'

'Well, that's one way of looking at it although they do say a million dollars isn't what it used to be. And one thing you learn in this job is that being hooked on money – or lifestyle – is no different from any other addiction: life revolves around feeding the habit. If you and your wife had gone your separate ways, she would've taken her earning capacity with her.'

Kiernan said, 'What evidence is there that my client was hooked on money or lifestyle?'

'Some of his colleagues certainly had that view,' said Sutton.

'Who?' I asked.

The last faint glimmer of humanity disappeared from Sutton's eyes. 'If you don't mind, Mr Souter, I'll ask the questions.' He bent over his notes again. 'Now I'd like to go through your movements in the week leading up to your wife's murder ...'

Kiernan sighed and produced his cigarettes and lighter.

Sutton glanced up. 'No smoking.'

Kiernan went ahead and lit up. He took three hungry drags, dropped the cigarette on the floor and stamped on it. From behind the smokescreen, he said, 'Let's stop fucking around, shall we?'

It was pretty straightforward: they reckoned I killed Anne and they reckoned they could prove it.

There was evidence that Anne wanted me out of her life: she kicked me out; she kept contact to a minimum; she changed her phone numbers and told her secretary to block my calls.

There was evidence that I became obsessive: I made nuisance calls; I staked out the house; I peeped in windows late at night.

There was evidence that I harboured violent feelings towards her: I hit her; I left angry messages on her voice-mail; I argued with her in the street. She told people I wasn't handling it well: I was acting weird and she was afraid of what I might do.

There was evidence that I underwent some sort of breakdown: I drank heavily; I holed up in Sarah's flat for days on end; I neglected my personal hygiene.

I had a double motive: her rejection and her money.

I didn't have an alibi.

Kiernan said, 'That's it?'

Muir was galvanised. 'Fuck, what more do you want?' He came around to my side of the table and positioned his head next to mine, as if he was going to whisper a secret. 'Come on, mate,' he said quietly, 'why don't you tell us what happened that night? You went round there and begged her to give you another chance, right? Promised you'd change, be whatever she wanted you to be? But she wasn't having any, was she? Told you to piss off, wished to christ she'd given you the boot years ago.'

I shook my head. Muir didn't appear to notice.

'She said a lot of other stuff too, didn't she? Shit that really got under your skin? Called you a loser, said she was sick of you embarrassing her, sick of looking at other men and thinking she'd drawn the short straw. Then she started in on the money: you'd bludged off her for the last time; you'd have to scrape by on your piss-ant salary while she'd be out there making mega-bucks. And just when you thought it couldn't get any worse, she really stuck the boot in. Said you were a dud in the sack, right? She was tired of giving you sympathy fucks and couldn't wait to get some decent sex.' His voice dropped, almost to a murmur. 'Well, fuck, how much can a man take? No-one should have to put up with that shit. The blinkers came off and you saw her for what she really was – a fucking bitch. A cold, scheming, dirty bitch who was giving you the flick so she could go out and fuck herself stupid.'

'Have you quite finished?' asked Kiernan.

He hadn't. 'You lost it, didn't you, mate? Something snapped and you planted that pillow on her face. You just meant to scare the shit out of her, right? Shut that vicious fucking mouth, make her think twice before she spoke to you like that again, make her show you a little fucking respect. It was good, wasn't it, watching her squirm, listening to her beg for a change? A real buzz. So you kept the pillow there a bit longer, to teach her a lesson she'd never fucking forget. And the useless bitch went and died on you. That's what happened, wasn't it, mate?'

Throughout this performance – which is what it was – I sat with my head lowered, staring at the table, remembering what Kiernan had said at our first meeting: cops don't approach investigations with an open mind. They walk into a crime scene, look around, and have déjà vu. Why should this one be any different? It looked like the husband did it. It felt like the husband did it. It fitted the pattern.

I lifted my head to meet Sutton's clinical gaze. 'Well, Mr Souter?'

'Anne wasn't a bitch,' I said, 'and I wasn't there that night. Apart from that, he was pretty much on the money.'

Kiernan chuckled. Sutton stood up. 'Charge him, sergeant,' he said.

Kiernan released a long, whistling breath and reached for his cigarettes.

I said, 'One thing.'

Sutton had his hand on the door knob. 'Well?'

'Didn't the pathologist say she'd had sex that night?'

Sutton nodded. 'What I didn't tell you was that the pathologist couldn't be entirely sure whether it happened pre- or post-mortem. I think that was your doing, Mr Souter – when you realised you'd killed her, you had a bit of a fiddle to give the J scenario some legs.'

Kiernan's mobile rang. He went and stood in the corner with his back to us.

'Just as a matter of interest,' I said, 'how hard did you try to find J?'

'Now you're clutching at straws. We're professionals, Mr Souter; we run a thorough investigation.'

Kiernan turned, flapping an arm. 'Just hold your horses,' he told Sutton. Then into the phone: 'Okay, run me through it again – slowly.'

A couple of minutes passed. Kiernan told the caller, 'Good work, mate.' Sutton and Muir eyed him suspiciously, wondering what smartarse legal shenanigans he had up his sleeve.

Kiernan came over and dropped a hand on my shoulder. 'And with one bound he was free.'

'What's going on?' demanded Sutton.

'Bullshit,' said Muir. 'He's full of it.'

Kiernan pointed at the folder under Sutton's arm. 'What did you get from the occupant of 20 Washbrook Avenue?'

Sutton looked to Muir, passing the buck.

Muir asked, 'That's the place directly across the road?'

Kiernan nodded.

'Single bloke.' Muir squinted like a contestant on a quiz show. 'Name of ... McKenzie.'

'McKechnie. Adrian McKechnie.'

'That's right.' Muir relaxed. 'We didn't get anything from him because he wasn't there. He was out of the country on business.'

'Did you check exactly when he left?' asked Kiernan.

Muir's eyes flickered to Sutton, then back to Kiernan. 'Get to the point.'

'All right.' Kiernan lit another cigarette. 'For the past couple of days, I've had people door-knocking in Washbrook Avenue – all part of the service. The bloke on the phone had just finished talking to McKechnie who's just got back from Japan. Turns out he actually left at the crack of dawn on Monday – after the murder, in other words.' Kiernan's grin blazed; this was as good as it got for him. 'Turns out he had an early night and got up at one in the morning to prepare for his trip. Turns out his study overlooks the street. Turns out that at around one thirty he saw someone leave the Souter house.'

Sutton came back to the table. He dropped the folder with a thud and stared hard at Kiernan. 'I presume you have a description?'

Kiernan's black eyes glittered. 'Male. Young. Tall. Gangly. And in case the penny hasn't dropped, bearing no fucking resemblance whatsoever to my client.'

Sutton chewed his lower lip. Muir swore. Kiernan clapped me on the shoulder again. 'Come on, mate, let's leave these clowns to it. They've got a killer to catch.'

CHAPTER 15

Kiernan suggested lunch at a place on the water in Rose Bay, one of Anne's favourites. They knew me there and they'd heard the whispers and read between the lines. Despite years of practice, the maître d' could barely force a smile. He tried to hide us in a corner but Kiernan was having none of it.

He called for champagne and proposed a toast to freedom and prosperity. Was it that cut and dried? I wondered. I'd come to feel like a devout gambler on a losing streak, privately aware that the law of averages was no longer operating on his behalf. I'd got so used to things going from bad to worse that it was hard to believe the trend could be reversed by one quick phone call. I, of all people, should have known how little it took to turn a life upside down.

Kiernan reassured me. 'This creep, whoever he is, was witnessed leaving the murder scene around the time of death. That's enough for a conviction right there.'

'Maybe McKechnie got his wires crossed.'

'You know him?'

'Just to say hello to.'

'Well, let me tell you a little bit about Adrian McKechnie: before he went into business, he was one of the big brains at the Reserve Bank – we're talking about a guy with a steel trap mind, okay? To put it in context, most witnesses in murder and mayhem cases fall into one or more of three categories: indecisive, unreliable or just plain cretinous. With McKechnie in our corner, the case against you is dead in the water and if Sutton doesn't know that yet, he soon will.'

'So where does that leave me?'

'Back in respectable society.'

'Respectable society mightn't be ready for me.'

He nodded. 'Yeah, you'd hope they nail this guy in a hurry. In the meantime, maybe we can do something to fast-forward your rehabilitation.'

'Like what?'

'Sutton's not the only one who knows how to work the media. So what are you going to do now?'

'Go back to work, I suppose.'

'You can afford not to although I wouldn't count the insurance money just yet. You can put the rent on those bastards stalling till the bitter end.'

'I've got to do something,' I said, 'otherwise life's just a matter of holding out till the sun's over the yardarm.'

'You're relatively young, relatively well-off, unencumbered – you can do whatever the fuck you want.'

That wasn't quite true. I couldn't turn the clock back.

Kiernan lunched like a man who'd called it a day and I had no reason not to keep up. He had a wealth of insider smut which he was keen to share but I steered him back to business. 'So you're sure this guy's the killer?'

'Got to be.'

'What do you think happened?'

He shook his head. 'No, mate, you don't want to go there.'

'Why not?'

'Because it's ugly and whichever way you look at it, it'll still be ugly. Let's talk about something else.'

'Read any good books lately – that sort of thing?' I said. 'I don't give a fuck any more.'

He lit a cigarette, looking miffed. 'I don't have a theory.'

'Okay, what theory will Sutton be working on?'

'How the fuck should I know?'

'Remember that little speech you gave me about how the cops operate – walk into a crime scene, déjà vu, Bob's your uncle? So who replaces the bitter male loser?'

'I'm beginning to see what Sutton was on about – you are an obsessive bastard, aren't you?'

'I put it down to losing my wife – twice.'

He fanned away the smoke and had a good look at me. Now that he was sure I wasn't a murderer, he was beginning to feel sorry for me.

Kiernan thought the cops would be looking at two scenarios: bad luck or Mr Wrong.

'Mr Wrong?'

'You know,' – he shrugged, embarrassed for both of us – 'she picked up some rough trade and took him home. Maybe she changed her mind and he went nuts or maybe he'd always wanted to kill a woman. You know your T.S. Eliot?'

'I know some T.S. Eliot: "Between the idea and the reality, between the motion and the act, falls the shadow."'

'I was thinking of Sweeney Agonistes,' he said. '"Any man has to, needs to, wants to, once in a lifetime, do a girl in."'

'If Anne had gone cruising for rough trade – which, I have to say, strikes me as pretty bloody unlikely – wouldn't the cops know about it? You heard Sutton – they went through her life with a fine toothcomb.'

'Yeah,' he said carefully, 'and who knows what they found? I'm not suggesting they would've deliberately disregarded evidence but they mightn't have paid much attention to it because they were so sure you did it. Then again, things slip through the net without it necessarily being their fault. Someone might've seen your wife with the killer but not everyone watches the news or reads the papers. If you don't know she was murdered, you wouldn't think twice about it: boy meets girl – happens all over town every night. Or maybe no-one noticed them because your wife slipped the guy her phone number on the sly. Or maybe it was the other way around: he picked her up when she was on her own and no-one was looking – in a supermarket, say, or even in the street. Predators tend not to operate in plain sight.'

'That strikes me as utterly unlikely.'

'You knew her, I didn't,' he said. 'But you should be prepared for the possibility that you didn't know her quite as well as you thought you did.' He watched me roll with the punch. 'This is what I meant – the deeper you go, the darker it gets.'

'What would qualify as bad luck?'

He put his elbows on the table and hunched forward, choosing his words carefully. He had a theory after all. 'Crossing paths with a psycho who selects his victims on a whim or prowls the night looking for an unlocked door or an open window. It's like driving home at six o'clock, stone-cold sober and doing everything by the book, and being cleaned up by some hoon running a red light. No rhyme or reason for it, just wrong place, wrong time.'

This was in the *Sun-Herald* the next day, under the headline 'Breakthrough in Souter murder':

Detectives investigating the murder of prominent Sydney public relations consultant Anne Souter are confident of an early arrest following what is being described as 'a major breakthrough'.

The official word from the officer heading the investigation, Detective Inspector Garry Sutton, was more cautious. He told the Sun-Herald *yesterday that 'significant new eye-witness evidence has come to light which has enabled us to narrow the focus of the investigation and concentrate our efforts and resources.' He indicated that the new evidence had provided the investigating team with a clearer picture of the nature of the crime and a detailed description of an individual who was now regarded as the prime suspect.*

Any decision to make this information public, he said, would depend on the progress of the investigation.

Since Ms Souter (38) was suffocated in her $1.5 million Woollahra home a week ago, Sydney's eastern suburbs have been abuzz with rumour. Extraordinary scenes followed Friday's funeral service at St Andrew's Anglican Cathedral when Ms Souter's estranged husband Nick was verbally and physically attacked by her father, Vaucluse businessman Roger Carew. Mr Souter, who moved out of the family home two months ago and is on indefinite paid leave from his teaching position at the exclusive boys' private school St Bartholomew's College, declined to press charges.

The Sun-Herald *understands that detectives interviewed Mr Souter several times last week. Asked whether the new evidence clarified Mr Souter's position, Detective Inspector Sutton said, 'Mr Souter is not our suspect, end of story.'*

There was a photograph of Anne, obviously cropped out of a group shot taken at a social function. She was whooping it up, glass in hand and arm around a man standing out of frame. I had enough third-hand knowledge of the media to know that there was probably a reason for running this photo as opposed, for instance, to one of her at a press conference. Why had they re-cast the career woman as a party girl?

A lot of people would have looked at that photo and thought, well, she obviously liked a good time. The pornographers would have decided that they knew what made her tick on the basis of her ovalled mouth. Me, I had enough second-hand knowledge of the PR business to be pretty sure that she was working.

I rang Sutton.

'Let me guess,' he said. 'You want to know if you can believe what you read in the papers?'

'No, but since you raised it ...'

'What I gave them is the current situation. We'll find this character your neighbour saw and we'll find out what he was doing there. If we're satisfied he did it, then that's that; if not, we're back to square one.'

'You mean back to trying to pin it on me?'

'I'm being straight with you, Mr Souter. I expect this character will turn out to be our man – I'll certainly take a lot of convincing otherwise – but we can't jump to conclusions.'

'Since when?'

Sutton had been doing this dirty work for too long to worry about a little grime under the fingernails. 'The suspect,' he said evenly, 'is fifteen to twenty years younger than your wife and a bit rough around the edges: could you see her having a relationship with someone like that?'

I said, 'No,' and mostly believed it. But the part of my mind which doubted everything and shrank from nothing wondered if that was why she couldn't bring herself to tell me the truth.

'So why did you ring?'

'I want to go home.'

'Let me find out if forensics have finished there. Anything else?'

I remembered Kiernan's talk of pick-ups and predators. 'Did Anne go out that night?'

'As far as we can tell, she went into her office at midday, got home late afternoon, and didn't go out again. Between six and seven she made a round of calls to journalists and she was at home when her parents rang just after nine. That's as much as we know.'

'Speaking of her parents, how did they take the news?'

'Well, Mr Carew had mixed feelings . . .'

'No kidding?'

'People in their position just want it resolved, Mr Souter. The waiting and the uncertainty are terribly hard on them.'

'Tell me, inspector: in what way, exactly, does their position differ from mine?'

Pretty straightforward question, wouldn't you think? Sutton didn't. 'I'll get back to you about the house,' he said and hung up.

Next day I moved back home. When people ask how I can live there, I just shrug. There's no point in trying to explain that it represents what we had as much as what I lost. Yes, the memories can be painful but they're better than nothing.

I got a bottle of wine from the cellar – which she'd barely made a dent in – and wandered around, glass in hand. I needed a gardener – that had been her department too, another thing for me to just sit back and enjoy – and a new cleaning lady. Even if the gabby old Uruguayan was prepared to accept that I didn't do it, she wasn't going back into that bedroom. I took down Anne's new pictures – whatever was she thinking? – bagged up some pointless glossies, and moved her clothes into the spare room. I made the bed and a mental note to replace the bed-clothes which were now and forever evidence. I dropped her contraceptive pills in a waste-paper basket.

The phone rang as I was brushing my teeth. Who could that be? I wondered. Someone who hadn't caught up with the news?

'Hello.'

'Nick, it's Fiona. How are you?'

Fiona? 'Well, you know ...'

'Yes, we've got a lot to talk about. How are you placed for lunch tomorrow?'

The venue was the upstairs private room of a restaurant favoured by the people who run things. You could tell by the chauffeur-driven Mercedes double-parked outside. It wasn't one of Anne's favourites.

Fiona arrived late, queening in unapologetically with the owner on her arm. Armand had laid on the private room, she explained, so we wouldn't be constantly interrupted.

'Or stared at,' I said.

'Exactly,' she said. 'That's not as much fun as it used to be.'

Armand left to organise Fiona's gin and tonic. We examined each other over the crystal. 'You've aged,' she said matter-of-factly.

'You haven't,' I said. 'What does that say about us?'

'That you can't be bothered disguising it.' The inspection continued. 'You've toughened up too.'

'You can tell just by looking at me?'

She nodded. 'It was either that or go to pieces, I imagine.'

'If the cops had left me alone,' I said, 'I probably would've gone to pieces.'

A waiter brought Fiona's drink and leather-bound menus. Without looking at it, she ordered poached salmon and a half-bottle of Mersault. I chose duck and passed on the wine just to prove that I could.

The night before, she'd had a quiet chuckle when I'd asked if Roger would be joining us. The question now was whether he knew who she was having lunch with.

'I have a system: I tell him what I'm going to do after I've done it. If he makes a fuss, I don't mention it again.' This was said with a completely straight face.

'Well, they say communication is the key to a happy marriage. So how is he?'

'You got a pretty close look at him the other day – what do you think?'

'He didn't look too good but then trying to kill someone with your bare hands can take it out of you.'

'He's not too good. Do you care?'

'Why should I?'

'No reason – he's certainly never given you any.' She paused and lifted her eyebrows. 'Perhaps you're thinking she's a fine one to talk?'

I shrugged. 'You weren't thrilled about having me as a son-in-law but you didn't take it personally.'

She pushed the half-finished gin away. 'Is that what Roger did?'

'You know it is. Harry put me onto it years ago – on our wedding night, in fact.'

'Harry did? What did he say?'

'That Roger was jealous because Anne was in love with me.'

She nodded. 'That was uncharacteristically perceptive of him. Poor Harry, he got a raw deal, really – most of our shortcomings and few of our redeeming features.'

'And what exactly would they be?'

'Now, now.'

'How about Anne? How did she fare?'

'Oh, she did all right out of us. In fact, I'd say she was about as good as Roger and I could do. But even the top models have a few built-in faults, don't they?'

Our food arrived before I could ask her what she meant.

We got onto what the neighbour saw. I passed on Kiernan's bad luck theory.

'Is that what you think?'

'Fiona, all I know for sure is that Anne was having an affair and I didn't kill her.' When she didn't respond, I added, 'Don't you believe me?'

'Would I be here if I didn't?'

'Does that go for the affair as well?'

She nodded.

'Did she say anything to you?'

'No, but I wouldn't have expected her to. She stopped confiding in me a long time ago.'

'Any particular reason?'

'There was a story about me going around – you know, Double Bay gossip. Anne asked me if it was true and I told her it was none of her business.' She shrugged. 'After that she stopped telling me her little secrets.'

'So how did she explain our situation?'

'Oh, the usual twaddle. My dear, I've seen an awful lot of marriages break up and seventy-five per cent of the time, there's a third party involved. Unlike Roger, I saw no reason why those odds wouldn't apply in our daughter's case.'

A waiter brought coffee. Fiona took a couple of sips and lit a cigarette. 'A few days before your wedding, I gave Anne some advice. I told her you'd make a perfectly good husband but sooner or later the time would come when that was no longer enough and the marriage would stand or fall on how she – or perhaps both of you – dealt with that. She wanted to know what made me so sure; I said the fact that she was my daughter. She looked me in the eye and said, "You've forgotten one thing – I don't take after you."' Fiona ground out the half-smoked cigarette. Nothing she had seemed to be worth finishing. 'That was the last time I gave her unsolicited advice and she certainly never asked for any.'

'What are you saying – that Anne was genetically predisposed towards infidelity?'

'I suppose I am,' she said. 'Do you want to hear it?'

'If you think it'll serve some purpose.'

'Only one way to find out. I wasn't a blushing bride – far from it, in fact. I didn't take that forsaking all others stuff seriously and I didn't think it was something Roger and I needed to talk about. I mean, he was a bit of a lad, as we used to say, and my reputation preceded me so I just took it for granted that we were on the same wavelength. Well, Roger turned out to be not quite as sophisticated as I thought he was. He expected me to renounce my wicked ways and become a good little homemaker while he continued to please himself. It was quite an adjustment for him.'

'But he made it?'

'Yes and no. You see, if you lined up every woman Roger's ever slept with – leaving aside the odd whore – you'd be hard-pressed to tell them apart. Once a snob, always a snob, I suppose. I wasn't so fussed about what school they went to.'

'What were you fussed about?'

She smiled serenely. 'That's not like you, Nick – you're usually quick on the uptake.'

'I wouldn't say that. I notice you used the past tense.'

'I'll be sixty-two this year.'

'So?'

She shrugged. 'Age changes everything. For one thing, it's harder to get in and out with your dignity intact.'

'Did Anne know? She certainly never mentioned it.'

'What was she going to say – "Oh, by the way, mother sleeps around"? I think she had a pretty good idea – there's always someone who's sure they'd be doing you a disservice if they didn't pass on information you could happily do without. And of course Roger in his cups can be a fount of information.'

'But she thought she was different?'

'Well, she was different, no doubt about that. The question is, how different?'

'Sutton asked me if I could imagine Anne having a relationship with someone like this character the neighbour saw – twenty-odd and rough around the edges. I said no.'

'Do you really think he meant a relationship? I mean, I can put my hand on my heart and say I've never contemplated a relationship with a man half my age. Sleeping with a man half my age – that's another matter.' I acknowledged this revelation with a stiff nod. Fiona's smile was as sardonic as I'd ever seen it. 'Am I shocking you, Nick?'

In my dream she'd morphed into an ear-licking wanton the minute Roger's back was turned. Where had that come from? A slow, semi-conscious processing of clues or suppressed desire?

'I'm pretty hard to shock these days,' I said. 'So why are you telling me this?'

She took her time selecting a cigarette. 'I thought it might help you understand – why Anne did what she did, why Roger is what he is. Both of them could blame me to some extent.'

'Martyrdom doesn't suit you, Fiona. Anne was a grown-up: she could think for herself. And as for Roger – are you seriously trying to tell me he was Mr Congeniality until you screwed him up?'

'No,' she said, drawing the word out. 'I'm trying to tell you that what happened between Roger and me influenced how he felt about Anne, which in turn influenced how he behaved towards you – and the boyfriends before you, for that matter.'

'I seem to remember there was one he didn't mind.'

'So there was – Alan.'

'What was his secret?'

'Alan was a boor with a one-track mind. From Roger's point of view, he never represented a serious threat.'

'What happened?'

She shrugged. 'Nature took its course. She wasn't giving him what he wanted ...'

'So he found someone who would?'

She held my stare. 'They always do.'

'Did you, by any chance, give nature a helping hand?'

'What I told Anne goes for you too: that's none of your business.'

'Begging your pardon, ma'am,' I said. 'All this candour's gone to my head.'

She flipped me a condescending smile. You don't know anything about anything, it seemed to say.

'As I was saying,' she said, 'Roger saw Anne as me without the flaws which was what he'd wanted all along. That's why he found it so hard to let go.'

'Is it just me or is that verging on unhealthy?'

'It's a sick world. And on the other side of the coin, perhaps that's why Anne was so secretive – she didn't want to shatter her father's illusions.'

Fiona had said her piece. She looked at her watch and went through the gosh-is-that-the-time routine. I let her pay the bill and watched her leave. She might have put herself out to pasture but she still looked as if she could raise a gallop. She still had some form.

Meet the Carews: Master Harry pimped his sister; now he's a coke-whore. Father behaves like a prize shit because he can't satisfy his wife; he drinks too much and has clammy thoughts about his daughter. Mother does whoever she pleases; even her daughter's boyfriend isn't off limits. And poor little Miss Annie: she tried so hard to get away but her genes just ran her down.

Did Fiona with her ruthless, if you've got an itch, scratch it sexuality represent one up for the pornographers? Her special pleasure was sleeping with men who weren't like her husband and rubbing his nose in it. The other day I read about a porn actress with the personalised numberplate STR82NL – straight to anal. I read about a woman who had sex with two hundred and fifty-one men in ten hours and called it feminism. I don't think these women are typical; I don't think you can base a theory of human behaviour on what goes on at the margins. For every doomed teenage junkie in the Cross, there are thousands of teenagers who yearn to be rich and famous and, eventually, old. Fiona's problem was that she didn't know the meaning of love and no matter how hard she tried to tar her daughter with the same brush, I knew that wasn't true of Anne.

I know what it's like to be loved.

CHAPTER 16

Two weeks went by. I found a cleaner and a gardener. Sutton and his merry men got nowhere. I saw quite a bit of Rosie and Julian. They were always there to prop me up, even when it looked as if they could do with some propping up themselves. They didn't come right out and say so but I could tell they worried about what would become of me.

I went out drinking with Jock who told me he was having an affair with the wife of one of his golfing buddies. The guy had asked for it. He swaggered when he won and sulked when he lost and pushed his luck at home. During daylight saving, he was in bed by nine, saving himself for a round before work.

Jock was pleased to be off the breakfast shift – sex first thing didn't suit his metabolism. Saturday afternoon was their window now. His friend's wife would go to see her eighty-three-year-old aunt, timing her visits to straddle the old girl's afternoon nap. Jock's wife Debbie was a joiner – of gyms, jogging packs, yoga classes, bridge clubs, reading groups – so it was easy for him. He'd sneak into the aunt's terrace while she was dozing upstairs and they'd go to it on the couch. Another middle-aged male who wouldn't go quietly.

'Tell you what,' he said, 'she's a handful, this one. In fact, I wouldn't be surprised if she's got a couple of other impact players coming off the bench.'

'How would you feel about that?'

'You mean would I be jealous?'

'Yeah.'

'Don't be fucking daft. It's not like I'm stuck on the tart; I'm giving her one – that's all there is to it. Speaking of which, when did you last bury the bone?'

'Before I moved out. What's that – two and a half months?'

'So what do you do – beat Pete?'

'You'll find this hard to believe but what with one thing and another, I really haven't been in the mood.'

Jock finished his beer and burped gratefully. 'Well, let me know when you regain feeling below the waist – I'm pretty sure I could tee you up with the golf widow.'

'I beg your pardon?'

'Yeah, the way I'd go about it, I'd acquaint her with your tragic circumstances. You know what women are like – if you can persuade them it's all in a good cause, you're home and hosed.'

He waited expectantly. I said, 'I believe it's your round,' and went to the toilet.

I went out drinking with Simon, a colleague from work. Simon was thirty-five, single, and blessed with television looks – regular but unmemorable. He was a theatre buff and had directed the school play, *The Doctor's Dilemma*, a joint production with a girls' school. According to classroom gossip, which invariably portrayed members of staff as sexual freaks of one stripe or another, he'd got his leg over the assistant director, a teacher at the other school, *and* the seventh form cutie-pie who'd played Mrs Dubedat.

Simon claimed that all he really wanted to do was settle down with Ms Right and raise a family. She was out there somewhere and he'd recognise her the moment he laid eyes on her. Until that happy day, though, he intended to keep it casual. Serious relationships were the worst of both worlds: all the restrictions of marriage without the rewards. And as often as not, when they hit the wall, they made just as much of a mess.

There was another option: the no-strings ongoing arrangement. The big attraction there was that it saved time and money: you didn't have to go on the prowl with your credit card every weekend. However, these arrangements were hard to come by and difficult to maintain. They tended to work best when the other party was married.

Recently, Simon had bumped into a woman he'd gone out with at university. They'd had a lot of fun, then something happened, as it does, and he hadn't seen her since. Now she had a wonderful husband and two wonderful kids.

They sat in a café and talked about old times. An hour went by in a blink, just like old times. A few days later they had lunch. After a bottle of chardonnay, she grabbed his hand. 'I know I shouldn't tell you this,' she said, 'but I'm going to anyway: sex with you was the best I've ever had.'

It was brilliant, said Simon. He didn't have to take her out, didn't have to ring her up, didn't have to factor her into his thinking. All she wanted from him was as much sex as they could cram into the time available. He wouldn't go so far as to say it was the best he'd ever had but it was up there.

Maybe there never was much romance. Maybe it was just me.

Three weeks after the *Sun-Herald* had talked up the prospects of a swift arrest, one of its columnists noted that we were still waiting. Word on the street, she claimed, was that the eye-witness evidence wasn't all it had been cracked up to be and the investigation was effectively back to square one.

By which Sutton had meant me.

Next day, he put out a statement: the investigation remained on track and his team was making progress on a number of fronts, *including* the process of identifying a man witnessed leaving the scene of the crime.

My italics.

School had started again so I went to see the headmaster. He was younger than me, a well-connected smoothie whose Oxford degree and stint at Eton had given the board the excuse they needed to overlook more obviously qualified candidates. He stroked the board, charmed the parents – especially the mothers, had as little as possible to do with the boys, and played favourites with the staff. I'd got no change out of him but then there are winners and losers under every regime.

He gave me morning tea in the Ridley Room. When I explained that I wanted to come back to work, he went over to the fire and poked around. With his back to me, he asked, 'Are you sure that's a good idea?'

'I think so. I think I'm in a fit state.'

'I'd be in for some pretty trenchant criticism if you weren't.'

'I think we're both entitled to a little leeway, headmaster. Toby Jenner's view is that you can't have staff using work as a form of therapy but as long as they're doing a reasonable job, why not? If a staff member's having a tough time of it, shouldn't the college be doing what it can to help him through it rather than making life harder for him? Assuming, of course, St Bart's still espouses all those fine old Christian principles.'

'Which you, of course, have instilled so diligently.' This was said with a practised wry smile. He came back to his armchair. 'Nick, your situation is only part of the story. You must be aware of the rumours.'

'Vaguely. I was rather hoping you'd attach more significance to the police's statement that I'm not a suspect.'

He put his tea cup down gingerly, as if he'd felt a twinge in his back. 'You must understand, Nick, it's not just a matter of what I think is appropriate – I've got to take the stakeholders' views into account.' He patted my forearm. 'Look, why don't we just hold off for a little longer? The police seem very confident and as soon as they make an arrest, the atmosphere will change. That way, you'll be coming back with the wind in your sails whereas, as things stand at the moment, you'd encounter some pretty stiff resistance. No point in pretending otherwise.'

'What if it drags on? What if, in three months time, they're no closer to solving it?'

'I'm afraid I can't answer that without knowing what the wider picture will be.'

'In other words, if the rumours are still going around, I'll still be persona non grata?'

'Let's be positive, Nick; let's assume they put this thing to rest pretty damn quickly.'

I was contemplating a nightcap when the phone rang.

'Hello.'

'Hello.' Unfamiliar female voice. 'Is that Nick?'

'Yes.'

'So you two worked things out, did you? That's great.'

'What?'

'You and Anne are obviously back under the same roof.'

'Who is this?'

'Sarah. Remember me? Old friend of Anne's with a flat in Darlinghurst?'

'Sorry, Sarah, I'm hopeless on voices. When did you get back?'

'Just this afternoon. Look, is this a bad time?'

We met next morning at a Darlinghurst café. India had left its mark on Sarah: the plumpness had gone along with the resolutely drab women's collective look. Her hair was oiled and scraped back from her brown, hollowed-out face and she had bangles up to her elbows. I put the red-rimmed eyes down to jet lag and grief.

I fleshed out what I'd told her on the phone and suggested she might want to check in with Sutton.

'Why?' She looked genuinely alarmed. Once upon a time I would have ridiculed such knee-jerk lefty paranoia. Not any more.

'I assume they'll want to talk to you. They've talked to everyone else.'

'Exactly. What can I tell them that they don't already know?'

'Probably nothing but there's only one way to establish that, isn't there? I expect the first question will be: did you ever see Anne with anyone matching the description of the suspect?'

'That's easy: no.'

'Did she ever talk about anyone like that?'

'No.'

'Okay, well then they'll probably want to know what she did talk about.'

'She talked about a lot of things, none of which, it seems to me, have any bearing on her being murdered.'

'Fine, just tell them that. It all helps to reduce the possibility that the murder was connected to something that was going on in her life.'

'Such as?'

'Well, I suppose an affair would come into that category. I keep telling the police she was having one but they don't believe me.' Sarah's newly bony face lent itself to conveying disapproval. 'You wouldn't happen to know anything about that, would you?'

'No,' she said, 'I wouldn't. I knew Anne practically all my life and I'd have to say I find it pretty hard to believe. That sort of thing wasn't her – she was too grounded. It wouldn't fit with her sense of who she was and what she was about.' She lowered her eyes. 'For all I know, this mightn't be any more palatable than the thought of her having an affair, but I think what happened was, you stayed where you were and she just grew away from you.'

So who was right? Fiona, who was tickled by the idea that infidelity ran in the Carew blood? Or Sarah, who was convinced that it didn't feature in Anne's high-minded scheme of things? The cynic or the hagiographer? I'd seen the note. As much as I wanted to, I couldn't put Anne on that high a pedestal.

A day doesn't go by without me wishing I'd never found the note. Having found it though, I should have kept it, not just because it backed up my story but for peace of mind. Sometimes I toyed with the notion that I'd imagined it or, worse, fabricated it. Could I have suffered some kind of breakdown and literally not known what I was doing? Was that why Anne withdrew? Once you start running from reality, it's tempting just to keep going. Any moment now I'll wake up and she'll be lying there beside me, sighing in her sleep like a soft machine. I'll revel in her body heat and gaze at that sweet, still face until I get a lump in the throat.

But this was my life and I couldn't daydream my way out of it. The note was real: I'd held it in my hand; Anne had tried to snatch it off me. And she'd admitted having an affair. The lies came later, in the detail.

So I had to favour Fiona. Sure, she had her own twisted reasons for wanting Anne to be a chip off the old block but she knew her stuff. A serial deceiver herself, forever open to temptation, she had an animal instinct for other people's susceptibility and secret agendas. Sarah, on the other hand, was an idealist. She saw things as they should be, not as they were.

So much time. Would it be easier knowing who J was and why Anne died or was it always going to be like this?

One of Rosie and Julian's specific areas of concern was my ability to manage my financial affairs. It was largely untested but on the assumption that I was as clueless in money matters as most arts graduates, Julian arranged for me to see an investment adviser.

He must have owed Julian a favour because he clearly had better things to do than explain risk and reward to a small-timer like me. Speculative investment, he said, was one step up from gambling and should be approached the same way: don't bet what you can't afford to lose. He talked about diversification and hedging and risk management. He showed me some snappy graphics on his laptop. He pointed out that I could sell the house, pay off the mortgage, buy a nice apartment, and bank two or three hundred grand. He pointed out that unless my investments were earning a higher rate of return than the interest rate on the mortgage, clearing the mortgage was a better use of my money. Then he loaded me up with brochures, prospectuses and analysts reports and sent me on my way.

In amongst this bumf was a brochure for the Metropolis. I'd thought it was a hotel pure and simple; in fact, it was a hotel within an apartment complex. The brochure was hawking the apartments as investment properties, promising high-yield rental income and juicy capital gain. The alleged appeal of these apartments from a resident's point of view was that you had twenty-four-hour access to the hotel's amenities – the gym, the pool, the tennis court – and services. Out of bubbly at two in the morning? Just whistle up room service.

So people actually lived – as opposed to stayed – in the Metropolis? Julian had seen Anne sneak through the lobby and get in a lift. She'd claimed she'd never set foot in the place and had a moment of panic when she realised she might have been seen. Depending on your level of trust, it was oddball or ominous behaviour but I hadn't dwelt on it because I couldn't see how to take it further.

The *Herald* covered residential property as if it was a branch of show business so I logged onto its web site and did a story search on the Metropolis. An early puff piece listed the notables who'd bought apartments there, the usual roll-call of Sydney nouveau-trash. The only name which struck any sort of chord was that of Christopher Jordan, merchant banker, but a search on him couldn't tell me why. He'd been involved in some big deals and owned a vineyard but that's what merchant bankers do, isn't it?

I sat up watching a remake of *Sabrina* with Harrison Ford trying to be Humphrey Bogart and a pretty English girl trying to be Audrey Hepburn. Neither of them got close but late at night when I've had a few, I'm a sucker for a happy ending. It took some doing but I managed to hold back the tears. I felt like if I got started, I'd never stop.

In the morning I found a note on the kitchen bench reminding me to ask Julian about Christopher Jordan.

Julian gave me more of the same – floats, capital raising, takeovers. When I grunted ungratefully, he said it might help if I explained where I was coming from. I told him Jordan had an apartment in the Metropolis.

'Oh.' There was a pause. 'And his name rings a bell, does it? You know, Nicky, he might've been a client – Anne could've been going to a meeting.'

'Yes, she could've.'

'And Jordan might've had some big hush-hush deal in the works – that would explain her behaviour.'

Or maybe there was no connection with Anne. Maybe Christopher Jordan was the name of a character in a book I read twenty years ago. *The Lady Vanishes* perhaps? No, that was a movie. How about *The Long Goodbye?*

Julian said he'd ask around. I dialled my parents-in-law's number, poised to abort if the wrong one answered.

'Fiona, it's Nick. Can you talk?'

'Till the cows come home – Roger's in LA.'

'What's he doing there?'

'Bringing our son back.'

'Harry's coming back?'

'He doesn't know it yet.'

'What if he digs his heels in?'

'When money talks, Harry listens – you know that as well as I do.'

'So what's prompted this?'

'What do you think? We've lost one child; we're not going to let the other one fade away.' When I didn't say anything, she said, 'You disapprove?'

'I was actually thinking better late than never.'

'Go to hell.'

'I'm sorry, Fiona, I didn't realise there was a sensitive soul beneath that worldly exterior.'

She chuckled. 'There's a lot you don't know about me.'

'I know more than I did a couple of weeks ago.'

'True.'

'But that's just the tip of the iceberg, is it?'

'That's for me to know and you to find out. You should take me out to lunch sometime – you never know, I might give you a glimpse of what's below the surface.'

'I can hardly wait. In the meantime, there's something you might be able to help me with: does the name Christopher Jordan mean anything to you?'

After a few seconds she said, 'Are you serious?'

'Yes.'

'You really have no idea who Chris Jordan is?'

'I know he's a merchant banker who owns a vineyard in the Hunter Valley . . .'

'Oh, he's much closer to home than that. Let me see, how can I put this? Well, Anne only ever lived with two men – Chris Jordan was the other one.' Jesus christ, the yuppie with the waterfront pad and the BMW. 'Placed him yet?'

'The guy she dumped for going to a whore-house.'

'That's the one.'

'And then took a while to get over.'

'Well, until she met you.'

No, it wasn't quite like that. She didn't meet me and not spare Christopher Jordan another thought. Even after we'd been going out for six weeks, she still went to him when she was alone in her bed.

'Are you still there, Nick?' Fiona couldn't keep the glee out of her voice.

'Yeah.'

'Why the sudden interest?'

'His name came up but I couldn't place him. It was bugging me, that's all.'

'Do you feel better now?'

'It's not bugging me any more.'

'Are you sure?'

'Why do you ask?'

'It just occurred to me that you might be wondering if it was Chris she had the affair with.'

'Sounds to me, Fiona, as if you know something I don't.'

She said, 'No,' but it sounded like, 'Maybe.'

I said, 'Take your time.'

'No, truly, I don't know any more than you do. As far as I'm aware, when they broke up, that was that. His name might've come up once or twice but she certainly never gave the impression they'd kept in touch. The only thing I would say is that Anne had her share of boyfriends before Chris but it was basically kids' stuff. He was the one who really made a woman of her; he pressed all the right buttons.'

She was almost purring. I imagined her lying back with her feet up on the sofa, stretching like a cat as she summoned her most stimulating memories.

'I thought she didn't confide in you?'

'She didn't but I've got eyes and a certain amount of experience in these matters; I recognised the signs. Personally, I fail to understand why any woman should go through life carrying a torch for the first man she slept with who was any good at it – I mean, if you shop around, you're going to find one sooner or later. But there's no doubt some women do.'

I thought of Simon's arrangement with his old flame. She'd been driven back to his bed by nostalgia for the best sex she'd ever had.

I remembered, from our very early days, Anne saying that one thing about Chris which had really got on her nerves was his habit of talking about himself in the third person, as people who take themselves terribly seriously are prone to do. What made it even worse was that he used his inevitable nickname: Jordy.

CHAPTER 17

Julian dropped in on his way home from work with a Christopher Jordan update. It was after ten and he looked as if he should have been in bed hours ago. The time of plenty was over; the gods were no longer pleased. Now Julian and his fellow wizards were having to drive themselves even harder to prevent the people losing faith in their magic.

Jordan was living at the Metropolis because his estranged wife was occupying the family home. If Julian's arithmetic was correct, this was his second wife who'd been the third party in the collapse of his first marriage. She'd changed the locks and called in the lawyers after discovering that Jordan was carrying on with a secretary.

I said, 'I see a pattern here.'

'A pants-man from way back,' agreed Julian. 'Did you find out if he was a client of Anne's?'

He made a pained face when I told him what I had found out. 'What now?'

'I'm going to front him,' I said.

'Where?'

'You tell me.'

Jordan's routine was to get up at six, trudge away on the treadmill, read the papers over breakfast at the café in the Metropolis lobby, walk to work, be at his desk by 7.30. Apparently you could set your watch by him.

I woke up tired when the alarm went off and was still yawning after two blasts of espresso. Jordan appeared at 6.55, Armani-suited and carrying a briefcase and a bundle of newsprint. He bantered with the staff and headed for a corner table. A waiter followed with his orange juice, latte and croissant.

I knew it was him because Julian had e-mailed me a head and shoulders photo. Four centimetre square mugshots tend to be inconclusive but he looked personable enough. In the flesh, though, it was a case of more is less. One prominent feature can give a face character but when they're all competing for attention, the effect is a little unnerving.

I went over to him. 'Christopher Jordan?'

He looked up quickly from the *Financial Review*. 'Yes?'

'I'm Nick Souter – Anne Carew's husband.'

His eyes went blank. I remembered a pseudo-intellectual politician telling the St Bart's sixth formers that none of the boys in his class had gone into business. The punchline, of course, was that he'd been in the top class.

Eventually he said, 'What do you want?'

'I'd like to talk to you.'

He shrugged. 'Okay.' He was puzzled but didn't seem like a man who'd been put on the spot.

I sat down and we had a good look at each other. 'Last I heard they were going to arrest you any day,' he said.

'I heard that too.'

'That was a while ago.'

'They seem to have gone off the idea.'

'So what do you want to talk about?'

Seeing he ran his life by the clock, I assumed he'd appreciate directness. 'Were you and Anne having an affair?'

He reached for his latte and finished it in three slow gulps. 'What makes you think that?'

'What does it matter? It's a pretty straightforward question, isn't it – yes or no?'

'It might be a straightforward question,' he said, 'but this isn't a straightforward situation. I mean, how the hell did you know I'd be here?'

'You seem to be having trouble focusing on the real issue,' I said.

He turned tough. It had taken all of three minutes. 'Listen, I don't know what your problem is and, frankly, I don't give a shit.' He checked a sports watch which bristled with technology. 'My day starts in twenty minutes and goes twelve hours non-stop. This is my down-time so I'd really appreciate you getting the fuck out of my face.'

I put Anne's mobile on the table. 'Suit yourself,' I said. 'But you won't mind if I pass your name on to the police? They're always interested in the grey areas in a murder victim's life. And you know what? I doubt they'll give a fuck how busy your day is.'

Jordan tried to stare me out while he thought of a way to back down without me noticing. He settled for pretending that he really didn't give a toss either way. 'What the hell?' he said with an exaggerated shrug. 'If it'll make you feel better.' He ordered another latte and called his office to prevent panic breaking out at 7.31.

Even though their worlds overlapped, Jordan had hardly seen Anne since they'd split up. They'd bumped into each other in the street a couple of times, both of them running late: a moment of frozen surprise then hi, how are you, must dash. Late last year he'd shown his face at a big law firm's Christmas drinks and there she was. And he fell for her all over again.

'The thing is,' he said, 'I was absolutely gutted when Anne left me. They reckon everyone has their heart broken at least once – well, that was my turn. When I saw her at that do, it all came back – it felt like seventeen days, not seventeen years.'

They had a long-time, no-see conversation. Jordan had been using the same PR outfit for years but then and there it entered his mind that perhaps it was time for a change. They arranged to have lunch and talk about it.

As it happened, they talked about everything but PR. Anne declared that she was happy and life was good. Jordan filed away two things: she'd met me on the rebound from him and we had a lot of miles on the clock.

Next day he rang her to point out that they hadn't actually got around to discussing PR which had been the whole object of the exercise.

She laughed. 'Really? I'd never have guessed.'

That sounded like an opening. 'So what did you think we were doing?'

'Indulging our curiosity.'

'Did you learn anything interesting?'

'Just that you haven't changed.'

'I don't know about that,' he said, 'but you certainly still have the same effect on me.'

She laughed again, longer and louder this time.

'I'm serious,' he said, as earnestly as possible.

'I don't think so,' said Anne. 'I think you're just trying it on. Either way, you're wasting your time.'

A week later he rang her to suggest a drink. She asked, business or social?

'Social.'

'Right answer: if you'd said business, I wouldn't have believed you. I'll have a drink with you on one condition – no more soppy stuff.'

Jordan went about it differently this time, taking an interest in her work, letting her talk him through how she'd built the business up from a one-woman band. But you can only talk so much shop over a glass of wine at the end of a long day.

She asked what happened to his marriage. He told her he'd had an affair.

'Why?'

'Why do people usually have affairs?'

'You tell me. I mean, did your wife make you unhappy?'

'No, we got on okay but we were really just ticking over – you know how you can love someone without being in love with them?'

'I would've thought most adults accept that that's on the cards if you're in it for the long haul.'

'Maybe some adults are more romantic than others.'

Anne laughed in his face. She'd done some checking up on him and knew about the secretary. 'That doesn't sound like romance to me,' she said. 'It sounds like another middle-aged man trying to turn the clock back.'

Jordan agreed that it wasn't his finest hour but the secretary was a hot little number who'd wiggled into his line of sight when he was feeling frisky. The trouble was, his wife took it personally. Unlike him, she didn't see any merit in the French attitude to sex and marriage which is that, at the end of the day, they are separate issues and to mix them up is to risk throwing the baby out with the bathwater. He told Anne about an article he'd read, quoting one of those straw people who have no existence outside glossy magazines and feature sections: Delphine (not her real name), forty-five, a Parisian marketing executive, liked steak au poivre but wouldn't want it every night.

Anne said fine if it worked both ways. Perhaps he should have asked his wife what was for dinner before he pounced on the secretary. By the way, how did his wife find out?

'Someone dobbed me in – she got an anonymous letter.'

'Did you flaunt it?'

'Shit, no, just the opposite. I thought I was careful to a fault.'

'Well, you know, Chris, you can never be too careful when you're playing with other people's lives.'

Next week they had another drink. (By now, I was pretty much convinced that this was the model for the fake relationship with Jason Swann.) They picked up where they'd left off. Jordan sensed that, ever since their reunion, Anne had been questioning her assumptions and was slowly coming around to Delphine's point of view.

Out of the blue, she asked him how he enjoyed apartment living. That seemed like another opening so he offered her a guided tour of his place. She didn't think that would be a good idea.

'Why not?'

'It's pretty obvious, isn't it?'

'You're afraid of what might happen?'

She nodded.

'What exactly are you afraid of?'

'One thing leading to another.'

'Would that really be so bad? I mean, what's the worst thing that could happen?'

'Theoretically? I could fall in love.'

Jordan couldn't keep the smile off his face. 'You're seriously worried about falling in love with me?'

'No,' she said, 'I'm seriously worried about stuffing up my marriage.'

Jordan wasn't discouraged. He was convinced each orbit was bringing her closer. Yes, it felt like two steps forward, one step back but that still represented net progress. Keep it up and you'll get there eventually.

He was working at home. A call was diverted through from his office, Anne wanting to know how he was placed for a quick bite of lunch. He took a punt: why didn't she pop over and he'd get room service on the job? She said she'd be there in half an hour.

He put a bottle of champagne on ice, slapped on some eau de cologne, did a quick tidy-up in the bedroom. It just went to show that if you believed in yourself, anything was possible.

The high lasted thirty-one minutes. This was the side of Anne he'd forgotten – steely, unbudging. She'd come to tell him that their little game was over: no more lunches, no more drinks after work. Maybe they could be friends down the track but he'd have to get there first. Jordan was stunned: What's going on? What's with the ultimatums? I mean, can't we even talk about it? There was nothing to talk about, she said: it was playing with fire and she was putting a stop to it before anyone got burned.

Déjà vu. He begged her to stay but she shook her head and walked out the door.

Jordan dropped money on the table and stood up. 'There you have it. That was the last time I ever saw her.'

'One last question: if you were writing someone a personal note, how would you sign it?'

His eyes went blank again. 'What?'

I repeated the question.

'It depends,' he said. 'Normally Chris Jordan but if it was someone I'd known for a long time, I'd sign it Jordy. That's what my old mates call me.'

As I was putting out the empties that night, a pizza delivery van went past, reminding me that I should have asked Jordan if he liked pizza. And that I should have told Sutton about Anne having one delivered.

Sutton couldn't recall any mention of pizza deliveries in the reports, not that he'd necessarily expect to. Working backwards, I narrowed it down to the Tuesday or Wednesday night of the third-to-last week of Anne's life.

He said he'd follow it up. I asked how it was going otherwise.

'Slowly.'

'No luck on the sighting?'

'Not yet. It's become a process of elimination – in other words, a typical murder investigation.'

'As opposed to an open-and-shut case?'

'Yes, we've pretty well given up hope of that.'

Rosie asked me to help out at her nine-year-old son's birthday party; she thought it would do me good. Crowd control for a swarm of pampered runts on a sugar jag wasn't my idea of therapy but, then again, what was?

I turned up with a couple of Tintin books and a video game which Julian Junior accepted as no more than his due. Desperate for attention on her big brother's big day, Arabella hurtled down the stairs to greet me.

A couple of mothers had pitched in: a ski-tanned Amazon in tight black leather pants and an elfin figure with huge dark eyes which had seen happier times. She empathised in gusts as the Amazon drawled condolences.

There was a magician and a troupe of clowns and a maniacal tantrum from a boy who didn't get his way in the seating arrangements. The women tried and failed to sweet-talk him out of it; that left me. It was like the moment in a western when the townsfolk finally accept that the desperados can't be appeased and pin the badge on the mysterious stranger. Teachers, like sergeant-majors, know the coercive properties of the sudden, lunatic scream so I frog-marched him into the corridor and let rip. He cowered as if I'd produced a meat-cleaver. Within minutes, he was wreathed in smiles and tomato sauce.

The Elf complimented me on my way with children and tittered gently when I told her, never forget that they are the enemy.

Stuffed to bursting point and limp from over-excitement, the guests offered no resistance when their look-alike mothers came to take them away. The Elf shook hands: if I ever wanted a chat, Rosie had her number. The Amazon made a slinky exit, confining herself to a fleeting, unfocused smile.

Julian Junior was holed up with his presents, Arabella and Maggie were in the rumpus room, under television's watchful eye, and the nanny was cleaning up. Rosie and I took our gins upstairs.

'So,' she said, 'what did you make of Liz?'

'Which one was she?'

Rosie rolled her eyes. 'The brunette. The blonde's Diana.'

'Tell me, what would Diana wear on a big night out?'

'Not much in my experience.'

'I'm a fine one to talk but I got the feeling Liz is a bit fragile.'

'That's probably got something to do with the fact that her husband died a few months ago.'

'Christ, what happened?'

'Cancer.'

'How's she coping?'

'Okay. She has her good days and her not-so-good days.'

'Lucky her. So what's with the I-feel-your-pain act? Hasn't she got enough of her own?'

'That's a joke, right?' said Rosie bleakly. 'I just thought there might be times when you felt like talking to someone who understands what you're going through. Excuse me for caring.'

'You're excused.'

'I mean, who do you talk to apart from me and Julian?'

'Well, there's the cops, there's my lawyer ...'

'Don't curl up in a corner, Nick; don't be a victim. I know you can't undo it but you don't have to let it dictate the rest of your life.'

I leaned over and hugged her. 'You won't let that happen.'

She hugged me back. 'You'll have to help.'

'I know,' I said. 'The nights are the worst times. Do you think Liz would be prepared to help me through the really bad ones?'

There was relief as well as mischief in Rosie's smile. 'I don't see why not. As long as it works both ways.'

The other item on her agenda was Christopher Jordan: was I still planning to confront him?

'I did – yesterday.'

'What did he say?'

'Basically that he and Anne met up again by accident and circled each other for a few weeks. He wanted to take it further but she backed out – said she didn't want to stuff up her marriage.'

'Did you believe him?'

Jordan had been convincing but that was neither here nor there. You don't get to where he was without being able to sell yourself and pitch a product you don't believe in. Even so and allowing for the way that all reportage trims and packages reality, I'd never felt that surge of certainty that I was being fed a line. If he had lied, it would have been to avoid getting sucked into the investigation but I was pretty sure it would have showed. He would have loved to tell me that Anne hadn't been able to resist him.

'On balance, yeah.'

'You don't sound too sure.'

'I'm not too sure,' I said. 'About anything. I just think that if they did have an affair, Jordan would find it difficult to sit there and pretend that he gave it his best shot but she knocked him back. Guys like him hate having to admit failure.'

Rosie's expression was carefully neutral. 'Well . . .'

'Well what?'

'I don't know, I just think most people in his position would lie, automatically.'

'You're assuming he had something to hide.'

'And you're assuming he didn't.'

'I get the feeling you think I'm in denial.'

She saw that my glass was empty. 'You spoke to him, not me,' she said, getting to her feet. 'And, besides, what does it matter now anyway?'

CHAPTER 18

Sutton brought news. I offered him coffee; he said he wouldn't say no. As I was making it, he asked if there was any particular reason the pizza delivery had stuck in my mind.

'Anne didn't like pizza.'

He examined this from all angles, like a child trying to figure out what makes a gadget tick. 'You suspected it wasn't for her?'

'It crossed my mind.'

'J?'

'Haven't we had this conversation?'

Sutton made a curious, sweeping gesture. In different circumstances, I would have assumed he was practising his backhand. 'Getting back to the pizza, can you remember anything about the person who delivered it?'

I shook my head. 'I was watching Anne, not him.'

'So it was a him?'

'Well, yeah.'

'How old?'

I was about to say I wouldn't have a clue but then why did I think of him as a delivery *boy*? 'I'd say late teens.'

'Short, tall or in-between?'

The mind is an attic, full of stuff we've bunged up there and forgotten about. 'Tall.'

'Male. Young. Tall. What about gangly? Would you say he was gangly?'

It had pretty well fallen into their lap. They went through Anne's phone records again: there were two calls to a pizza joint on Oxford Street, the first the night I was there, the second on the eve of her last weekend. The same kid did both runs: Aaron Cochrane was just nineteen, tall, gangly – and nervous. Muir watched him fidget and called Sutton to say it was game on.

They took Cochrane down to Police Headquarters City East and broke him in forty minutes flat. This is what he told them.

He was hooked the moment Anne opened the door. Personally, I didn't think the sweatshirt and leggings did a lot for her but then I wasn't seeing her for the first time.

The lights were on when he drove past at 11 the next night. He stopped and got out, thinking he'd just worship her from the shadows but the cracks in the curtains drew him across the road and through the gate. He sneaked around the back and got a show through the kitchen window: Anne in a bathrobe with a towel on her head, bent over the sink. The robe fell open but she had her hands full.

After that, he couldn't stay away. It was never quite that good again although he got flashes of her through chinks in the curtains. One night a peeper had got there before him, a clumsy fuck who knocked over a chair and had to run for it. Cochrane skipped a few nights in case she'd rung the cops and they'd put her place on their drive-by list. He made a day-trip, breaking in through the laundry window. She had a thrilling array of underwear. That settled it – she was hot. He stole a pair from the laundry basket and jerked off with them pressed to his nose.

He scored the second call-out to 17 Washbrook Avenue. She answered the door in a little black dress and a dizzying cloud of perfume. She recognised him, gave him a nice smile and a tip. As he drove away, it dawned on him that she'd been hoping to get him again. That was why she had her party gear on – she probably didn't even want the fucking pizza. He cursed his backwardness. She would have assumed he'd get the message and make the running; now she'd be sitting there with her pizza going cold wondering what she did wrong, thinking that maybe she just didn't do it for him.

He stopped the car and threw up in the gutter.

It seemed to help. He calmed down. It was only half-past nine: a smart lady like her would know he couldn't knock off that early. Unless she'd just wanted a quickie – no, she had too much class for that. And he didn't want that either, her bent over a sofa with her dress hoisted. He wanted to take his time, do it right. Now he understood the message: she was saying, 'I'll be here, ready and waiting.' She was telling him, 'Come and get me, baby.'

He got back ten minutes after midnight. The lights were off, the place was locked up tight. He was trying to make sense of it when he heard this noise. He wasn't sure what you'd call it – a moan? A cry? Definitely a woman, whatever it was. Coming from that open window upstairs – what was going on up there? Jesus, maybe she was being attacked; maybe that creep, that fucking peeper, had come back.

There was a ladder in the garden shed – he'd seen it on one of his forays. He positioned it under the window and went up quietly. The noises were louder now and unmistakable – little squeals and grunts, panting like someone running out of breath, hump, hump, hump, then the groans that went on and on . . .

Cochrane put the ladder back in the shed and left the mini-pizza he'd eaten on the way over on the footpath.

He stayed away the next night, churning on it. Part of him wanted to punish her for being a slut, part of him was even more turned on. After a while he understood what she'd been doing: in her mind, she wasn't fucking someone else – she would have had her eyes shut, fantasising that it was him.

Two guys called in sick on Sunday night so he didn't get off until just after one. The house was in darkness but this time she'd left the back door unlocked for him. He climbed the stairs hearing his heart pound. The light was on in the bedroom: she was in there waiting for him.

He pushed open the bedroom door. She was lying on the bed. She was dead.

I said, 'What?'

'Naturally, we don't believe that bit,' said Sutton.

'What about J? Do you believe in him now?'

He nodded slowly. 'It's possible we were wrong about that too.'

Aaron Cochrane was arrested and charged. People who'd gone underground started popping up like spring flowers, wafting sympathy and solicitude. I hung up on their airy overtures – 'let's catch up for a drink'; 'we'll have you round for dinner'; 'we must go out for a meal'. The headmaster rang to say ready when you are. I said I'd get back to him. Liz rang to see if I'd like to go to the rugby with her and her little boy. There was more than one problematical component in that package so I claimed a prior engagement.

And Harry rang to say no hard feelings.

'Are you asking me or telling me?'

'Telling you – you should've known better than to expect me to cross Roger.'

'You mean I should've known better than to expect help from a grasping little turd?'

Harry had his mother's low, rascal chuckle. 'Your apology is accepted. Have you got anything on this weekend?' It was a lead-in rather than a question. 'Course you haven't – you're a fucking recluse. Why don't you come up to the beach?'

'It's the middle of winter. What are we going to do – play Monopoly?'

'Well, I guess if we run out of things to talk about ...'

'I take it Roger won't be there?'

'Sadly, no. Rog's in Port Douglas, trying to get his tan back. You know, I still crack up whenever I think of you two rolling around on the ground like a couple of faggots at a picnic. Pity that cop had to poke his nose in.'

'You think so? Another minute or so and Roger probably would've had a heart attack.'

The silence must have lasted ten seconds. 'As I said,' said Harry, 'pity the cop had to poke his nose in.'

Harry's parents had presented him with a four-step plan: come home, say no to drugs, get a job, get rich when we die. Three weeks at a health farm had whittled Harry down and flushed him out. Maybe it was skin-deep – the military haircut certainly helped – but he looked like he was on the comeback trail.

His father was trying to jack up a stockbroking job for him but Harry had something speedier in mind: 'Pornography,' he said reverently. 'The industry of the future.'

'I could've sworn it was the industry of the present.'

'You ain't seen nothin' yet. Up till now, porn's basically been a substitute for the real thing, right? Something to jerk off over if you can't get laid for love nor money. Well, times are a-changing, my friend: porn's becoming an alternative to the real thing – and an increasingly goddamn attractive one.'

'Is that a fact?' I poured myself another glass of wine, my third; Harry had hardly touched his first. What lies had they told him at that health farm?

'You bet,' he said. 'Let's play the word association game. I say "sex"; you say ...?'

'Love.'

Harry shook his head. 'You sick fuck. You know what most normal people say? They say "AIDS" or some variation on "let-down", "disappointment", "overrated".'

'You wouldn't recognise a normal person if you tripped over one.'

'It's possible my sample was a little light on the 'burbs but even allowing for that, there's a trend emerging and it means happy days for the porno industry. Okay, AIDS was a lucky break for porno and sooner or later they'll find a cure but there ain't no cure for dissatisfaction. Take your average couple chugging away on autopilot: if they ever open their eyes, what do they see? He sees baggy tits and a saggy ass; she sees a beer gut, a bald patch, and arms like sticks of celery. What, on the other hand, do they see when they turn on TV or go to the movies or open a magazine? Babes. Hunks. Perfect tens. Stunning physical specimens who obviously have sensational sex lives. So they start to feel short-changed. Then they check out some porn and it's like, holy shit, so that's what sex is meant to be? Your average couple is turning to porn not because they're not getting any but because what they're getting sucks. What happens is, the more they're exposed to porn, the shittier their own sex lives seem, the more they prefer porn to the real thing. Porn's the last word in consumer capitalism – consumption creates dependency but it's legal, it doesn't give you cancer, and it gets you off.' He leaned across the table. 'Man, you're not going back to that fucking school, are you?'

'What's that got to do with it?'

'We could do this together.'

'What, go into the porn business?'

'Why not? I've got the contacts in LA, I could do the deals . . .'

'And what would I bring to the operation?'

'Seed money. Forget the fucking stockmarket, we're talking El Dorado here, we are talking serious, *serious* green. This isn't this month's half-assed get-rich-quick scheme – I've been thinking about it since I first got to LA. Australia's becoming the fifty-second state, right? Where the US goes, we follow. Well, porn's a cottage industry here compared to the States but it's only a matter of time and when the big boom happens, the guys who've tied up the best product – i.e. you and me – will be rolling in dough like fucking Scrooge McDuck. What do you say?'

'There's one small problem.'

'Small problems we can handle. What is it?'

'I don't approve of pornography.'

Harry rocked back in his chair, laughing hard. 'Man, you are the biggest fucking fruitcake I've ever come across – and that's saying something.'

As we were clearing up the lunch dishes, I asked Harry if Anne had ever mentioned Christopher Jordan.

'She did as a matter of fact,' he said with more than a hint of sadistic pleasure. 'Why do you ask?'

I shrugged. 'His name came up.'

'In connection with Annie?'

'Sort of.'

'And you put two and two together and got five? It wasn't him, Nick.'

'I didn't really think it was. What did she say?'

'Just that she ran into him and he was keen on a sequel.'

'Was she tempted?'

'Not really but she got a kick out of letting him think she was. It eats you up, huh – not knowing?'

'You could say that.'

Harry was about to say something when the doorbell rang.

Mandy and Beth were seventeen with round, bland faces and puppy fat. Harry had met them in some club, dropped LA names, and invited them up to his beach house. Mandy's parents thought she was sleeping over at Beth's and vice versa.

I retreated to the upper deck with the weekend papers but their shrieks and cackles flew up like arrows. I glared at Harry when he came up to say they were going for a walk on the beach; he just smirked and waggled his eyebrows, Groucho-style. They left behind a marijuana fug and a line-up of empties. Harry hadn't been brainwashed; he was just pacing himself. I thought of making a getaway but I'd had the best part of a bottle of wine. Give it an hour or two, I decided, then flee.

I was packing when they returned.

Harry came straight up. 'What the fuck are you doing?'

'What does it look like?'

'What's your problem?'

'You didn't tell me what I was letting myself in for.'

'Jesus, just chill out, why don't you? Go with the flow – you might actually have some fun.'

I zipped up the bag. 'What sort of fun?'

'Do I have to spell it out?' I picked up the bag; Harry stepped in front of me. 'Look, the chicks are going to cook dinner; we're going to pretend to enjoy it; we're going to drink wine, get high, listen to music, maybe watch a movie. What's so unbearable about that?'

'Then what?'

He shrugged. 'Then what happens, happens.'

'Harry, they're kids.'

'They're seventeen, for christ's sake. They've probably had more sexual partners than you have.'

'Great,' I said. 'Barely legal, will screw anything – just my type.'

As I walked around him, he said, 'There's something I was going to tell you – about Annie.'

I stopped. 'So tell me.'

'Not now, this isn't the time. Tomorrow, okay?'

I tossed the bag onto the bed. Harry beamed, revelling in his ability to manipulate me. 'Be cool, eh?' he said from the doorway. 'Maybe you haven't got much of an appetite right now but come the midnight hour, you might find those kids are looking good enough to eat.'

'I don't know what you plan to put in their drinks but I can't see that working both ways.'

'Don't try to second-guess them, man,' he said. 'You ain't qualified. Let me tell you, the only thing running through those little heads right now is the fact that it's Saturday and on Saturday night, girls just want to have fun. And don't discount the curiosity factor either – or, for that matter, the anything-you-can-do, I-can-do-better factor.' A troubling grin spread across his face. 'You owe it to yourself to give it a shot, amigo – most guys your age would kill for a slice of teen pie.'

'Well, as you pointed out, Harry, I'm a sick fuck.'

The grin faded and the banter left his voice. 'Get real, Nick: you're on your own now – no-one gives a shit what you do.'

I went with the flow. Dinner wasn't a complete success – perhaps the cooks should have had a lie-down before they attempted risotto – but Harry came to the rescue by storming the wine cellar. I guzzled vintage of the century shiraz and relived that weekend in the Blue Mountains.

After dinner, Harry got back on his hobbyhorse, playing the word association game – Beth said 'drugs and rock'n'roll'; Mandy said 'condoms' – and asking them what they thought of pornography.

Beth giggled. 'Why, have you got some?'

He stroked his chin. 'I have as a matter of fact – purely for research purposes. I'm thinking of getting into the business.'

'You mean stuff like *Penthouse*,' said Mandy, 'or the real thing?'

Harry darted me a look of triumph. 'Oh, the real thing – all the way with Jenna J.'

'Who?' I said.

'Jenna Jameson – the first lady of porn.'

Beth shrugged, exhaling extravagantly. She was what my pupils would have called a try-hard. 'I don't see why people make such a big deal of it,' she said. 'I mean, what harm does it do?'

'Exactly,' said Harry. 'It's just good, dirty fun.'

Beth vamped, squeezing his arm. 'Sounds like us,' she said. 'Bring it on.'

Harry said, 'Mandy?'

Mandy glanced uncertainly from Harry to me. She had enough sense to wonder where this was heading.

I stood up. 'I think I'll curl up with a good book.'

I woke up at two with a dry mouth and went downstairs to get a drink. Mandy was asleep on the sofa, down to her knickers and a baby-doll T-shirt. She'd nodded off watching Harry's porn video, presumably not for the first time. On the TV screen, three blondes with breast implants but without pubic hair were working each other over. Their ability to be simultaneously intimate and impersonal reminded me of the physiotherapist who treated my periodic bouts of lower back pain.

I drifted in and out of fragmentary dreams. In one, Mandy and I were on a train. When it entered a tunnel, she unzipped me, fished out my cock, and put it in her mouth. I woke up with a pulsating erection and mixed feelings.

I got back from a jog on the beach as the girls were leaving. Beth was hung-over and wouldn't look me in the eye; Mandy couldn't wait to be on her way; Harry was conspicuous by his absence.

I went up to his room. Harry lay on his back, tangled up in blood-streaked sheets. He opened his eyes when I yanked his foot.

'Had the painters in?'

He sat up. 'You won't fucking believe this – the Bethster was a virgin. Shit, if I'd sat down and made a list of the things I never expected to do again, popping a cherry would've been right up there with going to the Easter Show and jerking off six times in a day.'

'Well, I'm sure she'll treasure the memory.'

'Don't try to lay a guilt trip on me, bumfuck – it was her call.'

'Really? Was she capable of thinking it through and reaching a considered decision?'

'She came up here to get laid, you asshole – writing herself off was part of the plan.' He threw off the sheets and went into the en suite. Over the splashes I heard him say, 'You could've had Mandy, you know – Beth reckoned she was up for it.'

'Beth would say that.'

Harry reappeared in a bathrobe. He sat on the bed and lit a cigarette. 'Mark my words: one day you'll regret spurning that opportunity.'

'You said you had something to tell me.'

He nodded. 'You ought to give this shit up, you know – just close the book and move on.'

'Thank you, Sigmund, but that's easier said than done.'

'I'm not saying you've got to screw schoolies but . . .'

'You going to tell me or not?'

Harry stared at me. I didn't think he could hold a serious expression for that long. 'Okay. This came back to me when I was climbing the walls at that fucking health farm. You must've wondered about the logistics of it, right? Well, Annie had some arrangement. She didn't tell me what it was but she did say it meant compromising someone.'

He waited for a reaction. 'Well,' I said, 'you can't make an omelette without breaking an egg.'

He nodded reflectively. 'You know, that's exactly what I told Beth.'

By the time I got home, I was pretty sure I knew what Anne's arrangement had been. I was on my way out again when Kiernan rang.

'You probably don't want to hear this,' he said, 'but my snout down at City East tells me Sutton and co are getting a bit nervous.'

'Why?'

'Well, they can't have it both ways. If Cochrane killed your wife, you didn't; and if you didn't, why would you lie? You say she was seeing someone – someone who's chosen to lay low and who the cops have been unable to identify, let alone account for. Jesus, the kid's lawyer's going to have a fucking field day with that. Mate, how would you feel about appearing as a witness for the defence?'

The thought of being publicly grilled by a slippery, censorious lawyer out to create the impression that Anne led a sex-drenched secret life nauseated me. 'I couldn't think of anything worse.'

'You better get used to the idea,' said Kiernan, as always relishing the opportunity to tell it like it was. 'Here's something else: after he left your house that night, Cochrane rushed round to a mate's place to spill his guts. Next day, his mate left town to work on a cattle station in the Northern Territory – he's been completely incommunicado ever since . . .'

'But their stories match?'

'Word for fucking word. His mate also says Cochrane wanted to go to the cops but he talked him out of it.'

'How will all that go down in court?'

'Depends how credible Cochrane is. If the jury simply doesn't believe him when he says your wife was already dead, then he's gone for all money. If they're in two minds, they'll start paying attention to this other stuff.'

'So what exactly are the cops nervous about – not getting a conviction or convicting the wrong guy?'

'Not the latter, that's for sure. They've filed Cochrane under S for Psycho. As far as they're concerned, even if he didn't kill Anne Souter, it'd only be a matter of time before he locked onto some other poor bitch.'

Any man has to, needs to, wants to, once in a lifetime, do a girl in.

CHAPTER 19

I arrived at a bad time. Sarah was packing. She was moving out. She was trading up.

'A couple of months in India,' I said, 'a two-bedder in Potts Point – did you win Lotto or push a rich aunt down the stairs?'

'I saved,' she bridled. 'I went without things some people take for granted.'

'Sorry I asked.'

She retreated down the corridor. 'As you can see, I'm rather busy at the moment.'

'I won't keep you long.'

I followed her, squeezing past half-filled packing cartons. I was waiting for her to ask what brought me, wondering if she had an inkling or had even been half-expecting me. She went into the main room and resumed wrapping crockery in newspaper as if I wasn't there.

I said, 'So this is where it all happened, eh? This is where they got down and dirty?' She stopped wrapping. 'No offence, but it's not my idea of a love-nest.'

Sarah seemed to sway. She was thrown off-balance and possibly a little frightened. She might have thought I was capable of taking it out on her. 'I don't know what you're talking about,' she said in a strained voice.

'Yes you do.'

I wasn't the least bit inclined to take it out on her but I had no sympathy for her either. She wasn't the silly old softie I'd thought she was: when she'd had to decide, when she'd actually had to make a hard, personal choice, she'd come down on the side of convenience and self-interest, as people who like to moralise in big picture terms often do.

'Anne and her boyfriend needed somewhere safe,' I said. 'I believe "fuck-pad" is the technical term. You let them use this place. You might as well tell me the truth, Sarah – it's no skin off her nose now.'

She wouldn't look at me. 'Exactly – she's dead so why on earth can't you leave her in peace?'

'You'll have to do better than that.'

'What's wrong with you?' She cradled the half-wrapped bowl like a baby. 'You seem absolutely hell-bent on soiling Anne's memory. Well, you're not getting any help from me.'

'If I haven't heard from you by this time tomorrow,' I said, 'I'm going to the police. It worries them having a mystery boyfriend hanging over their case so you can rest assured they'll follow it up. You might think, so what? If I just deny it, what can they do? Well, probably not a lot unless money changed hands.' Sarah snapped to attention. 'Money did change hands, didn't it? Anne paid for your trip and there was enough left over for you to move up in the world. What did she do – write a cheque to cash or give you used twenties in a brown paper bag? Not that it matters – they'll go through her finances and your finances and they'll find the pay-off and then you'll really know what it's like to be compromised. So if you plan to keep protecting lover boy, you should ask yourself one question: how far are you really prepared to go for him?'

The phone rang as I was having a late breakfast. I was expecting Sarah; I got Liz. Assuming she still had therapeutic outings in mind, I greeted her cautiously, trying to remember what excuse I'd used last time.

'Nick, I really don't know how to say this,' she said shakily, lapsing into ominous silence.

Oh, jesus, I thought, she's going to get all emotional on me. 'Look, Liz, before you go any further, I know Rosie thinks it's high time I rejoined the human race but there are a couple of unresolved issues ...' A noise which could have been a choked-off sob came down the line; I hurried on. 'On top of that, the police are apparently having second thoughts about this kid they've charged ...'

'I'm sorry,' she said in a firmer voice. 'I should be better at this. I know from experience that it's pointless trying to soften the blow; you've got to be strong enough to just get on with it.' That didn't sound like groundwork for an invitation to McDonald's and the latest cinematic treat for the young and young at heart. 'I've got some awful news, Nick. Awful, awful news.'

One of the kids, knocked down crossing the road. Or worse, Rosie and the kids in a car accident. I thought those fucking Mercs were meant to be the safest things on four wheels ... Why us? Why now? Haven't we had enough?

Liz said, 'Julian's dead.'

'What?'

'Your brother-in-law, Julian – he's dead. I'm so sorry, Nick.'

I'd learned the hard way that death isn't always something that happens to other people so I didn't protest or refuse to accept the possibility. Now Liz just wanted to get it over with, say what she had to say and leave me to deal with it as best I could. Her voice grew more and more faint, as if she was ringing from a far-off land with a ramshackle telephone system. In fact, she was being drowned out by the bedlam inside me. Rosie was in shock, she said; she was at home, under sedation, being looked after by professionals. Our parents had been informed and were coming straight up. She was looking after the children.

When I asked what happened, Liz told me to check my e-mail. This time, she didn't try to stifle the sob.

Julian left home at 4.30 that morning. He went in to work and wrote notes for his partners. He sent Rosie and me an e-mail. He drove out to The Gap. He rang Rosie on his mobile. He jumped.

This is his e-mail:

Darling Rosie, dear Nick,

More than anything, you must be wondering why. What follows is an explanation and an apology. I hope it relieves your bewilderment and as for your grief, well, it should take care of that too. I should warn you, though, that you're in for more shocks.

I betrayed you both. Then I did something even worse.

I don't remember exactly when I first found myself attracted to Anne. Perhaps the spark was there right from the start. I think it's true to say that, from quite early on, we were both aware of what could have been. We never talked about it, let alone did anything about it. We were both happy with the choices we'd made and knew the dangers of dwelling on what if's. I guess we all have our secrets, we all think the unthinkable from time to time, we all imagine ourselves living other lives. It's okay to have these daydreams and fantasies as long as we can suppress them at will and as long as we remain committed to the lives we've chosen.

I know it sounds a bit like Greek tragedy to say we were doomed from the moment we broke those rules but that's how it seems now.

You'll remember the night. During dinner, I accidentally played footsie with Anne and we had a moment, as they say.

Rosie, you took yourself off to bed as soon as the other guests left. I persuaded Nick and Anne to stay the night. I didn't expect anything to happen and there wasn't a point when I consciously decided to try to make it happen. I just wanted to see how far I could push it and how Anne would react.

So Rosie went to bed and we got into the liqueurs. And Nick, who normally holds his drink so well and has a much better head for it than I do, you chose this night of all nights to let it get the better of you. And as you faded, the sexual sparring intensified. For the record, I was the instigator, I drove it. Anne took her cue from me; she trusted me to know when to stop.

The irony of it was that I suggested the spa thinking it would give you a second wind, Nick. You were having trouble keeping your eyes open and I was afraid that if you called it a night, Anne would feel obliged to follow suit. I was already in the spa when Anne appeared to say you'd got down to your boxers okay, then flaked out.

So there we were, sharing the spa in our underwear at 1.30 in the morning while our spouses slept. In my over-heated state, it seemed as if destiny was at work and once you get that idea in your head, weighing up the pros and cons seems wimpish and irrelevant — what is there to think about? I'd say Anne was confused; she still thought she could trust me not to go too far. But we'd worked ourselves up into such a state that one kiss was all it took. It was like throwing petrol on a bonfire.

So why, when we contemplated what we'd done in the cold light of day, didn't we simply agree that it could never happen again and do whatever was necessary to ensure that? Once again, I take responsibility. I was obsessed and did everything in my power to draw Anne into my obsession, to infect her if you like. And yes, it is true that the exhilaration and passion of a mad love affair are as addictive as any drug. For the first time in my life, I understood the appeal of sailing close to the wind. The sheer recklessness of it, the potentially horrendous consequences, added to the thrill. And the mind does have an extraordinary capacity to rationalise the irrational: the fact that we were prepared to risk everything showed how strongly we felt and if we felt that strongly, it had to be worth risking everything for. Perfect circular logic.

I'll spare you the sordid details. Suffice to say the affair involved all the lies, evasions, stratagems and compartmentalisation that go with the territory – and then some. I thanked my lucky stars that I'd ignored the rumblings about nepotism and manipulated the process to get Anne on board as our PR consultant – that provided the perfect cover. Obliquely at first, then more and more directly, we began to talk about where it was heading. We discussed setting a timeframe and letting nature take its course: if we still felt this way after a year, nine months, six months – it kept shrinking – we'd do whatever we had to do to be together.

And then Nick found the note. After the lengths we'd gone to, we were undone by an adolescent, spur of the moment gesture. I'd slipped it into Anne's pocket when she was in the shower; she didn't even know it was there.

Again, you must be thinking, that was their wake-up call, why didn't they heed it? Anne wanted to and if we'd pulled the plug then, there was probably a better than even chance of us all coming out of it intact. But of course she couldn't tell the truth. I helped her cook something up, suspecting that it would raise as many questions as it answered and that Nick being Nick, he'd find it difficult if not impossible to let the matter rest if he thought he wasn't getting the whole story. Remember, Nick, the analogy of the jumper? You shouldn't blame yourself, though: I was always in Anne's ear, exploiting your understandable anger and suspicion to turn her against you.

For a while there it all went my way: you moved out, things deteriorated between you and Anne, and she seemed resigned to the fact that your marriage was damaged beyond repair. So it came as a sickening shock when I went around there that night expecting champagne and sex only to be told that it was over. She said she'd come to realise that she could never go through with it because of all the harm it would do; that being the case, she planned to rebuild her marriage rather than prolong a relationship that had no future.

I pleaded with her but she'd made up her mind. I begged her not to end it that way, her presenting me with a fait accompli. I tried to talk her into one last night together, promising that if she still felt that way in the morning, I'd get out of her life for good. It was a trick, of course, an attempt to chip away at the edges of her resolve, and for a few moments there I thought she'd fallen for it. In fact, I was congratulating myself on having her in the palm of my hand when she pushed me off and told me go. She was emotional – so was I – and both the shove and the dismissal bordered on violent. Like the first kiss, it was petrol on the flames.

It finished like it started – with me losing control. I didn't make a conscious decision to kill Anne any more than I made a conscious decision to seduce her. But that's what I did and here's the real horror of it: inasmuch as I had a reason, I killed Anne to stop her going back to you, Nick. How many women and children have been killed by mad men deciding that if I can't have you, no-one will?

When I fully comprehended what I'd done, I'd have gladly died if that would have brought her back to life. If only. I tried to be a realist; I tried to bury myself in work and focus on my responsibilities. I even tried to be clever, leading Nick by the nose to Christopher Jordan. But it became harder and harder and now it's just too bloody hard.

My death won't bring her back but it will put an end to this nightmare and, hopefully, enable you two to get on with the lives you deserve. I'm not afraid to die. On the contrary, it will be a relief to escape from this torment which would have become even worse if I was to stand by and let an innocent young man's life be destroyed.

It breaks my heart to leave the children but I truly believe that they'll be better off with me gone rather than in prison for murder. If I was still around, this thing would never go away. They're young enough to get over me and grow up comparatively unscarred. Besides, I know that they're in the best possible hands. I have no right to ask you anything, Nick, but the children love you and I hope you can find it in your heart to be a significant figure in their lives.

I am sorrier than I can possibly say for what I've done. I don't ask for forgiveness. Some things cannot be forgiven.

Julian

Julian was generous and energetic, Julian had the garish sheen of extravagant success, but never in a million years . . .

He scorned the casual adulterers he worked with. They were fools and degenerates, jeopardising other people's happiness and security for the sake of a bit of variety and a marginally more intense orgasm.

He was like a brother – to both of us. He had far, far too much to lose – his perfect lifestyle, his perfect family. He and Rosie were meant to be.

What we don't know can't hurt us and what we find out can erase our certainties.

CHAPTER 20

It was the talk of the town for a while. A media hunting party set up camp on the footpath. I pulled the curtains, disconnected the phone, and waited them out. One morning I peeped through the curtains and the only person in sight was the doctor's wife from next door, simpering over their boxer as he laid a slimy coil a metre from my letterbox.

I rehashed endlessly, lingering over the moments when it could have gone either way. I studied Julian's e-mail like a cryptologist, always coming back to the comment that 'Nick being Nick, he'd find it difficult if not impossible to let the matter rest if he thought he wasn't getting the whole story.'

Don't blame yourself, he said – I turned her against you. Come on, Julian – credit where credit's due.

I wondered how many times he'd tried on the idea of suicide before he was sure that it suited him.

Rosie pulled through. Being a victim wasn't an option, she said – she had three children to take care of. The sub-text to this mantra was that it wouldn't do me any harm to shoulder some of that responsibility. Not that she was on her own: as well as the nanny and the likes of Liz, our parents were on the scene – displaced, fragile, sorrowful but, above all, needed.

Rosie and I barely touched on it. She asked me once how I remembered that night.

'Like a lot of those nights – had a good time, drank too much, woke up with a hangover.'

'So you were completely oblivious to what was going on?'

I shrugged. 'I was pissed and Julian was family.'

'But it happened right under your nose.'

'Maybe so,' I said, 'but I wasn't the only one who didn't see it coming.'

I thought she might take offence at that but she just shrugged and dropped the subject.

The coroner took Julian's word for it and Sutton closed the case.

Harry called in one night and we knocked off a few bottles of wine. He'd taken the stockbroking job to keep Roger happy but his heart still belonged to pornography. After he'd run his prospectus by me again, I said, 'You knew all along, didn't you?'

'What are you on about now?' Not everyone can be wary on a bottle and a half of wine. That's what living on your wits does for you.

'You knew it was Julian. Anne told you, didn't she?'

'What makes you think that?'

'You were the perfect confidant – detached, indebted and unshockable. Besides, I never really bought the idea of her dropping a hint here and a hint there. It would've been all or nothing.' Harry smoked impassively. 'Well?'

He kept me waiting for a few more seconds. 'Yeah, she told me. You can see why I didn't tell you?'

'You swore on the bible you wouldn't tell a soul?'

'Apart from that.'

'Roger would've disowned you?'

'Apart from that.'

'You thought I was better off not knowing?'

'Yeah, and I was right, wasn't I? Look at you.'

'What about me?'

'What about you? You're fucked up, that's what.'

'Look who's talking.'

'Whole different thing, dude. For a start, being fucked up is my natural state. I'm comfortable with it; I can live with it. Secondly, what fucks me up is money. Well, the world's fucking full of money. You can be on the bones of your ass, living on Jellimeat, but it only takes one deal, one lucky break, and you're back in the high life. But if you're fucked up because you've lost the only person who can make you happy, you're fucked up for the duration.'

'You couldn't resist giving me a clue though, could you? Just for the hell of it.' Harry smiled his unscrupulous smile. 'Well, you certainly set off a chain reaction – I worked out who was compromised, I went to see her, I put the wind up her, she put the wind up Julian, he baled out.'

'You know that for a fact?'

'No, but look at the timing: we had the conversation on Sunday morning, I saw Sarah on Sunday evening, Julian jumped first thing Monday morning.'

Harry leaned back in his chair. 'So in a way, I nudged the motherfucker off that cliff? Shit, I can't wait to tell Rog – if that don't get me the keys to the kingdom, what the fuck will?'

I bumped into Sarah in a bookshop. She still had the scraped-back hair and the bangles but her weight was back to pre-pilgrimage levels. She wanted to talk but I walked away. She just wanted me to tell her that it wasn't any of her fault.

I went to the doctor. Doctor, I said, what with these deaths in the family, I'm having trouble sleeping. That wasn't strictly true: I found that if I drank enough and stayed up late enough, getting to sleep wasn't too much of a problem. The doctor wrote a prescription for fourteen sleeping pills and indicated that there could be more where those came from.

Rosie took the kids and me to Fiji, calculating that a week of pool frolics and sandcastles would kick-start my career as a father-figure. I got into the swing early: beer for morning tea and at regular intervals thereafter, cocktails at sundown, wine with dinner, and a duty-free nightcap or two. It sounds a lot but it's hard to get wrecked at the beach. You sweat it out as fast as you suck it in and the swims clear your head.

The kids found other kids to play with which left Rosie and me to lounge by the pool with our paperbacks, keeping the bar staff on their toes. I rediscovered the knack of losing myself in a book; I dozed without dreaming; I covertly monitored the kittenish display of a couple of pert trophy wives. I felt the stirrings of the man I used to be.

One afternoon, Rosie nagged me into a walk on the beach to work up a thirst for the cocktail hour. It was a long beach and we went right to the end.

When we got there, she said, 'You know when I went to get that book from your room this morning?'

'Uh-huh.'

'I had to use the bathroom.'

'When you got to go, you got to go.'

'Your toilet bag was open and I couldn't help noticing you've got two full bottles of sleeping pills.' She seemed to be inviting inconsequential responses but my first effort didn't encourage me to try again. 'Then when I was looking for the book, I came across a copy of Julian's e-mail.'

'I assume this is all leading somewhere.'

'You tell me. I'm going to ask you a question, Nick, and I expect an honest, serious answer: should I be worried about you?'

'Well . . .'

'You know what I'm talking about.'

'I don't think so,' I said. 'Apart from anything else, I don't think I've got the guts.'

'God, I can't believe that even in your worst moments … Did you ever stop to think about what it would do to Mum and Dad?'

'Actually, I haven't got past the stage of thinking about what it would do to me.'

'What brought this on?'

'Come on, Rosie, you of all people …'

'No,' she said fiercely, 'me least of all. I don't get it: you coped with Anne having an affair, you coped with her kicking you out, you coped with the murder – so what is it you can't cope with? The fact that it was Julian?'

'No, the fact that it was partly my fault.'

'How do you work that out?'

'You saw what Julian said: Anne wanted to wipe the slate clean and start again but I kept putting obstacles in the way. She admitted she'd had a fling, she promised it wouldn't happen again, she said she loved me and wanted our marriage to survive but that wasn't enough – I had to know the truth.'

Rosie checked me by pulling hard on my arm. 'You really want to know the truth?' She put her hands on her hips and tilted her chin uncompromisingly. 'I hoped I wouldn't have to tell you this, Nick,' she said with no apparent reluctance, 'but I'm not going to stand by and let you do this to yourself. Most of what Julian said in that e-mail wasn't true. He was afraid the truth would be more than you could bear so he reversed the roles. It was the other way around – Anne started it, she pushed it, she was putting pressure on Julian to leave me. She was a selfish, destructive bitch, Nick; she had a plan all along and she didn't give a damn about what it would do to you and me.'

I felt dizzy and sat down on the sand with a bump, as if some prankster had whipped away my chair. Rosie knelt beside me, her crusading purpose giving way to anxiety. She'd told me for my own good, to save me from myself, but the proof of the pudding would be in the eating.

'Then why did he kill her?' My voice creaked with emotional exhaustion.

She put an arm around my shoulders. 'One thing at a time. Come on, let's get back and get a drink into you.'

That night, when the children were asleep, we went down to the beach with a bottle of cognac. Rosie lay in a hammock and explained what really happened.

Anne was the instigator. She cornered Julian in the spa and came on strong. Like most men, he was a sucker for a woman who took the initiative. He went into it thinking it would be an interlude, a quick, erotic time-out from the real world. Anne saw it differently; she saw it leading to something. She hinted that if he made a unilateral decision, she'd confess all to me and Rosie.

Julian's late finishes were getting later and more frequent. He was evasive about his movements, harder and harder to pin down; he'd disengaged from the children; he was drinking more and eating less; he'd gone off sex. It was a familiar story: Rosie had heard it often enough from friends who were now divorcees to know how it usually turned out. When she confronted him, he broke down and wept: he'd taken leave of his senses; he'd done something unforgivable; he'd jeopardised the things he treasured most.

Rosie went around to Washbrook Avenue to tell Anne it was over. Anne laughed at her. Dream on, she said, Julian's besotted. You should have been here earlier – he couldn't keep his hands off me. Sorry, darling, but I want your husband and I'm going to have him. I'd offer you mine but, last I heard, that was against the law.

Rosie grabbed a pillow and rammed it down on her face.

How would you react if your sister told you that she'd murdered your wife? And that she did it for both your sakes? I sat hunch-backed on a plastic chair, stunned into mute docility.

Julian crumbled again when Rosie told him. She managed to extract the information that they'd been ultra-secretive so there was a pretty good chance no-one else knew about the affair. She just hoped I had a rock-solid alibi. Worried about where my obsession with J might lead me, they laid the false trail which led to Christopher Jordan. They knew what Jordan would say – Anne had told Julian the whole story – but they assumed I wouldn't believe him.

When I became prime suspect, Julian raised the idea of him taking the rap. It was his fault anyway, he argued, and if the worst came to the worst, the children needed Rosie more than they needed him – the little ones can't do without their mother. The pressure eased when Kiernan's leg-man got McKechnie's evidence but that led to Cochrane. Rosie argued that seeing Cochrane didn't do it, he had to have a reasonable show of getting off so they should just sit tight.

They were driving back from visiting our parents when Julian got a call on his mobile. He said it was business but she didn't believe him – work stuff didn't rattle him like that any more. At home, he rang Kiernan who told him the police had their doubts about Cochrane. That's good, isn't it? said Rosie. Julian muttered that it wasn't that simple and disappeared into his study. He went to bed early. She stayed up watching TV.

Julian was asleep when she went to bed and gone when she woke up. His pillow was damp but that wasn't unusual: sometimes when she woke up in the night, she heard him crying softly. She was getting the kids up when he rang from The Gap.

'What did he say?' I asked.

Rosie lay on her back, admiring the stars. 'He said, "I'm going now. I've sent you and Nick an e-mail – you'll understand when you see it. Take care of the children. I'm sorry. I love you."' She could have been nominating her favourite songs.

I stood up. 'I'm going to bed.'

Without turning her head, she asked, 'Don't you have anything to say?'

'On the whole,' I said, 'I prefer Julian's version.'

Next day I flew home. I had to get away from Rosie.

She insisted on accompanying me to the airport. When she started talking about the children, I told her to shut up.

She waited until I'd checked in before asking what I was going to do.

'What would you suggest?'

'I'd suggest you put all this behind you and get on with life. That's what I intend to do.'

'I have a question,' I said. 'What happened in Berlin?'

'Aren't we the amateur psychologist? I fell in love.' I waited. 'He ran off with a friend of mine.' She shrugged. 'What do they say? All part of life's rich tapestry.'

I nodded. 'Well, we agree on one thing – a fair bit of what Julian said in his e-mail isn't true. But he lied to protect you, not me. That was the point of the exercise. The stuff about killing Anne to stop her going back to me – that just doesn't ring true. Not coming from Julian. I think he got that line from you. If you couldn't have him, there was no fucking way Anne was going to.'

She sighed and put her head on one side, like a mother trying to cajole a child. 'Look, Nick, I know this must've come as a hell of a shock but you and I have got to stick together ...'

'Why?' I didn't wait for her reasons; I didn't want to hear about what it would do to our parents. 'Here's what I think happened: you suspected Julian was having an affair. When I told you I thought the same about Anne, the pieces fell into place. You spied on them and it was even worse than you expected – Julian wasn't just fucking around. You confronted him and that was when he made the catastrophic mistake of telling you he was in love with Anne. What did he say? That he and Anne were meant to be? I can understand how that would've been hard to take. You couldn't bear the thought of being abandoned again so you decided the way to make him stay was to eliminate his reason for leaving.'

'Come on, Nick, you're not thinking straight . . .'

I turned and walked towards the departure gate. Rosie caught up with me. 'This is so bloody typical,' she blurted. 'You think you're the only one with clean hands, don't you? Like hell you are – if you'd been man enough to live with it instead of wallowing in self-pity, Julian would still be alive.'

I jerked my arm out of her grasp. Her eyes were devoid of any trace of remorse or self-knowledge. 'You've got it all wrong, Rosie – Julian's not dead because of anything I did. He's dead because he understood that someone had to answer for Anne.'

CHAPTER 21

These days I have as little as possible to do with Rosie. She's got a new man in her life, an ex-best friend's ex-husband. I hear via my parents that he's a significant figure in the kids' lives. Mum and Dad have never asked about the rift but they know it's somehow related to the rest of it, an aftershock from the whole inexplicable heartbreak.

I'm back at work. I see a fair bit of Liz and I guess you could say I'm a significant figure in her son's life. He's got me interested in cricket again. We're actually going down to Melbourne for the Boxing Day Test: Liz will make picnic lunches and we'll get there early and nab good seats in the Great Southern Stand, right behind the bowler's arm. After that, the boy's going to stay with his cousins while Liz and I do the Victorian wine tour. You could say she's rekindled my interest in a few things.

I like to walk the streets on cool, moist nights. The city smells a little cleaner and sparkles a little more brightly and there's something soothing about the hiss of tyres and the shimmer of headlights on the rain slick. I window-shop on Oxford Street or wander down New South Head Road to the Cross. There are a few sad sights on the street and I'm not just talking about the junkies and the deros, the fat old hookers and the stick-figure young ones with their doomed, glassy stares. Some people have an air of quiet despair, as if they've given up on the expectation or even the hope of achieving happiness. You get a sense of lives gone wrong – relationships gone sour, money gone west, health gone to the dogs, careers gone down the gurgler. Once these people had high hopes and things to look forward to; now they're just doing time. That's the way it goes: one false step, one miscalculation, one rush of blood, one fuck-up and life's promise can vanish like a bad investment.

Do I identify with these people? Less than I used to. Do I feel sorry for them? Yes I do. For what it's worth, I hope their luck changes. Do I cross my fingers for the shiny-eyed Asian honeymooners? Yes I do. What does that make me? Someone who never quite gave up, perhaps.

I try not to look back but you know how it is. The mystery sticks to me like my shadow striding behind me in the morning and rising to meet me in the evening, alert to any opportunity to buttonhole me yet again. What sort of woman was Anne really? How far did she fall short of my love-struck ideal? Did something happen to her or was she just a late developer?

I know the evidence backwards and I know it's flawed. The witnesses were untrustworthy; they all had private agendas. Some were protecting her; some were protecting themselves. Julian was protecting everyone but himself. I've come to see him as a kind of tragic hero, a Sydney Carton figure – 'It is a far, far better thing that I do . . .' He was, after all, a romantic at heart.

Some of them described the woman they wanted Anne to be. The pornographers, for instance, tried to portray her as one of them. Which is understandable. If women like her are coming on board, pornography's got it made; it can only be a matter of time before it puts paid to romance once and for all.

So I fall back on my memories and my instincts which tell me that Anne didn't have a dirty streak and didn't believe that sex has nothing to do with love. Which in turn leads me to think that the truth about Anne and Julian was that they both had times when they saw themselves having a life together, times when they wondered what the hell they were doing, and times when they flayed themselves with guilt. And I guess that where there's guilt, there's feeling.

Maybe even love.

ACKNOWLEDGEMENTS

The author would like to thank Susan Freeman-Green, Guy Launder, and Dr David Matthews for their assistance.

ABOUT THE AUTHOR

Paul Thomas is the author of five novels including *Inside Dope*, winner of the inaugural Ned Kelly Award for crime fiction. His work has been widely published and translated into several languages.